W9-BIC-413

The Watchmaker's Daughter

GLASS AND STEELE
#1

C.J. ARCHER

Copyright © 2016 C.J. Archer

All rights reserved.

Series by C.J. Archer:

Glass and Steele

The Emily Chambers Spirit Medium Trilogy

The 1st Freak House Trilogy

The 2nd Freak House Trilogy

The 3rd Freak House Trilogy

The Ministry of Curiosities

Lord Hawkesbury's Players

The Assassins Guild

The Witchblade Chronicles

Stand-alone books by C.J. Archer:

Redemption

Surrender

Courting His Countess

The Mercenary's Price

DEDICATION

To my fans. Your passion for my books is what keeps me writing.

CHAPTER 1

London, Spring 1890

There were several reasons why I fell in love with Eddie Hardacre, but seeing a painter put the finishing touches to "E. HARDACRE, WATCHMAKER" on the shop front that had been in my family's hands for over a century, I couldn't remember any of them. My former fiancé was worse than a pirate. At least pirates were loyal to their crew. Loyalty was a bartering tool Eddie employed whenever he needed to gain someone's trust. Someone like my poor, foolish dead father. And me.

It was time to tell Eddie what I thought of him. I'd kept my anger bottled inside for long enough, and if I didn't let it out, I would never heal. Besides, now was the perfect time, as a customer inspected one of Father's watches. Eddie loathed public displays of emotion.

I would give him the most public of emotional displays that I could.

I tugged on my jacket lapels, threw back my shoulders, and marched past the gentleman's shiny black coach and into the shop that should have been mine.

The entrance was as far as I got. The familiarity of my surroundings pinched my heart. The rich scent of polished wood mingled with the subtle tang of metal. The myriad *tick tocks,* which irritated so many customers after mere minutes inside, summoned a well of memories. The individual rhythms sounded chaotic when placed in one room together but they reassured me that all would be well, that I had come home. It had been two weeks since I'd heard their song. Two weeks since I'd stepped inside the shop. Two weeks since Father died.

It was time.

Nothing had changed inside. The counter top stretched across the back, as sleek as ever. Behind it, the door to the workshop was closed. I recognized every clock hanging on the walls and set out on the tables, and all the glass display cabinets seemed to be filled with the same watches, from the inexpensive open faced variety to those with elaborately designed silver cases, known as hunters. Even Father's ancient tortoiseshell and ormolu still ticked to its unique rhythm, but no one had bothered to correct it. It was three minutes slow.

"I'll be with you in a moment," Eddie said without looking up from the watch he was showing the gentleman. Such poor shop-keeping! One should always make eye contact with every customer. A warm smile and pleasant greeting never went amiss, either.

I was, however, glad that he hadn't seen me immediately. "Excuse me, sir." I addressed the back of the customer's dark head. He did not turn around, but I didn't let that stop me. "Excuse me, sir, but unless you wish to finance a liar and swindler, you should not purchase a thing from this man."

Eddie glanced up with a gasp. The color leached from his face. "India!" He spluttered a hasty, "Excuse me," to his customer and rounded the counter. Arm out to usher me to the door, the color flooded his face as quickly as it had left it. "How lovely of you to visit me here, but as you can see, I'm rather busy. I'll call on you later, my dear."

I ducked beneath his arm, turned so that I could keep him in my sight, and backed toward the counter. I wanted to see Eddie's face turn ruby red as I informed his customer of his despicable behavior. "I am not your *dear* anymore, and I cannot believe that I ever wanted to be." I used to consider him handsome, with his blond curls and blue eyes, and I'd once thought myself fortunate that he'd chosen me as his bride. My gratitude had been smashed to pieces, along with my future, two weeks ago. Now I thought him one of the ugliest men I'd ever seen .

"India!" He lunged for me, but I was ready for him and stepped behind the table holding the collection of small mantel clocks. "Come here at once." When I didn't, he stomped his foot on the floor like a spoiled child not getting his way.

I gave him a tight-lipped smile. "If you want me to leave, you will have to catch me first."

He glanced past me to the gentleman who must have been quite stunned by my shocking behavior. I didn't care what he thought. I had always been known as the prim and proper daughter of Elliot Steele, but recent events had changed me. Let the dusty old men gossip about me at the guild's dining table. It no longer mattered, since I was not connected to the guild through Father or the shop anymore.

Eddie suddenly dodged to the left. I swerved and moved farther around the table. He growled in frustration.

I laughed and inched closer, daring him to try again. Part of me wanted him to catch me, so that I could force him to act like the overbearing brute I knew him to be in front of a customer.

"You're making a scene," Eddie hissed.

"Good."

He licked his lips and his gaze flicked to the gentleman behind me again. He cleared his throat and squared his shoulders, attempting to look as if he were in control. "Come now, India, be a good girl and leave this gentleman in peace. He doesn't wish to witness your hysterics."

"I'm a little too old to be called a girl, Eddie, don't you think?"

"Quite," he said, his tone grating. "Twenty-seven is definitely past the flush of youth."

He might as well have announced that I was too old to wed. I was surprised he hadn't used it as an excuse to end our engagement, but then again, he'd known my age before he proposed. "Nor am I hysterical," I added.

Eddie smiled. It was all twisted cruelty. I braced myself for his next words. "India and I were once engaged," he said to the gentleman who had remained silent behind me. "Alas, her rather fanciful and forthright nature only became evident after our betrothal. I suppose I ought to be thankful that she didn't hide her true self until after it was too late." His laugh was as insipid as his pale blue eyes. "I had to end our engagement or risk our children becoming afflicted."

"You ended our engagement because you got what you wanted, and what you wanted wasn't me. It was Father's shop."

I only just heard the gentleman behind me clear his throat over the pounding of blood between my ears. Eddie must have heard it too, and he collected himself. He licked his lips again, a habit that I now despised.

"Sir, I do apologize." Eddie bobbed his head in imitation of the little automated bird that emerged on the hour from the cuckoo clocks. He looked as ridiculous as he was pathetic. "India," he snapped at me. "Leave! Now!"

I thrust my hand on my hip, smiled, and spun round to speak to the gentleman and make an even bigger scene. An extremely tanned man with dark brown eyes, striking cheekbones and thick lashes stood there. If it weren't for his scowl, and the signs of exhaustion around his mouth and eyes, he would be handsome. He was everything Eddie was not—tall and dark and broad across the shoulders. He wore a well-tailored black suit, untroubled by his impressive frame, a silk hat and gray silk tie. While his clothing screamed gentleman, his stance did not. He leaned one elbow on the counter as if he were half drunk and needed propping up. A gentleman would have straightened in the presence of a woman, but this man didn't. Perhaps he wasn't English. The deep tan would suggest not.

It took me a moment to remember what I'd been about to say, and in that moment, he spoke first. "I have business to conduct with Mr. Hardacre," he said in a flawed upper class English accent. It was plummy enough, but the crispness had been sliced off and replaced by a slight drawl. "Please take your argument with you when you leave." He held his hand out, showing me the door.

I remembered what I wanted to say all of a sudden. "Mr. Hardacre is a liar and a scoundrel."

Eddie made a strangled choking sound.

"So you already pointed out," the customer said. He sounded bored, but that could have been a result of his accent.

"Is that the man you want to give your custom to?" I pressed.

"At the present time, yes."

Eddie chuckled. My hand slid off my hip and fisted at my side. I swallowed down the sense of hopelessness that threatened to overwhelm me. My scheme to discredit Eddie was quickly unraveling before my eyes. "Then you're aiding and abetting a man with the morals of a rat. He doesn't care who he ruins to get what he wants, only that he gets it in the end, by whatever means necessary." I heard how pathetic and desperate I sounded, yet I couldn't stop the words from spilling forth anyway. I was tired of holding them in, of smiling and telling acquaintances that I would be all right. I wasn't all right. I *was* pathetic and desperate. I had no employment, no money, and no home. I'd lost my fiancé and my father, within days of one another, although I'd never really had the fiancé, as it turned out. Our engagement had been a ruse, a way to get Father to sign over the shop to Eddie.

"I am sorry, miss," the gentleman said, sounding genuinely sympathetic.

"I'm sure you are now. Eddie is no better than the muck on your boots."

He sighed and the tiny lines at the corners of his eyes deepened. "No, I mean I'm sorry for doing this."

Two long strides brought him to me so that I got to admire his impressive height and frame. But not for long. Two large hands clamped around my waist, lifted me, and tossed me over one of those brawny shoulders I'd been admiring.

"What are you doing?" I cried. "This is outrageous! Let me down at once!"

He did not. With one arm clamped over the backs of my thighs, he strode to the door as if I were nothing more than a sack of flour. The blood rushed to my head. My hat hung by its pins. I pounded his back with my fists, but it had no effect. I was utterly helpless and I did not like being so, one little bit.

Behind me, Eddie roared with laughter. I felt the gentleman's muscles tense and heard a sharp intake of breath. He didn't slow, however, but merely pushed open the door and deposited me on the pavement. I stumbled and he clasped my shoulders until I regained my balance, then he let me go.

"My apologies, miss," he said with a curt nod. "But your conversation was taking too long, and I'm a busy man."

I fixed my hat and straightened my spine, mustering as much dignity as I could. It wasn't easy with all the shopkeepers and their customers looking out of doors and windows to see what had caused the commotion. "I don't care!" To my horror, my voice cracked. I did *not* want to cry. Not anymore. I'd shed enough tears over Eddie and the things I'd lost. "I don't care if I make you late for an appointment, or if I cost Eddie your custom. You are a brute! A fiend! You may look like a gentleman, but you most certainly are not one!"

"Cyclops," the man said to someone over my shoulder.

I glanced around to see a giant figure with a black patch over one eye jump nimbly down from the coachman's perch and advance on me. I swallowed a scream and shrank away, but he caught my arm. I tried to pull free but he caught my other arm and his grip tightened. The red, lumpy scar dripping from beneath his patch stood out against his charcoal skin, the white of his teeth even more so as he bared them in a snarl.

7

"Let me go!" I screamed, pulling harder. "Mr. Macklefield! Help!"

Mr. Macklefield, the neighboring tailor, took one look at the giant and fled back inside his shop. Up and down the street, shopkeepers shut their doors. Folk I'd known my entire life cowered inside. Even the painter went very still on the top of his ladder, as if he hoped no one would notice him there. No one came to my rescue. I'd never felt more alone or so vulnerable.

I glanced up at the giant who held both my wrists and blinked back hot tears. "Please let me go," I whispered.

"Can't, miss," he said in a booming voice with an accent similar to the gentleman's but from the gutters rather than the townhouse. "You just stay out here with me and let Mr. Glass finish his chat."

I sniffed. "So you won't let me go, even if I promise not to go back inside?"

He shook his head.

"I won't be long," the gentleman behind me said.

"I see." I drew in a breath, let it out, and stomped my heel into the giant's boot.

He winced and his one eye widened, but he didn't let me go.

The gentleman laughed softly. "Good shot."

The giant grunted. "Not bad for a little thing."

I ought to have been frightened witless, but their light-hearted banter quelled my fear. Not that I felt safe and confident, but I no longer felt like the giant or his master wanted to hurt me.

"Sir, if you please," Eddie said in a sickeningly sycophantic tone. "We'll finalize our business inside."

"I need to ask you some questions first," the gentleman, Mr. Glass, said.

"Questions? About the watch? Of course."

"Sir," I said over my shoulder. I had only moments in which to ruin this for Eddie, as he'd ruined so much more for me. "Mason And Sons have a finer hunter minute repeater than the one you were admiring in...there." I couldn't bring myself to call it Hardacre Watchmakers. It was still Steele Watchmakers to me and always would be. "If you want my advice, you ought to spend your money at that establishment. Not only will you get excellent service, but you'll be supporting an upstanding family."

"India!" Eddie shouted. "If you don't calm down, I'll send for a constable." He clicked his fingers at Jimmy, the boy who occasionally ran errands for the shopkeepers in the street. He was the only one who'd not retreated indoors, but that would be because Jimmy wasn't allowed in the shops. None of the shopkeepers trusted him not to steal from them. None since Father had died and Eddie had evicted me, that is. He strolled over, hands thrust deep into his pockets, but hung back, clearly not willing to take Eddie's side but unable to do anything to help me.

"I've already been to Mason And Sons," Mr. Glass said to me, ignoring Eddie. "There was nothing to interest me there. I wish to look at *this* watch."

"Come, sir," Eddie said, grasping Mr. Glass's arm. Mr. Glass narrowed his gaze at him and Eddie let go with a loud swallow. "I'll give you a good price on the watch."

"You cannot have been to Mason And Sons," I said to the gentleman. "Mr. Mason truly does have a finer example of the same timepiece. I saw it late yesterday, and I doubt he has sold it already."

Mr. Glass turned a curious expression toward me. Where before he'd looked tired, he was now alert. It was as if he'd just realized something of monumental importance to him—and it involved me. His gaze focused on mine with fierce, driving intensity. It was an unnerving experience to be the object of it, more so than the physical presence of his coachman. If I weren't restrained, I would have left and been glad to have escaped—from what, I didn't know.

"You're familiar with Mr. Mason and his work?" he asked me.

"I am. He was both a friend and rival of my father's." Their relationship had been a complicated one. While they respected and liked one another, they had to compete for customers among London's elite. Fortunately there were enough wealthy in the city to keep them, and several other watch and clockmakers, in business. Mr. Mason had been the first person I'd gone to after Eddie had ended our engagement, but he'd not been able to employ me with three sons and a daughter of his own.

Mr. Glass closed his eyes and rubbed his forehead as if trying to remove an ache. It was so odd, coming after his intense glare, that I checked with his servant to see if he thought it out of character.

The coachman frowned at his master. "Matt?" He called his master by his first name? What a peculiar arrangement. "Er, sir? You need to...?"

"I'm fine," Mr. Glass snapped.

"Don't bloody look fine," the coachman muttered, sounding a little hurt.

"Your father is a watchmaker?" Mr. Glass asked me, lowering his hand. He patted his coat, as if feeling for something in the pocket. Perhaps it was snuff or a pipe that he wished to smoke to return the color to his cheeks. He looked quite peaky.

"Was." I spread my hands to indicate the shop windows with the watches set out on the lower shelf and the higher shelves filled with clocks of all shapes and sizes. "He owned this establishment under the name Steele until his death, two weeks ago." I swallowed the lump rising up my throat, but the tears welled nevertheless.

"He left it to *me* in his will," Eddie cut in quickly.

"Because you assured him that you would keep your promise to marry me, and my fool of a father believed you. I believed you," I choked out. I no longer cared what the gentleman or his servant thought of my behavior. Two weeks ago I'd been too sad and shocked to tell Eddie what I thought of him, but not anymore. I was still sad, but those two weeks had given me time to think. I wasn't shocked now, I was mad.

"I wasn't to know then that you were such a strong-willed creature," Eddie said. "If I had, I wouldn't have asked for your hand. Take this display, for example. One doesn't need further evidence of your willfulness."

Rage surged through my body. I felt like I was burning with it, from the inside out. "What I am is the daughter and assistant of Elliot Steele, watchmaker."

"No, that is what you *were*. Now you're just...pathetic. Go away, India. Nobody wants you here."

I gritted my teeth and pulled myself free from the man holding me. To my surprise, he let go. I barged up to Eddie and slapped him across the cheek before he saw my hand coming.

Eddie reeled back, clutching the side of his face. He stared open-mouthed at me, his expression caught between fear and shock, as if I were a ghastly and strange creature. I suppose, in some ways, I was. I certainly didn't feel like myself at that moment. I felt...lighter, liberated, and yes, very strange indeed.

Mr. Glass cleared his throat. "Miss Steele?"

I smiled at him and his one-eyed servant. The coachman grinned back. "Yes, Mr. Glass?" I said.

"Would you mind joining me this afternoon in the tea room at Brown's Hotel?"

"Me?" My smile slipped off. I stared at him. "But...why?"

"Yes," Eddie muttered. "Why her?"

Mr. Glass ignored him. "To discuss your father."

I was trying to decide if it was unseemly to drink tea alone with a strange gentleman in a salubrious hotel, and if I cared about that sort of thing anymore, when Eddie took advantage of my silence. "I can tell you everything you wish to know about Elliot Steele. I knew him well."

"Oh, do shut up, Eddie." It seemed I'd thought of something to say after all. "I will join you for tea, Mr. Glass. Thank you."

The brown eyes briefly flared and a small smile touched his lips. It quickly vanished, however, and his jaw went rigid. The muscle bunched and did not release. It was as if he were bearing down against a pain. Unease ate at my gut. I didn't know this man, and he had a rather frightening looking servant, yet I'd agreed to drink tea with him. It would seem today was a day to do things that were out of character for me. I pushed my unease aside.

"We can discuss watches," I said to Mr. Glass, simply to see Eddie's face turn red with anger again. "If it's a hunter minute repeater you're after then there are many fine examples in the city. Much finer than here."

"They were your father's timepieces!" Eddie cried. "That watch is exquisite."

"The regulator pins stick and it loses five seconds every twelve hours. I was never able to fix it."

"You mean your father couldn't," Eddie said smugly.

"No, I mean *I* couldn't. I've been doing all the repair work for three years, ever since Father's sight deteriorated."

"Well then, now it's my turn to repair them. Elliot left *me* all his notes."

"They're three years out of date. *My* notes were not part of the inheritance." I spun on my heel, gave a nod to Mr. Glass and another to his servant, and said, "Shall we say three o'clock?"

"Perfect," Mr. Glass said with a smile that momentarily banished the tiredness from his eyes. "See you then."

I walked up the street, feeling as if the entire city watched me. I turned the corner and doubled back, just in time to see Mr. Glass being driven away. He removed his gloves and studied something in his hand. He closed his fingers around it, tipped his head back, and breathed deeply, as if he were finally getting the rest he craved.

It wasn't this behavior that set my pulse racing, however. It was the object in his fisted hand, and the bright purplish glow it emitted. A glow that infused his skin and disappeared up his sleeve.

CHAPTER 2

"You told me yesterday that you would pay me," Mrs. Bray, my landlady, said as she stood in the doorway to my room. "And the day before, and the day before that." She folded her arms beneath her large bosom, pushing them up so that they were in danger of choking her, and peered down the length of her narrow nose at me. "I'm not a charity, Miss Steele."

She certainly wasn't. She wanted the rent for the tiny attic room in advance and reminded me every day, when I failed to pay her, that I would have to vacate if I didn't come up with the money. I'd managed to keep the room through a combination of charm and pleading, but I didn't think that tactic would work much longer. Going by the unsympathetic scowl on her pinched face, her patience had worn out.

The truth was, I hadn't anticipated staying in her lodging house long after Eddie threw me out of my home above the shop the day my father was buried— *the very day*. I thought I would have secured myself employment as a shop assistant with either a watch or clockmaker by now. But I'd applied in person to every single one in the vicinity, and none had any positions available, although some expressed their sympathies for my plight. Unfortunately I couldn't eat sympathy or sleep on it. I needed to work. Hence my applications to other shopkeepers. So far, three haberdashers, two drapers, four greengrocers, and a chemist refused to employ me without references. I was utterly weary of hearing the word no.

"I understand, Mrs. Bray," I said, mustering some sweetness from God knew where, "but I just need one more day. I'm going to apply to be a governess."

She snorted. "That's a laugh."

"Pardon?"

She hiked up her bosom with her folded arms. "Toffs employ other toffs as governesses. You're only a shopkeeper's assistant."

I had been a watchmaker and repairer, actually, but I didn't correct her. No one ever believed me when I claimed my father taught me everything he knew. Not even my friend, Catherine Mason, whose father and three brothers owned Mason And Sons. She'd told me that no honorable father would allow his daughter to get her hands dirty in the workshop. I liked Catherine so I didn't argue the point with her.

"I must try something different," I told Mrs. Bray. "I *need* employment."

"There's always the workhouse for destitute women."

I shuddered. The workhouse was for those with no roof over their head, no education, and no other possible means of supporting themselves. Employment there meant a bed to sleep on and food twice a day, albeit a lice-ridden bed and unpalatable gruel. It also meant long hours on the factory floor, risking life and limb with the dangerous machinery, and contending with depraved men who thought the poor women were no better than whores. A perfectly healthy woman I'd been acquainted with had wound up in one after her husband died. When I'd seen her again, a year later, she'd been at death's door, ravaged by syphilis and coughing up blood. The workhouse was a wretched place. It made Mrs. Bray's cold attic room, with the low roof and persistent odor of cat urine, seem like a palace.

If I couldn't find employment elsewhere, the workhouse was my only choice.

I collected my gloves and reticule from the bed, but she didn't let me pass. Her sizeable hips filled the doorway. "I have to go out for now," I told her, "but I'll be stopping by the Governesses' Benevolent Institution on my way back to see if there's any work for an educated woman like myself."

She rolled her tongue over her top teeth then made a sucking sound. "I told you, you won't find anything. You're not the right sort to be a governess."

"I must try."

"You're persistent, I'll give you that." She sucked the air between her teeth again. "But you have to pack your things and take them with you."

I gasped. "Are you evicting me?"

"I've had inquiries from a gentleman wishing to lease this room." She backed out of the doorway and headed to the stairs in her awkward, rolling gait. "You have fifteen minutes."

"But I have nowhere else to go!"

"You've got friends. Ask that pretty girl who called on you last week to help."

I stood at the top of the stairs and stared at her retreating back. The Masons couldn't afford to support me, not with so many of their own mouths to feed. I would have to sleep on Catherine's floor. They would try to help me if they knew my plight, but I couldn't bring myself to beg. Pride was all I had left.

"Please, Mrs. Bray. I'll have the money by the end of today."

She stopped at the bottom of the stairs and shook her head. "How?" she called up. "You've got no job and nothing more to sell. Even if you find employment today, you won't be paid for weeks. I need that money now, Miss Steele. I've got to eat too." She walked off. "You've got fifteen minutes or I fetch the constable and have you arrested for trespass."

Arrested! From the look on her face, she was serious.

I headed back into my room and numbly packed my bag. Having sold as many personal items as I could to pay for food and rent for the last two weeks, my few remaining belongings amounted to very little. I possessed two changes of unmentionables, a nightgown, one other dress, a coat, and a hairbrush, hand mirror and combs that had belonged to my mother. My bag was so light that I had no trouble getting it down the stairs.

Mrs. Bray saw me out and shut the door the moment I crossed the threshold, almost hitting me in the back. I walked as erectly as possible down the steps to the pavement, my battered leather valise in hand. It had been a gloomy, damp house anyway. I would find somewhere better to live, just as soon as I secured myself employment. In the meantime, Catherine Mason's floor would have to do.

I wouldn't rely on the Masons' charity for long, however. I wouldn't need to. I was eminently employable, if only someone would give me the opportunity to prove it without references. After meeting with Mr. Glass, I would apply at the Governesses' Benevolent Institution. I could even ask him if anyone in his circle was in need of the services of an educated woman. Indeed, this meeting with Mr. Glass could prove quite fruitful. I had a good feeling about it.

I walked from the lodging house near King's Cross Road to Mayfair. It took almost an hour, but the air was reasonably clear, allowing some spring sunshine to leak through the gray pall. I knew the way well enough, having delivered timepieces to wealthy customers who lived there. I'd even delivered an exquisite watch to a foreign prince when he'd stayed at Brown's Hotel. Nevertheless, the colonnaded façades of the grand buildings never ceased to amaze me and make me feel small.

My valise no longer felt light by the time I reached Albermarle Street, and my shoulders and arms ached. The liveried porter of Brown's Hotel opened the front door for me. I ignored the questioning arch of his brows and his pointed glance at my simple dress and valise, and strolled inside with what I hoped was an air of confidence. I wanted to at least look like I knew where I was going, even if my stomach had tied itself into knots. The porter stowed my valise away in a back room and directed me to the tearoom.

I received more curious stares as I scanned the faces for Mr. Glass. Plain shop girls didn't usually mingle in the tearoom at Brown's with ladies and gentlemen of good breeding. I felt like a drab piece of sackcloth amid colorful silks and delicate laces.

I spotted Mr. Glass at a table near the window. He rose and greeted me with a dashing smile that I couldn't help but return, despite my knotted stomach. He must have had a good rest since we last met, because there was no sign of tiredness in his eyes. They were as clear and warm as his smile. There was also no sign of the purplish glow on the skin of his bare hand. It appeared quite as it should—tanned, strong, and entirely normal.

"Thank you for coming, Miss Steele," he said, pulling out a chair for me.

"Thank you for the invitation, Mr. Glass, although I'm still unsure what it is you want to ask me."

"I have questions about your father."

"So you said, but what do you want to know about him?"

We were interrupted by the waiter, and my awkwardness returned. Not only was I unsure if I was expected to pay for my afternoon tea, but everyone at the surrounding tables still stared. Was I the oddity or was Mr. Glass, with his good looks and somewhat lazy way of sitting? Or was it the both of us together? None knew me, but it was quite possible that Mr. Glass's acquaintances were among the other patrons and his meeting a woman like this was about to become the gossip of the week.

"Your finest tea, please," Mr. Glass asked the waiter, "and your best cakes and...things," he added with a dismissive wave of his hand. "I don't care what. Do you, Miss Steele?"

"Er, no." As long as I wasn't expected to pay for them. Despite the strangeness of Mr. Glass and his relaxed manner, I did peg him as a gentleman, and no gentleman would invite a lady to tea and then ask her to pay her share.

The waiter retreated and Mr. Glass sat forward. He picked up the small silver fork and twisted it between his fingers. "You must think my request to meet with you odd," he said.

"No odder than my acceptance of it. I'm not in the habit of taking tea with strange men."

He held up the fork in surrender. "Of course not. I can see that you're a respectable lady."

"You saw that in our brief encounter this morning? The encounter in which I berated my former fiancé, attempted to ruin his business, and stomped on your servant's toe?"

"To be fair, Cyclops deserved it. I didn't think he would grip you that hard." He let the fork go and placed a hand to his heart. "I deserved it more. Please allow me to apologize most sincerely for my treatment of you. I was...not myself. I'm not ordinarily so rough with women. It was uncalled for, and I can only apologize for it again and again."

"Apology accepted. I admit to being somewhat shocked at the time, but I wasn't harmed. I do suggest that you refrain from hauling women around like a caveman next time you are not feeling like yourself. Others may not be as forgiving."

He grinned, which I hoped he would. I did so like his smile with his perfect white teeth against his smooth brown skin. It made his eyes twinkle too. "I will try to restrain myself, although I do have a temper and I'm unused to the delicate sensibilities of English women."

"Women approve of being manhandled where you come from?"

"Not many, no. They usually stomp on toes, and more, if they find themselves in such a situation." He picked up the fork again and toyed with it. He seemed to have a problem sitting still. He must be a man of action. That sort rarely sat in tearooms with ladies. "I like your directness, Miss Steele. It's refreshing. I was beginning to think all Englishmen and women spoke in roundabout ways without saying what they truly felt."

"I'm not usually so forward, but this morning I'd reached the end of my tether." The dam had finally burst after seeing Eddie's smug smiles and listening to his inane laughter. My anger had nowhere to go but out. It wasn't until later, when I sat quietly in my attic room, that I realized my anger was largely directed at myself now—anger that I'd ever accepted a proposal from a man I didn't love and never could. "Where are you from, Mr. Glass? Your accent is unusual."

"My accent is a mix, so I've been told, thanks to the different heritages of my parents and our travels. I'm recently from America."

"America? How thrilling."

He chuckled. "Not particularly."

"It is when the furthest you've traveled is Cheshunt."

He gave me a blank look.

"It's a little north of London."

The waiter arrived with a silver tea-stand laden with slices of cake, sandwiches and pastries. I'd never seen so many all at once before, or presented so prettily. My stomach growled. I hadn't eaten since that morning, and then only a slice of moldy bread that Mrs. Bray had been about to throw out.

Mr. Glass eyed me from beneath long lashes but didn't comment. He waited until the waiter poured our tea and left us with the pot before urging me to fill my plate.

I took a delicate pastry and ate it in two bites before he'd even begun. He nudged the cake-stand a little closer to me and I took a slice of cake and ate that. At his further prompting, I shook my head.

"I'm quite full, thank you," I lied. My mother had always told me not to make a pig of myself, and I mostly followed her advice. I tried not to look at the cakes for fear of showing my regret, however.

"That may be so, but I can't possibly eat all of these on my own," he said. "Please, assist me, or they will go to waste."

If he was going to be so gentlemanly about it, then I might as well.

He sipped his tea, and I had to suppress a giggle. He looked out of place in a room full of mostly women, a pretty floral teacup in one hand and a pastry in the other. I wondered if he did this sort of thing in America. If I had to guess, I'd say he was a gentleman farmer with those brown hands of his.

"Do you mind if I start asking you questions now?" he said.

"Go ahead. It's why I'm here."

He set the cup down carefully, as if he were afraid he'd break it. He stared at the contents for a moment, and when he looked up, that intense stare he'd given me earlier in the day returned. A shiver trickled down my spine and chilled my skin. I couldn't make up my mind if I liked being looked at in such a way. "How old was your father?" he asked.

That was an odd question to begin with. "Forty-nine. Why?"

He sat back in the chair with a softly muttered, "Damn it."

"Why?" I repeated. "And why do you want to know about my father anyway? What has it got to do with buying yourself a new watch?"

His lips twitched at the corners, but he didn't break into a full smile. "A full stomach makes you curious."

I arched my brow and waited for an answer.

He leaned forward again and picked up his teacup. "I'm trying to find a man I met five years ago. He was a watchmaker and made a watch for me that now requires fixing."

"Has it stopped working?"

"It's slowing down."

"You've tried winding it?"

"Do I look like a fool?"

"My apologies." I sipped my tea and kept my eyes averted. I heard him sigh again and he shifted in the chair, as if he were regretting asking me to tea. "Why didn't you show your watch to Eddie?" I asked. "He might have been able to fix it."

"Not this watch."

"Why not? Is it American? Some American watches are different to ours, but a good watchmaker can work out what needs correcting without damaging the mechanisms. Eddie isn't a bad watchmaker, he's just limited in the types he can repair. He wasn't apprenticed to my father. Would you like me to look at it? I can assure you, I may be a mere woman, but I was apprenticed to the best watchmaker in the city, perhaps the country. The only reason I wasn't allowed into the guild and am not able to call myself a master watchmaker is because of their archaic rules that don't allow female members. It was why—"

"Miss Steele." He held up his hand for me to stop. I bit my tongue. "Thank you for your offer, but this watch is a special one. The original maker is the only one in the world who can repair it."

"That's rather arrogant of him, to make such a claim."

"Nevertheless, I'd like to find him."

I was about to press him to show it to me, but decided against it. It made no difference to me if he thought only one person could repair it. "Tell me about this arrogant watchmaker. So far, he fits the description of several men in the guild."

He seemed to find that amusing. He smiled, and his shoulders relaxed. "I admit that I've been running all over London without really knowing what I'm doing and where I'm going." He sat forward. "Would you mind helping me narrow my search?"

"I would be delighted. I take it you don't know his name."

"He called himself Chronos."

"The Greek God of Time? We can add ridiculous to arrogant. Go on."

His eyes crinkled at the corners. "I met him in a saloon in New Mexico, five years ago. He was English and told me he came from London." His eyes suddenly shadowed, and he turned serious as he studied the teacup. "He was an old man then, so it couldn't have been your father."

"Father has never left England anyway. He's lived above that shop all his life, as his father did, and his father too. Now Eddie has it," I spat.

His gaze sharpened. "Your grandfather is a watchmaker?"

"He was. He's dead."

He stared at me, unblinking. I shrank back from the force of it. "When did he die?"

"Before I was born, so he couldn't have been your mysterious Chronos either."

He passed a hand over his eyes and down his face then blew out a breath. It must be a very special watch indeed to elicit such a reaction. I could feel his anxiety from across the table.

"Let me see if I have this correct," I said. "Five years ago, you were given a watch by an Englishman in America who claims that no one else can fix it. You refuse to let anyone else attempt to fix it, so you traveled all this way to find him. You don't know his name, or where he lived in London specifically, and you only know that he must be old."

"You have it," he said, absently patting his coat pocket.

I did not mention the fact that he could be dead. No doubt he'd thought of that, and I didn't want to see disappointment shadow that handsome face. "Then you have come to the right person. I know every important watchmaker in London, and most unimportant ones too."

"I had a feeling you would be able to help me," he said. "I'll pay you for your time, of course. It may take several days to locate the right man."

Pay me! Ah, now I understood why he'd chosen me instead of Eddie, or anyone else. He must have sensed my desperation this morning and guessed I had the time to devote to such a scheme. "If you insist," I said as graciously as I could manage while trying to hold back my smile.

"What is the current wage for a shop assistant in London?" he asked.

"One with experience could hope for a pound. I don't know about any other sort of assistant."

"A pound then." He held out his hand. "Deal?"

I shook his hand firmly, as my father had always taught me when shaking a man's hand after a particularly lucrative transaction. "Deal," I repeated, mimicking his accent.

He laughed softly. "Have another cake, Miss Steele. Then let's begin."

I ate a slice, touched my napkin to the corners of my mouth, and washed it down with a gulp of tea. I wasn't being very ladylike, but I was no lady and he didn't seem to notice.

"Most watchmakers are traditionally located in Clerkenwell and St. Luke's," I said, "but you'll find some scattered elsewhere. My ancestor set up his premises on St. Martin's Lane and we've been there ever since."

"Until your former fiancé took it from you."

I couldn't meet his gaze. It had been one thing to air my dirty linen when I'd been mad at Eddie, but it was quite another to be reminded of my shocking behavior, and by a gentleman too. "My father thought that only a man could manage the business." I don't know why I wanted to explain the situation to him. It seemed important that he know that Father loved me, but he'd been duped. "He liked precision, organization, and neatness, so he changed his will when I became engaged, thinking that Eddie could be relied upon to keep his word. No one expected him to die suddenly before the wedding. And to be fair to Father, Eddie was very sweet up until then. It wasn't until the funeral when he showed what a nasty little worm he was."

Mr. Glass remained silent, and I wished I hadn't blurted out my problems all over again. He must think me as pathetic as I felt. "My mother used to tell me that God would punish people like that after they're dead," he said.

"I wish Eddie would get his come-uppance in *this* lifetime where I could see it and enjoy it."

One corner of his mouth kicked up. "You and I think alike." He lifted his teacup in salute. Finding it empty, he refilled both mine and his.

"Will you be staying in London long after you've found the old watchmaker?" I heard myself ask with a hint of breathiness in my voice.

He shook his head. "I've business to take care of back home."

Pity. "Tell me what your watchmaker looks like," I said. "Aside from being old, that is."

"He had blue eyes, white hair, and was otherwise non-descript. I got the feeling he was running away from something or someone."

"Why do you say that?"

"Because most folk who end up in Broken Creek, New Mexico, are usually running away from something or someone."

"Is that why you were there, Mr. Glass?"

His eyes twinkled but no smile touched his lips. "I visited for the scenery."

"Is it beautiful?"

"To some."

He didn't elaborate, and I got the feeling he no longer wanted to discuss his past in Broken Creek.

"So tell me which watchmakers you've visited already," I said. "That will narrow our search."

"My lawyer informed me that most live in Clerkenwell, as you yourself noted. I began there this morning." He listed a half-dozen whose names I recognized, although I knew none personally. "I decided to stop in at Masons' and Hardacre's on my way home. Indeed, I was told that it was named Steele's and was surprised to see the painter changing the sign. I'm glad you were there, Miss Steele. Our meeting has an air of fortuitousness about it."

I smiled. "I agree. I've had a good feeling about it ever since our encounter."

"Even when I manhandled you?"

"Perhaps it started after that."

We discussed returning to Clerkenwell's watchmakers, but in the end, decided to investigate the better class of horologists elsewhere in the city. Mr. Glass insisted the man he'd met five years ago had been educated with a middle class accent and not a slum one. After spending most of the morning in Clerkenwell, he'd already learned the difference.

Fortunately I knew most of those watchmakers well, since Father had been friendly with them back when he still liked and respected the guild members. A twang of guilt over my role in his falling out with the guild twisted my gut. He'd fallen out with the other members over *my* application.

Once the teapot was empty and most of the delicious confections gone, Mr. Glass patted his jacket pocket and stood. The waiter brought hat and gloves, and Mr. Glass paid for the both of us. He escorted me to the hotel entrance, but I hung back to retrieve my valise. I had planned on waiting until he'd gone, but he seemed to be waiting for me to exit first.

"Are you staying here at Brown's?" I asked him.

"No, I have a house not far away," he said.

I didn't ask how someone who'd never set foot on English soil until two days ago could possibly have a house, but perhaps there was a family link somewhere. It would explain part of the accent and the fact he had a lawyer.

"Thank you, Miss Steele. I enjoyed your company today," he said.

Oh dear. He wanted me to leave first. Should I go and come back for my valise after he'd gone, or let him see it and know I was now homeless?

The decision was made for me by the porter I'd met upon entering. He deposited the valise at my feet. "You almost forgot your luggage," he said with a wicked gleam in his eye.

My face flared with heat. "Thank you. So kind of you to collect it for me."

He bowed and left. With a clenching of back teeth, I turned to Mr. Glass. He was frowning at my valise. Since the cat was out of the bag, I might as well give it a further nudge. I had nothing to lose.

"Mr. Glass, may I be so bold as to ask for an advance against wages? It's just that I have expenses, you see, and no other employment at present."

He blinked slowly. "Of course. I'll give you the entire week's wage now. Will that cover expenses?"

An entire week! What a generous fellow. "Most assuredly. Thank you."

He glanced around. "Pretend to grow teary," he said quietly.

It took me a moment to realize he wanted to conduct the transaction in a way that would protect my reputation. I sniffed and touched my finger to my lowered eyes while he surreptitiously folded some coins into his handkerchief. He handed it to me, and I used it to dab away my fake tears before dropping it into my reticule. The transaction was all very clandestine, and I was quite sure no one had noticed and come to the wrong conclusion—or the right one, as the case may be.

"Miss Steele, am I correct in assuming that you're on your way to a new abode today?" He nodded at the valise.

"I'm going to my friend, Catherine Mason's, house." It wasn't quite a lie, and it would be too embarrassing to tell him that I'd been thrown out of the lodging house I'd been staying in for the last two weeks.

"Is that Catherine Mason of Masons And Sons?" he asked. "Does she live above the family shop?"

"Next door. Her eldest brother now lives above the shop with his wife and child. It won't take me long by omnibus."

"If you'd like to wait here, I can have Cyclops drive you."

"Thank you, that is very generous, but I can't possibly impose on you any further. The advancement of wages is more than enough. Besides, the omnibus route isn't far and it's a pleasant day for a walk."

He glanced through the front window at the sky. "You call this a pleasant day? The sky is gray and I feel it's so close that I'll be smothered by it."

"It wouldn't be a London sky if it was blue and high." I picked up my valise and the porter held open the door for me.

Mr. Glass followed me outside and down the steps. "I'll collect you in the morning from the Masons' house," he said, brushing his thumb over his jacket pocket in what struck me as an absent-minded motion.

It was at least the third time he'd done it this afternoon. Whatever was in there must be important—perhaps that strange glowing object.

"Be careful of pick pockets," I said.

At his frown, I nodded at his jacket pocket. He placed his hands behind his back. "There's nothing in there," he said stiffly. "Just a handkerchief."

"You carry two?"

"Teary eyed women are common in America."

A bubble of laughter almost escaped, but I swallowed it down. He looked quite serious and more than a little annoyed. I couldn't think how my warning would annoy anyone, but I shrugged it off.

"What time tomorrow?" I asked.

"Is nine too early?"

"Not for me." Clearly he wasn't like other men of his ilk who slept in until noon.

He gave me a curt nod and I went on my way. I couldn't help stealing a glance from the street corner, but Mr. Glass had already left. The omnibus route was indeed close, and I didn't have long to wait before one rattled by. Fortune was smiling on me that afternoon because I managed to get a seat inside, facing a gentleman reading a newspaper. When Father's eyesight deteriorated, I read him the newspaper every evening, but I hadn't bought one since his death. I'd needed to save every penny.

I quickly scanned the front page for something interesting. There were several articles, but one headline stood out above all others: AMERICAN OUTLAW SIGHTED IN ENGLAND.

My chest tightened. My blood ran cold. No, surely not. Surely the handsome and gentlemanly Mr. Glass wasn't an outlaw. Surely his recent arrival here and that of the man depicted in the newspaper's sketch with WANTED printed above it was just a coincidence.

It was difficult to tell if they were one and the same from the black and white drawing. The outlaw had a scruffy beard and moustache, and wore a large hat pulled down over his face. *That's* what an outlaw looked like. He wasn't well dressed and cleanly shaved. Wild West outlaws were filthy and crude. They behaved like...cavemen.

Oh God.

What had I got myself into?

CHAPTER 3

I read as much of the article as I could before the man and his newspaper alighted from the omnibus. It claimed that very little was known about the outlaw, not even his name. He'd been dubbed Dark Rider by the *Las Vegas Gazette* because no one had seen his face and his crimes were committed during the night. Dark Rider had held up stagecoaches, stolen horses, and murdered a lawman who'd tracked him down. A colorful account of the aborted arrest took up most of the article, but what caught my eye was the final paragraph. A reward of two thousand dollars was being offered for his capture. I didn't know how much that was in English money but it was an impressive number. It had to be more than the pound's worth of coins now sitting in my reticule. I couldn't stop thinking about it and the outlaw the rest of the way to the Masons' house.

"Of course you can stay," Catherine said, when she led me to the kitchen. "Can't she, Mama?"

Mrs. Mason smiled a weak greeting then pounded her fist into a mound of dough. "As long as your father doesn't mind."

"Why would he mind? India is my oldest friend, and she needs us now." Catherine squeezed my hand and rolled her eyes.

"He'll be home shortly," Mrs. Mason said, giving the dough a particularly heavy beating. The Masons kept no maid, and whenever I saw Catherine or her mother, they wore aprons and could be found in the kitchen. Their house was perpetually full of delicious smells.

"I don't want to be any trouble." I nibbled on my lower lip. Perhaps my coming here had been a mistake. The Masons didn't have much charity to offer. "It'll only be for the night. I'll sleep on the floor and eat the scraps from the table. Oh, and I can pay you. My new employer gave me a week's wages in advance."

Mrs. Mason stopped kneading. "A penny or two would help to ease Mr. Mason's mind." She smiled, more genuinely this time. "You're a sweet friend to our Catherine and always welcome here. It's just that..." She shook her head and glanced at the door.

"What is it, Mama?" Catherine prompted.

"You're a young woman, India, and we have two impressionable young men in the house still. That's all."

"Oh. I didn't think about that," I said.

Catherine laughed. "Ronnie and Gareth don't interest India in the least, Mama. She can do quite a bit better than my dull-witted brothers."

Her mother returned to her dough. "Even so."

"Ronnie and Gareth are like brothers to me," I said. Hopefully it was enough to reassure her that I wasn't about to trap her sons into marriage. Admittedly it stung that she thought I would. She must also know that her sons would have no interest in me, no matter what methods I used to trap them. Like Catherine, the

Mason boys were all attractive and fair. They could have their pick of girls. I was too old for them, and too plain with my straight brown hair, short stature and a waist that refused to shrink to a more fashionable size no matter how tightly I pulled my corset laces.

Catherine led me by the hand up the stairs to her room. She shut the door and tossed herself onto the bed. She patted the mattress beside her. "Ronnie heard a rumor that you confronted Eddie. Is that so? Tell me what happened." Her long pale lashes fanned over her big blue eyes in innocent wonder. It was not surprising that she had several suitors vying for her hand. A few years younger than me, and quite a lot taller and prettier, the youths always followed her about like puppies. She seemed to enjoy the attention, but I expected it must get tiresome after a while.

"I tried," I told her. "I did manage to ruin a transaction with his customer." Although I was no longer sure if Mr. Glass was there to purchase a watch after all.

Catherine giggled into her hand. "Good for you. That horrible little man is...well, he's horrible. Father is refusing to send any custom his way now, even if it's something we don't stock and he knows Steele's—I mean, Hardacre's—does."

"Your father is an honorable man."

She placed her hand over mine on my lap and gave me a sympathetic smile. "I'm glad you still think so. I know it wasn't easy to forgive him after the guild made their decision, but he had to go along with the majority."

"I don't blame him."

I must have sounded convincing because she seemed to believe me. The truth was, I did blame Mr. Mason for not standing up to them. Father had said he'd sat quietly and not said a word during the meeting among the senior guild members at which my application for membership had been tabled. A mere week before that, Mr. Mason had urged me to apply. The about-face baffled me. The relationship between our two families had never been quite the same again, although my friendship with Catherine remained unchanged, thank goodness. I knew so few other women of similar age that the loss of her friendship would have been worse than my broken engagement to Eddie.

"Tell me about your new position," Catherine said. "Does it involve watches?"

"In a way."

"Good. You've got a knack for fine repair work, so Father says. He was quite impressed by how quickly you learned everything. He used to hold you up as an example of why women ought to be allowed to perform men's work if they chose." She screwed up her nose. "Sorry, India, but I am glad he stopped all that. I began to feel quite inadequate next to your perfection."

"I'm hardly perfect," I scoffed.

"Father has always appreciated brains over beauty." She patted her bouncy blonde curls. "Some men do, you know," she added, as if such men were a rarity.

"Most prefer a little of both," I said, laughing, "but not too much of either."

She broke into giggles again.

"We'd be quite the combination if we were one person," I said, still smiling. "With your looks and my watchmaking skills, we'd have all the gentlemen for miles around purchasing our watches."

"Stop putting yourself down like that, India." She nudged my elbow. "You're pretty. I don't know why you think you're not."

"Because next to you, I'm not."

"Bollocks." She giggled at the crass word. "That Eddie Hardacre has a lot to answer for, always putting you down the way he did. I don't know what you saw in him."

"Nor do I," I said on a sigh. "I suppose it was because he was the first man to pay me much attention and the first to ask me to marry him."

"He was only the first because you intimidate most other men."

"I do not!"

"You do. Ask Ronnie and Gareth. You frighten them to death."

"That's because I don't fall at their feet and run hither and thither to please them like other girls."

"That and your quick tongue. They think you're going to tease them."

I rolled my eyes, but her words were quite a shock. Did men truly find me intimidating? All men, or just pretty brainless twits like her younger brothers?

"Where's the shop located?" she asked. At my blank look, she added, "The shop where you'll be working?"

"It's not a shop. It's a short-term commission to help a gentleman find a certain watchmaker he met some years ago. I know it sounds odd," I said when she blinked back at me. "But the gentleman seems very nice and he's paying well. The work won't be much, and I can continue to make inquiries for further employment while I'm driven to every watchmaker in the city."

"See what I mean. I would never have thought of that. How clever of you. Soooo..." She nudged me again. "Is this gentleman handsome?"

"Very. He's also amiable and wealthy. We had tea at Brown's."

She gasped. "Then you must wear something prettier than that old dress." She jumped up and opened the drawer where she kept her gowns.

"Catherine, I won't fit into any of your clothes."

"Oh." She closed the drawer and regarded me with a critical eye. "Then we'll do something with your hair. I've been wanting to modernize your style for some time."

I sighed and succumbed to her ministrations. She plucked out the pins and ran her hands through the tresses.

"Your handsome gentleman employer will be surprised to see you tomorrow. I think we can cinch your waist a little more, too."

I groaned. "He's not a prospect, Catherine."

"Every unattached man is a prospect." She paused, her hands in my hair. "He isn't married, is he?"

"He didn't mention a wife, but I didn't ask."

"You must find out for certain, first thing. Now, what else can you tell me about him?"

I told her his name and that he was American with possibly some English heritage. She oohed and aahed as I thought she would and bounced on her toes when I told her he had a house in Mayfair. I told her everything I remembered from our conversation.

I didn't tell her there was quite a good chance he was a Wild West outlaw on the run.

***

"She shouldn't stay here." Mr. Mason's hissed voice could barely be heard over the clatter of pots and pans in the kitchen as Mrs. Mason washed dishes. He had dismissed all of us except his wife after the evening meal. Throughout dinner, he'd cast odd looks my way, as if he were seeing me in a new light. It was so strange that I'd almost asked him if something was amiss, but decided against it. He must simply feel peculiar having me stay in his house without Father, and perhaps he missed Father's company too. I'd returned to the kitchen for a drink, but stopped upon hearing Mr. Mason's whisper.

"She's too close to Catherine," he went on.

"India's a good girl, sensible," Mrs. Mason said. "Catherine could learn a thing or two from her."

I leaned closer. "You don't understand," he said heavily. Although I couldn't see him, I pictured him sitting at the table, running his hands over his bald head.

"Then explain it to me."

"I...I can't."

A chair scraped and footsteps approached. I hid in a dark recess and waited for him to leave before I returned to Catherine's room. My feet felt like logs, my heart sore. Why didn't Mr. Mason want me here? Was I truly a threat to his sons? Did he think me no longer a virtuous woman now that my father was gone? I could think of no other reason—nothing else had changed since I'd last seen him. So why did he no longer want me near his family?

"You didn't bring up the jug," Catherine said when I returned to her room.

"I'm no longer thirsty."

***

The noses of the entire Mason household were pressed against the front window when Mr. Glass arrived in his carriage. The men tossed out words like coupler, shafts and axles as if they were coachbuilders not watchmakers, while the women argued about how much he must earn a year to own such a handsome conveyance. I opened the door and went out to greet him.

"Good morning, miss," said Cyclops from the driver's seat. "Forgive me for not coming down, but I only got one good foot left and I don't want to risk it."

He flashed a grin as wide as his face and tugged on his cap.

Someone smelling of bacon sidled up behind me. "India," Mrs. Mason whispered in my ear. "As a respectable woman and good friend to your poor departed parents, I feel that it's my duty to make sure you know what you're doing."

"Why now? You were aware that Mr. Glass was collecting me yesterday."

"Yes. Well. Now I've seen his coachman and I'm having doubts. Are you sure he's not a pirate? He's only got one eye."

"I don't *think* pirates have such nice smiles." My flippant response may have been to tease her a little, but in truth, my heart was hammering. It wasn't in my character to ride in carriages with strange men. If my parents were here, they'd disallow it or insist on coming along. I knew the Masons wouldn't treat me the way they'd treat their own daughter, but it was kind of Mrs. Mason to act as my conscience. On this occasion, however, I was going to ignore it. I couldn't afford to be cautious. It wasn't just the pound that was at stake anymore, it was the two thousand American dollars.

Mr. Glass's long legs unfolded from the cabin and he stepped onto the pavement. "Good morning, Miss Steele. Mr. Mason," he added, holding his hand out to Catherine's father. "Pleased to see you again, sir."

Mr. Mason had avoided me all morning. Well, perhaps not *avoided* me. He'd gone to his workshop before I'd woken. While I wanted to know for certain why he no longer thought me a good influence on Catherine, I also didn't want to be told to my face that I was a poor example. My stretched nerves couldn't take any more strain. Besides, I was grateful not to have been thrown out of the house.

Mr. Glass shook the hand of each member of the Mason family as the head of the household introduced them. "You're still looking for your watch's maker?" Mr. Mason asked.

"I am," Mr. Glass said.

"My offer from yesterday still stands. I'll see if I can repair it for you."

"Thank you, but I prefer the original watchmaker himself to do it."

"Most watches don't differ greatly from one another, you know. I'm sure I can manage to work it out if it's one I haven't seen before." He laughed a little nervously, making his jowls shake.

"Not this watch." Mr. Glass folded the carriage step down for me then held out his hand. "Where to first, Miss Steele?"

"Oxford Street, at the Marble Arch end," I said. "Do you know where that is, Mr. Cyclops? It's not far from Mayfair."

Cyclops studied a dirty and much crumpled map spread out on his lap. "I know it. And it's just Cyclops, miss, no mister."

Mr. Mason clasped the button edge of his waistcoat over his stomach. Mrs. Mason was an excellent seamstress and could modify a great many items of clothing, but she couldn't make her husband's waistcoat larger to fit over his increasing girth.

"What makes this watch particularly special?" Mr. Mason pressed. The nervous laughter had died, and he now seemed anxious to catch every word that fell from Mr. Glass's lips.

Mr. Glass bestowed a smile on him, but his shoulders had gone quite rigid. "If I knew that, I wouldn't need to find the original watchmaker."

He climbed in and Gareth folded up the step and closed the door. Cyclops had the horse pulling away from the curb before Mr. Mason could speak another word. The poor man stood there, his mouth open, his eyes darting between Mr. Glass and me. He'd gone a little pale, which hadn't escaped his wife's notice. She clutched his arm but he seemed not to register her presence.

I waved to Catherine through the window and tried not to show her how anxious I felt. By the look on her face, she was anxious enough for us both.

Mr. Glass angled his legs so that they did not touch my skirts. "I hope you're refreshed, Miss Steele. We've a lot to do this morning."

"There are several watchmakers in and around Oxford Street," I said. "Cyclops can remain near Marble Arch and we can walk from there. It will take longer than the morning, however. As you said, there's a lot to do."

He leaned his elbow on the window ledge and rubbed the back of his finger over his lips in thought. Shadows flickered through his tired eyes. "We can return this afternoon after luncheon."

"There are some excellent chop houses in the area. We can dine at one of those and resume our investigation immediately."

"I prefer to return home for an hour or two."

I was about to protest that no one needed that long to eat luncheon, but held it in check. Perhaps long lunches were an American custom. It wasn't my place to disagree with him when he was paying me. Nor was it my place to ask him why he was so tired this morning, although the curiosity would probably force me to at some point during the day.

"As you wish, Mr. Glass," I said. "But we do have quite a lot of watchmakers to visit, and I require some time to myself."

"For shopping?"

"For making inquiries at employment agencies, as well as lodging houses."

He arched his brows. "You're not staying with the Masons?"

I had to tell him at some point that he wouldn't be collecting me from there tomorrow morning, but I hesitated nevertheless. In the end, I could only do it while not looking directly at him. "I don't want to inconvenience the Masons any more than I have."

He was silent a long time in which I could feel his gaze on me as I pretended to take interest in the passing scenery through the window. "You can stay in my house for the duration of your employment," he finally said.

I gasped and snapped my gaze to his. I was lost for words, something that happened rarely.

He smiled, sending my already rapidly beating heart plunging. "Well?" he prompted.

"I... I..." I sounded witless, but I couldn't think of an excuse to refuse him. Live under the same roof as a foreigner who was quite possibly a gunslinger? I'd be mad to consider it. "I shouldn't. It wouldn't be proper."

"You don't seem like you're in a position to worry about what's proper." At my second gasp, he merely shrugged. "Are you?"

"No-o," I hedged, "but it's not polite to point that out to a woman in reduced circumstances."

"My apologies. The rules surrounding politeness here are numerous. I'm not familiar with them all yet."

"You're forgiven."

"So is that a definite refusal of my offer?"

I should say that it was without hesitation. I ought to insist on finding my own accommodation.

But it would be wonderful not to have to worry about it for the week. And living in the same house as Mr. Glass would make it easier to spy on him and learn

42

the truth. If I locked my door at night and slept with a knife under my pillow then I ought to be safe. Besides, the newspaper article didn't say the outlaw attacked women, only stole horses and robbed stagecoaches— aside from the murder, that is. I had nothing of value for him to steal, and I wasn't a lawman. If I learned something that connected him to the man in the newspaper, I would tell only the police and not give him so much as a hint of my suspicions.

"I'll stay with you only if I live in the servants' quarters and you tell everyone that I am your housekeeper or maid," I said.

"I employ charwomen, not maids. My female cousin came over with me and is staying in the house. Does having another woman present make you feel more at ease?"

"Yes, it does."

"Then consider yourself a temporary guest of number sixteen Park Street, Mayfair."

The speed at which the decision had been made was dizzying. It took a moment to sink in that I was about to live like a duchess in one of London's best addresses for a week. When it did finally sink in, I had to bite the inside of my lip to hide my smile.

Mr. Glass didn't hide his. "It's a nice house," he said, his tone teasing. "It's a little larger than what I'm used to, but I like it."

"Thank you," I said. "It's very kind of you. Oh, that reminds me." I opened my reticule and removed his handkerchief. "Thank you for this. I don't know where I'd be without it."

"Glad I could be of assistance."

The way he said it didn't make me feel at all wretched for my situation. On the contrary, I felt like I'd done him a favor by accepting his offer of work. I supposed I had. The only other people who could point out all the watchmakers in the city were already in gainful employment and wouldn't be available for the time-consuming task.

He pocketed the handkerchief and, as his hand moved away, he went to touch the coat pocket that he'd touched several times the day before, only to check himself. He glanced at me and smiled again, but I wasn't fooled. He was looking to see if I'd noticed. I smiled back, pretending that I hadn't.

Cyclops pulled to the side of the road near Marble Arch and Mr. Glass assisted me from the coach. "No more than three hours," Cyclops called down. "Sir."

Mr. Glass held up his hand in dismissal and waited at the curb for the traffic to ease. After a moment, I said, "We'll have to take our chances in that gap."

With one hand holding onto my hat and the other picking up my skirts, we dashed across to the Oxford Street side. "Is the traffic as bad as this where you're from?" I asked as we passed by a draper's shop where a lovely red silk had been displayed to best catch the morning light.

"No," Mr. Glass said.

I tore my gaze away from the silks at his curt answer. It took a moment before I realized he wouldn't want to give me too much information about himself if he were an outlaw. The notion both thrilled and worried me.

"Do you live in a city or village?" I pressed on nevertheless.

"A large town at present, but I've lived all over the world."

"Really? Where, precisely?"

"France, Italy, Prussia, and now America."

"Where in America?"

"Here and there." He sidestepped around a boy carrying an empty crate on his shoulder and waited for me to catch up. He shortened his strides to keep apace with me.

"You mentioned a place in New Mexico," I went on. "Broken Creek, was it?"

"Yes."

"How long did you live there?"

"I didn't live there."

"Then where did you live?"

"You ask a lot of questions, Miss Steele."

"I'm naturally inquisitive, but if I am to live in your house, I'd feel more comfortable if I knew you better." There. That didn't sound at all suspiciously nosy, simply cautious.

"This looks like our first stop," he said, nodding at the sign jutting out from the doorway still some shops away. He was definitely avoiding answering.

Mr. Thompson's shop was not unlike my father's or Mr. Mason's, although somewhat smaller. Rent was higher on Oxford Street and there was no space for a workshop at the back. I happened to know that Mr. Thompson no longer made watches or clocks, but sold ones manufactured in Clerkenwell factories.

Mr. Thompson looked up from the cabinet, where he was rearranging watches, and smiled at Mr. Glass. He turned to me and the smile faded. "Miss Steele! What are you doing here?" He backed away and rounded the counter bench, placing it between us.

"Good morning, Mr. Thompson," I said, stepping up to the counter.

He moved to the side, away from me. I followed, but he moved a little farther again and made a great fuss over the selection of watch chains laid out on a velvet mat. His gaze slid sideways, watching me. I hadn't seen Mr. Thompson in two years, and clearly I hadn't changed or he wouldn't have recognized me. He'd been amiable to me back then, so why this odd behavior now?

"This is Mr. Glass," I said. "He's looking for a particular watchmaker who went to America some five years ago."

Mr. Thompson glanced at Mr. Glass and nodded a greeting.

"He would be older than you are, Mr. Thompson," Mr. Glass said. "Do you know of any watchmakers who were in America around that time? He would be quite old now. Your father, perhaps?"

Mr. Thompson, who was about my father's age, shook his head. "My father was a chandler not a watchmaker. And I don't know anyone who has been to America. Do you wish to purchase a new watch, sir? Or clock?"

"Not today."

Mr. Thompson cleared his throat, looked at me then pointedly at the door. He couldn't have been clearer if he'd shouted, "Get out!" at the top of his voice.

I marched out of the shop, Mr. Glass at my heels. I puzzled on Mr. Thompson's greeting until we reached the next watchmaker, a narrow shop of little more than a door's width wedged between a jeweler and tobacconist.

Mr. Baxter, the proprietor, had been a friend to my father and one of the few to come to his funeral, although he'd not stayed after the ceremony. I expected a hearty, friendly greeting at least, as he was a blustery, generous man whose character was as big as his barrel chest. Yet he too stood behind his counter to speak to me, as if it were a shield to hide behind, if necessary. Unlike Mr. Thompson, Mr. Baxter could hardly look at me, and seemed quite ill at ease, something that I would never have associated with him.

We asked our questions, he gave brief answers, and Mr. Glass and I left without being any closer to finding Chronos. We had to cross busy Oxford Street to get to the next shop on my list, one that I'd been dreading before and felt even more anxious about now, after being received so strangely by both Mr. Thompson and Mr. Baxter. I couldn't even describe their receptions as frosty. It was as if they were wary of me. Perhaps they expected me to argue with them over their refusal to allow me into the guild. They had, after all, voted against my admission, along with the other members.

But it was the next watchmaker on my list who'd been most vehement in refusing me, according to Father after he returned home the night of the vote. Mr. Abercrombie was president of the guild and had held the position for the past few years because no one dared speak against him. He had inherited a fortune as well as the shop from his father and so could afford the best tools and supplies. The queen had purchased a clock from his father some thirty years ago, and Mr. Abercrombie had made an excellent living off the claim ever since. He now boasted the custom of princes and lords and had four staff working for him in his shop alone. He wielded power within the guild, with every other member bowing to his wishes. If he didn't want a watchmaker to belong to the guild, then he wouldn't be allowed in. Every member would vote as Mr. Abercrombie advised. And if a watchmaker couldn't belong to the guild, he couldn't legally sell watches in England. It was why Father had been so upset when my application had been refused—and it explained why he'd given the shop to Eddie instead of me. Eddie, as a man, was admitted.

Abercrombie's Fine Watches And Clocks was triple the size of Mr. Thompson's shop and occupied a prominent corner. Mr. Glass held the door open for me, but I shook my head.

"You go in and ask your questions without me," I said. "My presence is not required."

He glanced back across the street to Baxter's, frowned slightly, then nodded. "Very well."

I watched through the window. The slender figure of Mr. Abercrombie stood in the center of the shop, his hands at his back. With his oiled moustache and pince-nez perched on the edge of his nose, he looked as respectable as any of his royal clients. He directed one of his staff to take Mr. Glass's hat and coat, but Mr. Glass refused. He spoke and Mr. Abercrombie responded with a quizzical expression. He spoke, presumably to offer to look at Mr. Glass's special watch instead. Although his back was to me, I could see Mr. Glass heave a sigh. He must be tired of hearing the same responses.

Mr. Abercrombie spread out his hands to indicate all his wonderful wares. My gaze followed the motion, and I couldn't stop staring at the lovely mahogany long-case clock with the brass dial displayed behind the counter. It was quite a spectacular piece.

Movement caught my eye, and suddenly Mr. Abercrombie came marching through the door. He caught my arm before I could run off.

"It *is* you!" He peered over the top of his pince-nez at me. If the rabid look in his eye didn't make me shrink away, his stinking breath certainly did. "What are you doing here, Miss Steele?"

I swallowed and tried to pull away from him, but he held me too tightly. "I'm just shopping, Mr. Abercrombie. Let me go, please, or I'll scream."

"Go ahead and scream. I'll tell everyone you stole from me."

I gasped. "Why would you do that? Why do you hate me so?"

His only response was to dig his fingers in more. I winced as the nails bit through my sleeve to my skin.

"Unhand Miss Steele," came the low growl from behind Mr. Abercrombie. I hadn't seen Mr. Glass emerge from the shop, but he now appeared over the watchmaker's shoulder, a dark scowl scoring his forehead, his eyes as black as thunderclouds.

"You know her?" Mr. Abercrombie said, not letting me go. "What is this? What's going on?"

"I said, unhand her. *Now*."

If I were Mr. Abercrombie, and Mr. Glass had spoken to me in such a fiersome way, I would have done what he'd demanded—and quickly. But Mr. Abercrombie didn't. "Tell me what it is you really want or I'll accuse her of theft," he said.

"You can't accuse me of stealing when I've nothing of yours," I snapped. "Let me go, Mr. Abercrombie. You're hurting me." The blood had indeed stopped flowing to my lower arm and hand. My fingers throbbed.

Mr. Abercrombie pulled me against him, grinned in my face, and slipped something inside my pocket. I didn't need to look to know that it would be a watch.

"Thief!" Mr. Abercrombie cried. "Someone fetch a constable! I've caught a thief."

CHAPTER 4

Mr. Abercrombie's cry stoked the shoppers and shopkeepers into action. One woman screamed, another pulled her small child to her hip, and doors shut firmly. Three men, however, charged toward us. One, a butcher going by his bloodied apron, held a knife.

"I'm not a thief!" I shouted, desperately trying to pull myself free of Mr. Abercrombie's grip.

His lip curled into a sneer, and Mr. Glass punched that sneer off his face.

The watchmaker's fingers sprang apart, letting me go. He stumbled to the side with a groan of agony, clutching his jaw. Before I could gather my wits and my skirts, Mr. Glass snatched my hand and hauled me away in a sprint. His other hand pressed against his coat, over his inside pocket.

"Stop! Thief!" someone behind us bellowed.

I didn't dare glance over my shoulder. It was difficult enough keeping up with Mr. Glass's pace, as he dodged around those attempting to stop us and other obstacles in our path. The voices behind didn't grow further away, however, no matter how fast we ran.

And I couldn't run any faster. My blasted corset made it impossible to take a deep breath. My chest ached with the need for air. My face felt like it would explode from heat and my throat constricted. I didn't dare ask him to slow down, however. If I were caught, I would go to prison for God knew how long. London's prisons were little better than lice infested, disease soaked hells.

The pedestrians and obstacles thinned as we left the shopping precinct. We found ourselves in a narrow street filled with stables behind Mayfair's grand houses. Coachmen driving empty coaches glanced down at the men still chasing us but didn't stop to help.

A stable boy stepped onto the street ahead and raised his fists. Mr. Glass could have easily pushed the scrappy lad aside, but he darted left under an archway—straight into a yard with no other exits.

He swore in a strong American accent and called London more confusing than a "honeycomb designed by drunken bees". I would have admonished him for his foul language if I had the breath. As it was, I had to fight for every one. My vision turned black at the edges too, and I had to grip his hand tightly to remain steady. Part of me was relieved to stop, yet I knew it meant the end. We were trapped.

The butcher and two others stood beneath the arch, grinning like foxes. "Got you now," the butcher snarled. With his bloodied apron and monstrous knife in hand, he looked as if he were preparing to carve us into bite-sized pieces.

"Turn around now and no one need get hurt," Mr. Glass said in that low, commanding voice he'd used on Abercrombie. It hadn't worked then and it didn't work now. The butcher and his colleagues approached at a steady pace.

I backed up against a brick wall, Mr. Glass at my side. "Can you run?" he murmured.

My breath had not yet returned and little stars danced before my eyes, but I nodded. I had to run. There were no other choices.

"I'll distract them while you slip away," he said. "Skirt around the edge to the archway. Turn left and then right. Wait for me there."

I squeezed his hand, hoping he would understand that I wanted to ask him how he planned on meeting me with three men in the way. But he didn't understand the squeeze, and only pushed me aside to safety.

The butcher and one of his friends closed the distance on Mr. Glass. The third man prowled toward me. Sweat dampened his face and hair, and he breathed heavily. The look in his eyes wasn't one I'd ever seen before. They were glassy, glazed, the pupils taking over most of the whites. He seemed unaware of the fight breaking out near him, and completely focused on me. There was no point trying to tell him there'd been a mistake. I couldn't reason with someone in the grip of feverish madness.

I stumbled backward, but somehow maintained my balance. With arms out at his sides, he licked his lips and advanced on me. I could try to go around, as Mr. Glass had suggested, but I wouldn't be fast enough. I had to engage him and somehow get the upper hand physically.

My best chance was to trip him over. With any luck, momentum would propel him into the wall behind me. To do that, I needed to encourage him to come toward me at a run.

I picked up my skirts and darted to my left. With a twisted grin, he came after me. I ran a little, looking over my shoulder. When he was almost upon me, I dashed to the side and thrust out my foot.

He fell over but didn't hit the wall. I didn't wait to see if he recovered. I ran out through the arch and turned left, then right, where I pressed my back to a wall and gasped as much air into my lungs as I could.

A moment later, running footsteps approached. I got my foot ready again, but it was Mr. Glass. He held the butcher's knife. Without a word, he clasped my hand again, and we ran together down the street.

No one followed. There were no footsteps behind us, only the sound of my breathing—not his—and the distant rumble of carriage wheels. If I'd not been holding Mr. Glass's hand, I would have run into things. The stars in my vision had turned to black spots. As it was, my shoulder bumped a wall as we rounded another corner.

I stumbled, only to be caught by Mr. Glass. My head swam and I couldn't quite see him through the black haze. I felt myself falling and landed on the pavement. Or perhaps he had lowered me. I couldn't be sure of much anymore, except that I needed to breathe or I would pass out altogether.

"Unbutton your waistcoat," Mr. Glass demanded.

I tried to say, "Pardon?" but all that came out was a strangled gasp.

"Unbutton your waistcoat. The dress too."

When I simply stared ahead at his blurry silhouette, hoping that I was somehow conveying my shock at his suggestion, he clicked his tongue. Strong nimble fingers undid my waistcoat. I batted them away, but my swat was ineffective.

Mr. Glass finished with my waistcoat and moved on to the line of buttons down my dress. They proved more difficult to undo quickly and he gave up being delicate with a grunt and a tug. Buttons flew off in all directions, raining on the pavement beside me.

"My apologies, Miss Steele, but if you don't breathe, you'll faint. Or die." He must have removed his gloves at some point because his bare fingers skimmed the swell of my breasts above my corset.

My chest tightened further. Little veins of heat spread across my skin, centering on the place where his fingers lingered. I coughed, and he set to work untying the corset laces at my back. Delicious air rushed into my body, expanding my chest like a balloon. I sucked in breath after breath until slowly the blackness retreated and the dizziness dispersed, leaving me very aware of the man crouching before me—the smooth skin of his cheeks, the warmth of his breath, the flecks of gold in eyes, which continued to watch me with earnestness and something else I couldn't quite read.

His thumb stroked my skin, close to my breast. Part of me wanted his hand to explore, to have it touch me everywhere, to feel his arms around me. The thought of our heartbeats meshing together sent mine racing all over again, but not from lack of breath this time.

Those thoughts were sheer madness. Clearly I was affected from all that vigorous exercise.

"Thank you, Mr. Glass." A whisper was all I could manage.

He blinked rapidly, then removed his hands. Cool air rushed in to replace his warmth, but I could still feel the impression his hands had made on my skin. "Are you well enough to continue?"

"I won't faint, although I need to fix my attire." I quickly reached back and re-tied my corset laces.

"Of course." He collected the buttons and my reticule, which I must have dropped at some point. "I do apologize for..." He cleared his throat. "For everything."

"It's quite all right, but if I hear you mention this to anyone, I'll not only deny it, I will castrate you in the night while you sleep."

He laughed softly. "There's no need to go to such extremes. I would have given my word."

I wasn't sure if the word of an outlaw was worth very much, but kept the quip to myself. He'd saved me, after all.

He tipped my buttons into my reticule as I arranged my jacket over my undone dress as best as I could. I looked up to see him patting his pocket. When he saw me looking, he stopped and gathered up his gloves and the butcher's knife. He held out his hand to me and we stood together.

He quickly turned his head away and touched his fingers to his temples, but not before I saw how pale he'd gone.

"Are you all right, Mr. Glass?" I asked. "Did you overdo it too?"

"I'm fine. Don't fuss."

"I hardly call a little inquiry into your health fussing, particularly when you look peaky."

He huffed loudly. "I'm fine. Let's go. We should move quickly." He handed me the reticule and tucked the knife into the waistband of his trousers. "But there's no need to run. I think we're closer to my house than we are to Cyclops and Marble Arch, so we'll head there."

"Do you know where Park Street is from here?" I asked.

"I do."

"You've been down these streets before?" Since we were still among mews, stables and the businesses that serviced horses and carriages, I was doubtful. Not too many gentlemen would bother to come back here.

"My sense of direction is excellent. We need to go this way."

Since I didn't know Mayfair too well, I let him lead the way. He was still pale, except for the dark circles that had appeared beneath his eyes. He'd seemed well enough only a short time ago, so I didn't think our encounter with the butcher caused it. Rather, he looked as if he hadn't slept properly in days.

"Did you scare those fellows away after you took the butcher's knife?" I asked, looking behind us. There were no sounds of anyone following.

After a few steps, he said, "They were in no condition to follow us."

I gasped. "You hurt them?"

He looked at me sideways. "Does it matter?"

"I...I don't know. They were just law-abiding innocent men, trying to stop someone they thought was a thief." And there were three of them and only one of him. *How* had he beaten them?

"They were vigilantes," he said. "Their kind of justice is never innocent and is rarely law-abiding."

"Perhaps in your country."

He walked on apace and I thought the conversation ended, when he said, "They would have had their sport with you, Miss Steele, before they handed you over to the authorities."

"How do you know that?" But even as I said it, I knew he was right. I'd seen it in the eyes of the man who'd approached me. I shivered and folded my arms over my chest. "Thank you, again, for helping me escape."

"There's no need to thank me."

"There is. I'm also sorry you got involved."

"If it wasn't for me, you wouldn't have been there in the first place. It's as much my fault."

His logic was a little broken since he couldn't have known the reception I'd get. "I still don't understand why Mr. Abercrombie would do such a thing. Why accuse me of stealing?"

"That's what I'd like to know," he muttered so quietly that I almost didn't hear.

"I haven't seen him in years and the whole guild saga resolved itself in his favor. I ought to be the angry one, not him."

"You'll have to explain this guild system to me at home. It's not the first time you've mentioned it."

We entered Park Street and checked up and down the street before advancing.

"Thank goodness you're not known here," I said. "Or the police would be knocking on your door by now." I was safe while I resided with Mr. Glass and kept away from Oxford Street, but once our business was concluded, I would need to be careful. While the Masons wouldn't believe Abercrombie if he told them I stole, I didn't want to involve them if I could help it. "I hope Mr. Abercrombie doesn't get it into his head to search for me and continue with the ridiculous accusation of theft."

"I'll take care of Abercrombie," Mr. Glass said.

"Take care of him how?"

"Leave it to me."

Did he mean to harm Abercrombie? Or threaten him, Wild West style?

I didn't get a chance to ask again. We'd reached number sixteen, a red and cream brick townhouse that stretched up to the gray sky. I peered over the black iron fence running alongside the steps down to the service entrance. The blinds were down and no light rimmed them. It mustn't be the charwoman's day.

Mr. Glass's knock on the main door was answered by a footman or butler. I couldn't tell which because only his head appeared around the door, as if he were hiding the rest of himself.

"It's only you," the man said, opening the door wider. "Just as well. I ain't dressed proper yet."

"Why not?" Mr. Glass said. "It's almost midday. What if we'd had callers?"

"We ain't."

"But we might have." He stepped aside to allow me to pass.

The man, who wore trousers, a shirt and waistcoat only, straightened to his full height. He was only a little taller than me, with a blocky build, square face, and a crooked nose. His two small eyes sparkled like sapphires as they scanned me from head to toe. I felt very conspicuous with my unbuttoned dress beneath my waistcoat.

"Is that her?" he asked in an accent similar to Cyclops's.

"This is Miss Steele, yes. Miss Steele, this is Duke, my butler. Or footman."

"Both?" I said, smiling. "Pleased to meet you, Mr. Duke. Is that a first name, last or title?"

"It's just Duke." He grunted. "Why'd you bring her back here?"

Mr. Glass pushed past him. "Butlers and footmen don't ask questions."

Duke gave another grunt and eyed me from beneath a ponderous brow.

"Miss Steele will be staying here until her work with me is complete."

"But—"

"It's not up for discussion." Mr. Glass rounded on him. "Is that understood? Not a word."

Duke's lips pressed together, but only for a second. "You look dog tired, M— sir." He glanced at me again, focusing on my chest. I hadn't laced myself tightly and my gown was still undone beneath my waistcoat. He must know. "You were supposed to inquire about the watchmaker, not frolic with the lady who's supposed to be helping you."

"Duke!" Mr. Glass snapped.

"I said frolic, not fu—"

"DUKE!"

Duke chuckled. I did my best to look shocked, but it was difficult to keep a straight face. Mr. Glass looked terribly embarrassed, and I'd never witnessed a servant speak so insolently to his master. I didn't think his behavior could be put down to being American. The more servants of Mr. Glass's I met, the more convinced I was that he wasn't truly their employer, but merely acting a role. Perhaps he was their gang leader.

That thought wiped the smile off my face. I swallowed heavily and folded my arms over my chest again. I was beginning to have serious doubts about staying in the house. It had been one thing to sleep under the same roof as Mr. Glass, knowing that Cyclops probably slept in the stables, but quite another knowing this ruffian wouldn't be far away from my bedroom either.

"You've offended Miss Steele," Mr. Glass said to Duke. "Apologize." When Duke hesitated, Mr. Glass whipped out the butcher's knife.

I swallowed my scream and covered my mouth with my hands.

Duke merely grunted again. "Apologies, miss. It was just a joke."

Mr. Glass tossed the knife to his man. Duke caught it easily by the handle. "That might come in handy in the kitchen," Mr. Glass said.

Duke inspected the blade. "There's blood on it."

"Not mine nor Miss Steele's."

"Only you would go out to make simple inquiries and come back with a knife as big as my forearm." He studied Mr. Glass's face closely, then glanced at the long case clock. "You look tired and it ain't quite time to."

"Time to what?" I asked.

"Nothing," they both said.

"Go and fetch Cyclops," Mr. Glass directed his man. "He's waiting for us at Marble Arch."

Duke looked like he would protest, but thought better of it. He plucked a hat off the hat stand then moved past us to the front door.

"When you get back, prepare a room for Miss Steele," Mr. Glass said. "And be sure to dress properly from now on. We have a guest."

"Aye, aye, sir." Duke saluted. "Will there be anything else? Tea, cake, and a watchmaker to go with 'em?"

"Lunch, and stop being an ass. Where's Willie?"

Willie? There were more ruffian servants? God, help me.

"Out," Duke said. "Don't know where." He nodded at the clock. "You better go...rest. I'll see to Cyclops and the room." It was the most sincere he'd sounded since we walked in, like he was genuinely concerned about Mr. Glass getting rest.

He must be ill, or exertion wouldn't have done this to him. He looked even paler now and the shadows under his eyes stood out in bas-relief. Creases had appeared across his forehead and around his mouth where before there'd been none.

"You do look very poorly," I said to him as Duke left. "Please, go and rest. I'll wait in the, er..." I glanced at the door leading off from the entrance hall.

"Drawing room." He gave me a grim smile and indicated the room. "I'll be with you in a few minutes. Make yourself at home, since it will be, for the near future."

I made my way to the drawing room but stopped inside the door. He headed up the stairs, his gait laborious, his head bowed. Once he was out of sight, I followed quietly, looking out for other servants. Mr. Glass stopped at the top of the landing. He seemed out of breath, as if that brief climb had exhausted him. Yet he'd hardly looked like he'd raised a sweat immediately after attacking three thugs. What sort of illness had a delayed onset?

It was all very odd, but it was none of my affair and had nothing to do with my reason for following him. I wanted to find out where his private rooms were located so that I could return another time and look through them for evidence of his occupation in America and his reason for coming to England. There was no better time. He was too ill to notice me and the servants were gone.

I peeked around the corner on the third level and had to dart back quickly. He'd stopped near the end, with his hand pressed against a door and his head lowered. The three flights of stairs had done him in.

When I looked again, I expected to see him gone, having entered, but he was sitting on the floor, his legs stretched out before him, his back to the wall. He held a glowing object in the palm of his hand and a chain dangled from his fingers. It was like he held a small sun and its rays infused his hand with purple light. The light spread along the veins and up into his sleeve, as I'd seen it do in the carriage the day before.

I continued to watch, both fascinated and terrified by the strange phenomenon. Mr. Glass seemed to know what he was doing. He showed no fear. Indeed, he seemed to bask in the object's rays and grow more healthy by the second. Suddenly his chest expanded as he took a huge gasp of air, and the color in his face returned. It no longer looked bloodless, but full of life as the bright glow crept out of his collar and up his neck, to his chin, cheeks and finally his forehead. His face and hands—perhaps his entire body—was a map of fiery, glowing veins.

With another deep breath, he snapped the lid of the object closed, extinguishing the light. He held it up by its chain then tucked it into his inside pocket. Even from a distance, I could see it was an ordinary silver watch.

No; not ordinary. It might look like a simple watch, but there was nothing ordinary about that glow.

Mr. Glass stood and disappeared into the room. He hadn't seen me, thank goodness. I wasn't ready to face him over this secret. For it had to be a secret, or why not tell me about it in the first place, since it was most likely also linked to the watchmaker he wanted help finding.

"Who're you?" The harsh female voice coming from behind me made me jump. My heart almost burst out of my chest. I went to turn to face her, but she grabbed both my elbows and jerked me back against her body. She smelled like tobacco and lilacs, an odd combination to say the least. "And why are you spying?"

CHAPTER 5

"Let me go." I struggled against her but she was damnably strong for a woman. "I've had quite enough of being restrained today." I went to smash my heel down on her toes, but she predicted my move and jumped back without letting me go.

"I said, who are you and why are you spying?" The deep, almost masculine voice, coupled with the smell of tobacco, made me wonder if she was in fact a he after all.

"My name is India Steele and I'm not spying. I'm a guest of Mr. Glass's and I'm looking for the privy."

Her grip loosened enough for me to wriggle free. I turned on her, unsure whether a smile or admonishment was in order. In the end, I couldn't control my wide-eyed stare.

She was definitely a woman. Her figure was as curved as mine and certainly couldn't be mistaken for a masculine one. Yet she wore loose men's trousers and a man's leather waistcoat over a plain white shirt. Her black hair had been arranged in a relaxed style on top of her head, as if she'd slept with it like that. Even dressed in masculine attire, she had a pretty oval face, despite the scowl and pursed lips.

"The privy's that way." She jerked her head in the opposite direction to Mr. Glass's room.

"Thank you." I tried to edge past her, but she caught my arm.

I shook myself free and matched her scowl with one of my own. "I really have had enough of being waylaid today, thank you. Kindly allow me to pass."

She merely folded her arms and widened her stance. "I'm not sure I should until I've spoken to Matt."

"Matt?"

"Matthew. Mr. Glass." So she was on a first name basis with him too. I supposed I should have suspected.

I decided to change tactics and thrust out my hand. "Since there's no one about to make introductions, shall we just introduce ourselves?" I smiled. Her scowl deepened. "My name is India Steele."

"So you said."

"And you are?"

"Not trusting you."

I withdrew my hand. "May I ask why?"

Her scowl disappeared. She cleared her throat and looked somewhat less sure of herself. "You talk like a proper English lady, but you don't dress like one."

I didn't tell her that *she* talked like a woman and dressed like a man. Until I knew how she would accept such quips, it was best to keep them to myself. Particularly since I was in something of a precarious situation while living in the house of a man I didn't trust.

"What do you mean?" I asked.

"You're loose in the general area of your pups."

"Pups?"

She indicated my chest.

"Oh." My face heated and once again I found myself folding my arms over my breasts. "That's why I need the privy. I'm in need of a sewing kit and a private room."

She considered this by twisting her mouth to the side. Hands on hips, she turned and walked off. A few paces away, she stopped and looked over her shoulder at me. "Come on, then."

I followed her. "Thank you, Miss..."

"Willie Johnson. Call me Willie, not Miss Anything. Got it?"

"Er, yes, you stated your wishes very clearly."

She stopped and rounded on me, her face only an inch from mine. "Are you having a joke at my expense?"

I tried not to splutter at the stench of tobacco on her breath. "Not at all." I hoped she believed me. She may be a woman, but I didn't feel any safer with her than with Mr. Glass's other servants. She seemed fiercer than Duke. "Tell me, Miss— Tell me, Willie, are you the housekeeper here? Or the cook perhaps?"

She blinked at me then burst into raucous laughter that had me stepping back to avoid her breath. "Me, cook? Not likely. They'd rather starve than eat my cooking. As to cleaning, no thanks." She snorted then wiped her nose with the back of her hand. I was beginning to wonder if she'd been raised by wild bears. "There you go." She jerked her head at a nearby door.

I opened it but didn't go in. "That's not the privy."

"It's my room. Or one of them. Matt gave me the lady's suite, as he called it, even though I said I didn't need this much space." She indicated I should go in ahead of her. "My needle and thread are in there, but I've thought of something better."

I went in ahead of her. The room was a large sitting room with chaise longue positioned beneath a window, a table, two armchairs by the fireplace, tea table on wheels, a writing desk and empty glass display cabinet. The sage green and cream striped wallpaper matched that of the sofa, and it all matched the tiny green flowers on the curtains and cushions. It was far too feminine for the woman standing beside me. Perhaps that was why it looked like it wasn't used. It smelled like it too, all stale and close. No tobacco, though.

Willie closed the door. "Come with me to my bedroom and undress." She indicated an adjoining door. "Go on, don't get all prim and missish now."

I followed her to the bedroom door, but didn't go in. This room didn't smell unused. Indeed, the scent of lilacs was quite strong here. "I'm not being prim, I'm simply wondering what you have in store for me."

Willie rummaged through a large trunk at the end of her bed and pulled out a brown cotton dress with a lace cream falling collar. She shook it out and held it up for me. "It's real ugly, but it'll fit you."

We were of a size, true, and while the dress wasn't overly pretty, it wasn't ugly either. It had no embellishments whatsoever except for the large collar. It was certainly in a better state than my button-less gown. I would guess it had never been worn. "You're loaning it to me?" I asked her.

"Keep it. I don't wear dresses, corsets and ladies' things. A girl can't run in them, or holster a gun on her hip."

"True, but they're excellent if you want to trip someone over." She gave me a blank look. "Your feet can't be seen beneath these skirts." I gave her a demonstration.

"I'd rather run or fight."

I sighed. "Sometimes, so would I."

I took the gown and she left me alone to change out of my dress and into hers. It fitted well, although was a little short. My ankles were visible. My mother would have made me change out of it if she'd been there, but she was long dead. Besides, beggars couldn't be choosers.

I was checking over my gown to see if any damage had been done to the fabric when Willie walked back in without knocking first. "Christ, it's just a dress. What's taking so long?"

"I'm finished."

Willie scanned me head to toe. "It's still an ugly dress, but it looks better on you than me."

"Er, thank you. I think."

"Leave your outfit in my sitting room and collect it later. I suppose I should be offering you refreshments seeing as you're a guest and all."

"Thank you! A cup of tea would be lovely." I was parched after my exertions, and now that I once more felt suitably attired, I was ready to face the household over a cup of tea.

I only hoped Mr. Glass didn't rest for long. I liked his company, and felt more at ease in his presence. His servants—or whatever they were—made my nerves jump.

Willie led the way back down to the drawing room then disappeared after ordering me to "Wait here." She managed to infuse the words with steel, so that I didn't dare move. She clearly didn't trust me.

And I didn't trust her. Or any of them.

But I would bide my time, for now, and continue investigating later. It wouldn't be wise to get caught outside the drawing room again.

I strolled around the room, which was as pretty as Willie's rooms, although done in blue and gold colors. It too had a stale smell to it, however, that had me wanting to open the windows. After a few minutes of idly inspecting the knick knacks up close, I couldn't stand it any longer. I unlatched one of the window sashes and opened it.

I breathed deeply and watched the glossy black coaches rumble past with distinguished looking gentlemen inside. Elegant ladies dressed in fine gowns walked with parasols in hand to protect themselves from the spring sunshine, and nannies pushed perambulators along the pavement. Nobody hurried. No shopkeepers shouted about how wonderful their wares were, and delivery carts didn't jostle one another for space. It was quite lovely here in Mayfair.

A coach pulled up out the front of number sixteen and Duke hopped down off the coachman's seat where he'd been sitting next to Cyclops. Cyclops spotted me and waved, but Duke, following his gaze, frowned.

"What'd you open the window for?" he called out.

"Fresh air," I called back.

"You call this air fresh?" He looked skyward and screwed up his nose. "You English are mad."

I heard the front door open before he'd even reached it. I leaned out the window to see who'd opened it for Duke, but couldn't quite see.

"Better?" Duke asked.

"Stop fussing," came Mr. Glass's response. "And keep quiet around Miss Steele."

I couldn't hear if Duke warned him that I was standing at the open window or not. The door closed and a moment later, they both strolled into the drawing room. Mr. Glass looked much refreshed. His eyes were bright and his skin had returned to its normal color, not pale or lit up by veins of purple light. He smiled at me. I smiled back, wondering if Duke was supposed to be quiet about the strange watch or something else.

"I see you've changed, Miss Steele," Mr. Glass said. "You must have met my cousin."

I felt the heat in my cheeks rise again at his reference to my attire, even though he didn't mention the reason behind the need to change. Yet I was glad, too, that he'd acknowledged my change of clothing without dwelling on the matter. Indeed, he'd managed to seamlessly change the subject. It was a smooth transition, and I wondered if it had been designed that way to alleviate my embarrassment over our earlier encounter.

"*Willie* is your cousin?" I asked.

"On my mother's side."

"She didn't tell me that. Indeed, she didn't tell me much at all. I thought she was a servant."

Mr. Glass looked pained. "Did she threaten you?"

"In a way. But then she gave me this dress so I suspect everything is fine between us now."

"Wouldn't wager the ranch on that, Miss Steele," Duke said. "She hates dresses. Way she'd see it, you're doing her a favor."

"Then perhaps we can be friends since friends do one another favors."

Duke burst out laughing. "She ain't never had a friend. All the girls are scared of her back home, and most of the men, too."

Mr. Glass nodded. "It's true. She terrifies even me when she flies into a temper. But don't worry, she's rarely home. It's unlikely you'll see much of her while you're staying with us."

"Speak of the devil," said Duke, as Willie walked in carrying a tray laden with teapot, cups and slices of cake. "And look at that! She's gone all womanly on us, too, and made tea. Must be the influence of having a real lady in the house."

"You're lucky I'm holding this tray, Duke, or I'd clock you for that." Willie set the tray down with a loud clunk that rattled the delicate china.

Duke chuckled. "I got a room to make up and lunch to prepare. Come and help me, Willie."

"Do it yourself. I ain't the maid."

"Do *I* look like *I'm* wearing an apron?"

"Duke," Mr. Glass snapped. "Enough. Willie...do whatever you want. As usual."

Duke left, chuckling, and Willie served the tea. The small smile on her lips suddenly faded and she straightened, even though she hadn't finished filling the second cup. Tea spilled onto the saucer from the spout.

"What does he mean, prepare a room?" she asked.

"Miss Steele is without lodgings at present," Mr. Glass said. "I offered her a room here until our business is concluded and we leave London."

She glared at him then turned that glare onto me. "Did you force him into this?"

"No!" I protested, eyeing the teapot. Her white knuckled grip on the handle looked ominous. It wouldn't surprise me if she used it as a weapon.

"You're a dang fool, Matt." She thrust the teapot in his direction, causing the tea to slosh around inside. "A chit bats her eyelashes and flashes her puppies and you're falling over yourself to help her."

Mr. Glass's nostrils flared. "Don't," he growled.

"Well, it's true." Willie sniffed, but some of the wind had been knocked out of her sails. "Even more true when she's all helpless, like Missy here."

"Excuse me," I said, rising. I wasn't tall, but I was taller than Willie. Unfortunately, my superior height didn't concern her. She watched me with an air of amusement, as if she thought my attempt at intimidation was laughable. "First of all, I am not helpless. While I may be without steady employment or accommodation, I can assure you that it's only temporary. Secondly, I didn't *flash* anything at Mr.

Glass. And batting eyelashes is ridiculous. No self-respecting woman would do it."

Willie smirked. "Seems we agree on something."

"I'll finish pouring the tea," Mr. Glass said. "You may go."

Willie folded her arms and sat heavily on the sofa. She sprawled on it with her legs apart, as if she were trying to take up as much space as possible. Considering I'd been sitting on it, I suspected her aim was to force me to move. I squashed myself into the corner, my skirts brushing her knee as I did so.

"I'm staying here," she announced. "You might need saving from her."

"Willie," he growled. "Get out or I'll cut your allowance in half."

She sat forward, hands on her knees, then pushed herself up. "No need to be so mean. I'm only looking out for you, like you done for me so many times."

He sighed and dragged his hand through his hair. It was the most harried I'd seen him all day, and considering what a day it had been, that was quite surprising. "I know, Willie. But right now, I need to speak with Miss Steele. We've got work to do, and I'd rather not waste another minute."

Willie bit her lip then suddenly threw her arms around her cousin. The sudden burst of emotion surprised him as much as me. His brows rose and he took several seconds before he gingerly patted her shoulder as if she were a dangerous animal he wasn't sure how to pet.

"I'll be helping Duke if you need me," she said, pulling away from him.

"Try not to pick a fight with him."

"I will if he will."

Mr. Glass sighed as she walked out of the drawing room.

"She's quite a little whirlwind," I said.

"More like a tornado." But he smiled as he picked up the teapot and continued pouring. "I am sorry for her behavior, Miss Steele. Willie is...difficult."

"She's certainly a unique character."

"Her upbringing wasn't ideal for a young woman. I didn't meet her until we were both fifteen, and by then, it was too late. She was already set in her ways."

"She's been dressing like a man since before she was fifteen?" While Willie's age was difficult to gauge, I gathered Mr. Glass to be in his late twenties when he was in good health. Earlier, before he'd gone upstairs, he'd looked much older.

"She has, and acting like a man, too."

"Why?"

He handed me the teacup but didn't meet my gaze. "She found it's easier to be a temperamental, foul-mouthed man than a temperamental, foul-mouthed woman."

I sipped my tea and set aside thoughts of Willie. They were replaced with thoughts of my new employer and his remarkable recovery. He couldn't have slept in the brief time we were apart, so his restored health must be due to the glowing watch.

"I'm glad to see you looking much better," I said. "I didn't expect you to be up and about for some time. You looked very ill earlier." If he didn't tell me about the watch now then he must certainly want to keep it a secret.

"I keep a tonic in my room," he said, his gaze holding mine. "A little swig and I'm cured." He smiled easily. If I hadn't seen the scene with the watch, I would have been completely taken in by his charming manner. "I know it's not my affair," he continued, sitting down in an armchair opposite me, "but since I'm a sort of accomplice, I'd like to know what that business with

Abercrombie was about. You claimed not to know why he accused you of theft, but surely there must be a reason."

"I don't know. Truly, I don't. The whole episode was very strange and troubling. Father never liked him, I do know that. He called Abercrombie a pompous prig, full of self-importance. Abercrombie's quite rich, you see, and wields a great deal of influence in the Watchmakers' Guild as its master."

"What is this guild?"

"It's one of several craft guilds that have been in operation for centuries here in England. The official title is the Worshipful Company of Watchmakers, but no one calls them that nowadays. There's an Engineers' Guild, a Tailors' Guild, a Carpenters' Guild, a Jewelers' Guild and dozens of others. Everyone who creates something and sells that creation must belong to a company. It's the law. No membership, no license to sell. Don't you have them in America?"

"There are organizations in different states, but they're not as controlling. Is the guild's only function to determine who can and can't sell their goods?"

"They also take care of the widows and families of deceased members with hardship funds, and issue awards for quality workmanship. A member is only eligible for the award if he enters, of course, and there's a fee for entry, but the winners' names are published in all the major newspapers and journals. The custom that generates can be enormous."

"Who decides on a winner?"

"The guild master and other members elected to the committee, which is known as the Court of Assistants. It may not surprise you to learn that Mr. Abercrombie has won both the Best Watch and Best Clock award for the last three years."

"Did he cheat?"

"He probably bought votes or made threats."

"Is that why your father disliked him?"

"One of the reasons." I swirled the tea slowly around my cup and tried to suppress the well of despair that always threatened to spill over whenever I thought about Father, the guild, and losing our shop to Eddie. "When Father became ill, he encouraged me to apply for membership. He knew that in order to keep the shop operating on my own, after his death, I would have to belong to the guild. They refused my application."

"Did you have the necessary qualifications?"

"Of course. I'd been Father's apprentice for years. The entry test requires the applicant to disassemble a watch mechanism and put it back together again. It's very simple, and I would have passed easily, but I wasn't given the opportunity. They threw out my application without even considering it."

"Why?"

"Because I'm female."

He considered this with a frown. "But I've seen female shopkeepers here who I'm sure make their own wares—dressmakers, jewelers, milliners. Don't they need to belong to their respective guilds too?"

"They do, but their companies allow women. The Watchmakers' Guild doesn't."

"Why not?"

"You ought to ask them. It's ridiculous. I'm an excellent watchmaker, but they seem to think I would make an inferior product and devalue their reputation." It still made my blood boil to think about it. Their logic was flawed and archaic, but there was nothing I could do. An overhaul of their bylaws could only be started if all members agreed to a vote.

"Ah. I see, now," he said.

"See what?"

"Why your father left the shop to Hardacre. He must have seen it as the only way to keep the shop for you, assuming you would soon marry him."

"Except that we didn't marry," I bit off. "Eddie tricked Father, and me too." I would never be tricked again by a two-faced, lying little turd.

"He must have been quite believable," he said quietly.

"He was, but it doesn't excuse my own blindness." The truth was, I'd wanted to believe that Eddie loved me. I was twenty-seven and had never known the affections of a man. A year ago, I'd given up hope of marriage and embraced spinsterhood. And then Eddie breezed into my life with his easy smiles, handsome face, and eagerness to please. Nothing was too much trouble or too dull, from accompanying me to the market to watching me fix a clock in the workroom.

Yet he'd never laughed at the jokes I laughed at. I should have taken that as a sign that he wasn't for me, at the very least. A lifetime without laughter would have been sheer drudgery. It was a testament to my desperation that I agreed to marry him, despite his lack of humor.

Mr. Glass set his teacup down and shifted in his chair. The silence stretched uncomfortably, and I wished we hadn't raised the subject of Eddie at all. I concentrated on sipping my tea until finally Mr. Glass spoke.

"Does the Watchmakers' Guild keep records of previous members?"

"I suppose so, but I'm not sure how helpful their register would be in finding your watchmaker when you don't know his name. I think we can be quite sure it isn't Chronos."

"Agreed." He sighed. "Shall we discuss the route we'll take this afternoon?" He pulled a folded piece of paper out of his pocket and moved his teacup aside to make space on the table. The paper turned out to be a map of London.

"Are you sure you're up to going out again this afternoon?" I asked.

His shoulders tensed. "Of course. There's nothing wrong with me."

"But—"

"The map, Miss Steele. Please point out where you think we should go next."

I sighed and studied the map. "We'll try the area south of Hyde Park and over to Westminster," I said, drawing a circle with my finger around the area. "That should be enough for today."

"Out of the way of Oxford Street," he said with a nod of agreement.

"Yes," I said quietly. "Well away."

"We'll stop by the Masons' and retrieve your belongings while we're out."

"And mention the trouble Mr. Abercrombie is trying to stir up. I couldn't bear it if they heard the rumors from another source first, or if Mr. Abercrombie approached them looking for me."

"He won't pursue the matter." He folded the map and returned it to his pocket.

"You can't be sure of that."

He gave me a crooked smile that was full of mischief and mystery. "Yes, I can."

***

The afternoon's visits brought us no closer to finding Mr. Glass's watchmaker. Fortunately, I was neither attacked nor snubbed, although that could have been because I remained in the carriage most of the time. I only got out at Mr. Healy's shop, to stretch my legs and see how he fared. He'd been a good friend to Father and kind to me on the day of the funeral. I wanted him to know that I was well. I was relieved when he greeted me with a smile.

We stopped at the Masons' home in the late afternoon, and Mrs. Mason welcomed us with a cup of tea and slices of walnut cake. "Gareth, take this to your Papa and brother in the shop," she said, handing her son a tray laden with teapot and cake.

Gareth disappeared and a few minutes later, Mr. Mason returned alone, carrying his teacup. He greeted us with strained smiles and shook Mr. Glass's hand.

"Any success?" he asked.

"Not yet," Mr. Glass said. I was glad to see that he wasn't overset with tiredness this afternoon. He looked quite well. "But Miss Steele assures me we've only scratched the surface. I had no idea London was so large."

"It's Europe's grandest city," Mr. Mason said with a puff of his chest.

"Aside from Paris," Catherine said dreamily. "I do so wish to see Paris one day, don't you, India?"

"I've never thought about it before," I said. "I suppose so, but I doubt I'll ever leave London. I only speak English, for one thing, nor do I know anyone outside this city."

Catherine huffed out a small breath. "You're so conventional all the time."

I blinked at her. By conventional, I suspected she meant dull. Was that how she saw me? As a prim spinster with no dreams, no ambitions or hopes? Was that how *everyone* saw me?

"Paris is indeed a beautiful city." Mr. Glass's rich, deep voice broke into my self-centered thoughts.

"You've been there?" Catherine leaned forward, her teacup pausing on its way to her lips.

"I lived there, many years ago."

"How thrilling."

"That's enough, Catherine," Mr. Mason chided. "Mr. Glass has more important things to discuss than your flights of fancy. Paris is not for the likes of you."

Catherine slouched back against her chair with a pout. I gave her a sympathetic smile, but she looked away.

The conversation stalled, so I decided to get to the point of our visit. "Mr. Glass has offered me lodgings in his house," I told the Masons. "I've come to collect my things."

Catherine's jaw dropped but she quickly recovered. "Marvelous! Come upstairs and we'll fetch them together."

Mrs. Mason *tsk tsk*ed. "I'm sure the arrangement is all very respectable," she said, "but I feel I must protest. What will people think?"

"India knows what she's doing," Mr. Mason said quickly. "Don't fret, my dear."

His wife glared at him. He sipped his tea.

"They won't think anything, because nobody I know will find out," I said hotly. "Even if they do, does it matter? My future is already ruined. Eddie saw to that. A little scandal won't taint me further."

Mrs. Mason *humph*ed and bustled about, collecting teacups and plates, her cheeks pink. No doubt she was contemplating all sorts of lurid scenarios involving Mr. Glass and myself. They were probably similar to the ones I'd contemplated myself, particularly after the corset incident. Sometimes my skin still felt as if it bore the impressions of his hands.

"I understand your concerns," Mr. Glass said. "And I'm glad Miss Steele has good friends in you both. But rest assured, my cousin, Miss Willemina Johnson, is staying with me and will act as chaperone. She's a respectable, responsible woman of high moral character and will insure that Miss Steele is treated with courtesy at all times. Miss Steele, would you say my description of Willie is accurate, based on your first impressions?"

They all looked to me. Fortunately my cheeks no longer felt hot, but I had a devil of a time keeping a straight face. Willie probably would have fallen over with laughter herself if she'd heard her cousin's description. "She's all that and more," I assured the Masons. "She's very sweet and kind."

Mr. Glass smiled at me. Hopefully I was the only one who noticed the wicked gleam in his eyes.

"I intend to look for more permanent lodgings and employment in the coming days," I said. "I don't want to burden your good selves any further."

"You're no burden, India," Catherine said, touching my knee.

"Not at all," Mrs. Mason said, after an awkward moment. Her husband sipped his tea.

"That's settled then," Catherine said, standing. "Come, India, let's get your things."

Up in her room, she helped me pack while I told her that the hem of my dress had come down so Willie had loaned me one of hers until I could repair it later. She hardly seemed to be listening.

"He's so lovely," she eventually said, closing my valise and fixing the clasp in place.

"Mr. Glass? I hadn't noticed."

"Tosh! Of course you have. And to think, you're going to stay with him in his house. What an opportunity!"

"I know what you're referring to, Catherine, and I think you've gone mad. I am not going to throw myself at Mr. Glass."

"Perhaps he'll throw himself at you."

That had us both laughing until we collapsed on the bed, out of breath.

Once recovered, we headed back down to the parlor with my valise. I touched Catherine's hand before we went in, wanting some sort of reassurance from a person I knew and trusted. Despite our laughter, I was anxious about staying in Mr. Glass's house. He and the other members of his household were nothing like us. They were bold and brash, and they talked about holsters and...pups. They could be outlaws. I could be walking into something too deep to dig myself out of.

Catherine squeezed my hand in sympathy, although she didn't know the real reason behind my anxiety. She must think me nervous about the possibility of ravishment.

Catherine and her parents walked us to the door. I hugged each of them in turn and promised to see them again soon. All except Mr. Mason hugged me enthusiastically. "One other thing," I said before we left. "Has Mr. Abercrombie been here asking after me?"

"Miss Steele, there's no need," Mr. Glass said with a hard glare and shake of his head. "It'll be taken care of by the morning."

"Abercrombie?" Mr. Mason said. "No. Why?"

"It's of no consequence," Mr. Glass cut in.

"Actually, it is," I said. "He tried to have me arrested for theft."

"Good lord!" Mrs. Mason pressed her apron hem to her chin. "That's awful."

I briefly explained the event and assured them I hadn't stolen anything from him. "I just wanted you to know from me before you heard it from someone else." Although Mr. Glass had assured me everything would be taken care of, I couldn't see how. I needed to protect myself, and that meant involving the Masons.

"Of course, of course." Mr. Mason nodded excessively, which only set his jowls off like a bowl of jelly. He looked quite worried, and that had me worried.

"If Abercrombie does come here looking for you, we won't tell him where you've gone," his wife said.

I smiled at her and tried to catch her husband's eye but he wasn't looking at me. "Thank you."

Mr. Glass stored my valise at the back of the coach while I climbed inside. He climbed in after me and the coach lurched forward.

"It wasn't necessary to mention the incident with Abercrombie," he said. "I *will* see that he doesn't trouble you again."

"I don't see how you can do that. Perhaps if you shared how you would see to it, I might have more faith."

He plucked off his gloves, finger by finger. "I have some influence in this city."

"But you've never been here before!"

"That's irrelevant."

I clicked my tongue. It was easier to get answers from statues. "Forgive my doubt, Mr. Glass, but I find it difficult to trust someone who doesn't give satisfactory explanations."

His brow crinkled. His gaze locked with mine. "I hope that's not true, Miss Steele." His low, deep voice rumbled from his chest. "I don't want you to feel unsafe in my home."

"Oh." I waved off his concern. "That's another matter entirely."

"I know Willie, Duke and Cyclops are...different to you English folk, but you have my word that they won't harm you."

"I'm glad to hear it."

"Unless you cross them."

I went very still. Did he know that I suspected him? Was he warning me not to act on my suspicions?

He smiled, and I didn't detect any falseness in it; not that I was an expert at reading people. Look at how I'd been taken in by Eddie.

We arrived back at Mr. Glass's Mayfair home and I was glad to see that my room was ready. It was spacious and decorated in wallpaper of pink climbing roses with matching cushions on the bed. It commanded a pretty view over the street, way down below. I'd never been up so high, and looking out the window made me feel uneasy. I stepped back but kept it open for the air. The room, like many of the others, smelled stale. It would seem the house had been shut up for a long time before Mr. Glass's arrival.

Someone had laid my dress on the bed so I emptied my reticule of the buttons. I found my sewing kit in my valise, but quickly ran out of thread. With a deep breath to fortify my nerves, I left the room to go in search of Willie. I hoped she wouldn't accuse me of spying again if she came across me outside my room.

I headed down a flight of stairs to her suite, but no one answered my knock. She was probably in the kitchen, preparing the evening meal, or helping Duke. I gazed up the corridor toward Mr. Glass's door, but decided against knocking. He might be resting.

I made my way down the winding staircase to the ground floor and peeked into rooms. All empty. The kitchen was below ground level, and I finally found the door leading to the service stairs hidden in a wall near the back of the house. Voices filtered up to me, first Willie's then Mr. Glass's. I paused on the last step upon hearing Willie's stinging words.

"I don't like her," she said. "She's a hoity toity miss who thinks she's better than all of us."

"You're being childish," Mr. Glass chided. "Miss Steele isn't like that at all."

Willie snorted. "Why'd you bring her *here,* anyway? You could have paid for lodgings somewhere else. She didn't have to come under *our* roof."

"I agree with Willie," said Duke. "Letting the Steele woman live here is dangerous. She might see something she shouldn't."

"Or Matt might do something *he* shouldn't," said Cyclops with a deep chuckle.

"Shut your trap, Cyclops," Willie snapped. "Matt ain't interested in the likes of her. What's she got to offer him that other ladies don't?"

Cyclops's low chuckle filtered out to me. I wished I could see the others' reactions, particularly Mr. Glass's.

"I wanted her here for a reason," Mr. Glass said. "Not that reason," he added quickly. "There's something about her. I can feel it. Or, rather, the device can."

"The device can?" Duke echoed.

"When she's nearby, the watch becomes warmer. I can feel it through my shirt."

"That's ridiculous," Willie said. "It can't do that."

"How would you know?" Duke sneered. "But Matt...is that all? Does it glow or something?"

"No, but I'm convinced she's more than a simple watchmaker's daughter. She *must* be, or why would all the other watchmakers in the city be afraid of her?"

Afraid of me? That was overstating it a little. They did seem unnaturally wary of me, however, for reasons I couldn't fathom. Even Mr. Mason. The only one who treated me as he'd always done was Mr. Healy.

"She's staying here," Mr. Glass announced, "because she's of use to me. So be nice. *All* of you, Willie."

Was that why he was being gentlemanly to me? Was that why he'd saved me from Mr. Abercrombie's clutches? Because he suspected I was useful to him? While I'd never expected to become friends with him, I had thought we shared an amiable connection. Now, I wasn't sure what I felt or whether I could trust his pleasant manner. It sounded like it was all an act to lull me into trusting him.

But to what end, I didn't know. I had nothing worth stealing and there was certainly nothing special about me, no matter what he thought. Nothing special at all.

CHAPTER 6

Dinner was an unusual affair. Duke had prepared sole, followed by roasted pork, potatoes, salads, and finishing with jelly. The unusual part was that he and Cyclops dined with Mr. Glass, Willie and myself in the dining room instead of the servants' quarters.

"This is delicious, Duke," I said, casting him a smile.

His cheeks flushed and he concentrated on his plate of food. "Thanks," he mumbled.

"Should be," Willie said, stabbing a slice of pork with her fork. "He spent all afternoon on it to impress you."

Duke rolled his eyes. "It takes all afternoon to prepare something like this. Not that you would know. You burn everything."

"Where did you learn?" I asked quickly before the conversation descended into an argument between them.

"Here and there." He stuffed his mouth full of potato. I gathered that meant he didn't want to answer any more questions about his cooking.

"Cyclops, did you collect our tickets?" Mr. Glass asked his coachman.

"Aye, after I brought you back here, I went to the booking office," Cyclops said.

"Finally!" Willie licked pork grease off her lower lip. "I was beginning to think we were going to stay in this miserable country forever. When are we going home?"

"Next Tuesday." Cyclops's one clear eye focused on Mr. Glass. "As long as all goes well and we find him."

"We will," Mr. Glass said, cheerfully. "Won't we, Miss Steele?"

"I, er, hope so," I said. Unless the watchmaker was dead, or living elsewhere. The more I thought about all the reasons why he wouldn't be in London, the more doubtful of success I became. He could be anywhere in the world. "But what happens if we don't find him in a week? Will you still return to America?"

The resulting silence was so complete that even chewing ceased. Duke, Willie and Cyclops all glanced at Mr. Glass. Mr. Glass studied his wine but did not drink.

"You'll find him, Miss Steele." Willie pointed her knife at me. "Or else."

"Willie," Mr. Glass said with effort. "If we fail to find the watchmaker, it won't be Miss Steele's fault."

Willie sniffed then gulped down the contents of her wineglass. "Just find him," she growled, setting the glass down hard. "You can't afford not to."

Again, nobody spoke, and again Mr. Glass pretended not to notice everyone staring at him. Cyclops looked worried, Willie seemed angry, but Duke's reaction interested me most. His eyes moistened. When he saw me watching, he quickly lowered his head, and shoveled another potato into his mouth.

"Goodness me," I said, brightly. "You all seem rather distressed by the thought of not finding the watchmaker." I hoped I wasn't stirring a bees nest, but

I would seem more suspicious to them if I *didn't* say something at this juncture. "Your watch must be very special indeed if only one man in the world can fix it, and the thought of not finding him elicits such concern."

"It is," Mr. Glass said with a flat smile. "Now, Miss Steele, please tell us about yourself."

His sudden change of topic didn't surprise me, but turning it on to me did. "There's nothing to tell. I'm quite dull."

"I find that hard to believe. The watch and clock business here in London seems lively. Everyone seems to know everyone else. Is that how your parents met? Was your mother from a watchmaking family?"

Ah, now I understood. He was fishing for information about my other grandfather, in the hope he might be the watchmaker he sought. It would seem I was only of interest to Mr. Glass in relation to his glowing watch. It stung a little to realize that, but I shouldn't have been surprised. My life *was* dull, and so was I, by extension. "My mother's father was a confectioner. He had a shop near where my father lived growing up. Father bought sweets every day just so he could speak to her."

Mr. Glass smiled and opened his mouth to say something, but Willie got in first. "Delightful," she said in a dreadful attempt at an English accent. "Now, if you'll excuse me, I'm going out." She wiped her mouth with the back of her hand, plucked the napkin off her lap, and stood.

"Is that wise, Willie?" Mr. Glass asked darkly.

"Nope, but being wise is for virgins and dullards." She tossed me a smile.

"It's also for the living." I smiled back at her. "And those who wish to remain so. Enjoy your evening, Willie."

Instead of looking offended, Willie's grin broadened. She squared up to face me. "Care to join me, Miss Steele? I could teach you how to win at poker."

"No," Mr. Glass snapped before I got a chance to speak. "Miss Steele does not care to join you for poker. Nor should you be out playing all night. It's not safe, and it's not seemly. Things are different here in England."

She snorted. "That's true. But one thing is the same, Matt—I am a free woman who can do as she pleases. Goodnight, all. Enjoy your evening of reading and polite conversation. I'm off to win me some English money."

"If you're not back by dawn, I'm coming to fetch you," Mr. Glass called after her.

She gave him a rude hand gesture that I'd only ever seen youths give to constables behind their backs.

"Forgive me, Miss Steele," he said once Willie was out of earshot. "I shouldn't have answered for you."

Yet it had seemed like a natural thing for him to do. Perhaps he was used to giving orders and having them obeyed. Except by Willie.

"I don't have to watch my cousin back home," he said. "She plays poker with a group of regulars, most nights. None would dare harm her."

"Why?"

His mouth worked, but no words came out.

Cyclops answered for him. "They're scared of Matt."

I blanched. I'd expected to hear that they were scared of Willie, not her rather charming cousin. I tried to think of something to say, but in the end, I simply kept silent.

Mr. Glass laughed and waved off Cyclops's answer. Cyclops scowled in return. "I'm worried Willie's smart mouth will get her into trouble," Mr. Glass told me.

"She seems like the sort who can get herself *out* of trouble well enough," I said.

"You should let her hear you say that. She'd like you more for it." He sighed and passed a hand over his eyes. "The class of men she's playing against here are more cunning than the cowboys she's used to. They act all charming and gentlemanly, but they're not. They're devious."

I wondered if he was speaking from direct experience or observation only. He hadn't been on our shores long, but he'd clearly come into contact with charming gentlemen who turned out to be devious.

The similarity to himself struck me like a blow. He may not be English, but he was acting the part of a gentleman around me. The more I got to know him, the more I suspected it was all a charade. Few open, innocent gentlemen could thrash three armed thugs, or instill fear in American cowboys. An outlaw, on the other hand, could.

"Willie'll be fine," Duke said to Mr. Glass. "If she gets arrested, we'll just crack her out of jail like we did that time in Tombstone."

I gasped. "You broke her out of jail? Or a cemetery?"

"Holding cell," Cyclops said with a shrug. "Tombstone is a town."

"Strange name for a town."

"Willie was innocent," Duke assured me.

Good lord. I felt as if I'd stepped into a sensation novel.

"Apologies, Miss Steele. I see we've alarmed you," Mr. Glass said.

"Not at all. I'm not easily alarmed."

"So I've seen," he said with a hint of admiration and a warm smile. "Few women would have had the presence of mind to trip a man up when she was cornered. Indeed, most would have spent the rest of the day recovering from the ordeal you endured this morning."

"I suppose." I couldn't look at him. His praise was too much, and that intense look in his eyes was back again, as if he were reliving the moment he'd parted my corset and laid his hands on my bare skin.

"A brave lady," Cyclops said, raising his glass in salute. "You'd be well suited to the Wild West, Miss Steele."

"Thank you, but it sounds a little too wild for my tastes."

Mr. Glass rose. "Perhaps I should go with Willie."

"No," both Cyclops and Duke said. They both glanced at me.

"Check the time." Duke nodded at the broken clock on the mantel. The hands hadn't moved all night. "It's late. Isn't it, Cyclops?"

"Too late for someone who's been unwell," Cyclops agreed.

Mr. Glass came around the table and held his hand out to me. I took it and rose. "I have to go out anyway."

"Why?" Duke asked.

"To make sure Abercrombie doesn't pursue his foolish claim of theft. Miss Steele is innocent, and I intend to make sure nothing comes of his accusation."

I gaped at him, but he merely smiled. His thumb stroked my hand in a most intimate fashion, sending my heart into little somersaults in my chest. I decided against protesting yet again over his need to do anything about Abercrombie. It was in my best interests to let him think that I trusted him.

"May I take that clock to my rooms tonight?" I asked instead. "I'd like to try and fix it."

"Of course." He plucked it off the mantel and handed it to me. "I wound it, but it still refuses to work."

I returned to my room with the clock and pulled out the pieces of the mechanism, laying each of them carefully on the table. I fished out the toolkit from my valise and cleaned each wheel, lever, and pin with a cloth. I took my time, finding comfort in the soothing task that came so naturally to me. I'd been cleaning mechanisms for as long as I could remember. After nearly an hour, I discovered the culprit—one of the springs had snapped. The clock couldn't be fixed until a spare had been purchased.

I set the pieces aside and contemplated what to do next. With Willie and Mr. Glass out, and Cyclops most likely driving him, I decided to go about searching for proof that Mr. Glass was the outlaw mentioned in that newspaper article. If I wanted the reward, I must earn it before anyone else did. Besides, I also wanted a knife.

Candlestick in hand, I headed downstairs, not quietly or suspiciously but as though I had need of a cup of tea. I found Duke snoring loudly on the sofa in the drawing room, his boots off and his arms across his chest. I continued on to the kitchen and removed a knife from the drawer. I'd just slipped it up my sleeve when someone cleared their throat behind me.

I spun round, my gasp caught in my chest. Mr. Glass stood in the doorway, one shoulder against the doorframe, arms and ankles crossed. He looked as if he'd been there for some time.

"You're back," I said lamely.

"I am." His face was in shadow, but I could just make out the curve of his lips as he smiled. It was not a warm smile designed to reassure me. It was roguish and knowing, as if he was warning me that he knew what I was up to.

I swallowed hard. "Did you speak with Abercrombie?"

He pushed off from the doorframe and prowled into the kitchen. "I never said I was going to speak with him."

"Oh." I backed away as he came closer. His smile widened ever so slightly. "What about Willie?"

"She can take care of herself for one night. I wanted to come straight home."

He kept advancing, and I continued to back away from him, although my retreat was pointless. There were no exits behind me.

"Oh," I said again. My voice sounded breathy, girlish. "I was about to put on some tea," I said, more boldly. "Would you like a cup?"

"No, thank you."

I felt the warmth of the range behind me and stopped. I needed to face up to this man and show him I wasn't afraid, or he might wonder *why* I was afraid. "Can you point to where the teacups are located?"

"Are you sure you want tea?" His voice was a purr that I found mesmerizing. "Or did you come down here looking for something else?"

"Tea," I said, weakly. "Definitely tea."

He was very close now, his feet touching the hem of my skirt. I only came up to his shoulder. My candle may have been on the table now behind him, but I could still make out the fierce intensity in his gaze as it locked with mine. I couldn't look away. Didn't want to.

My heart hammered against my chest, drowning out all sensible thoughts, leaving me only with mad ones. Ones where I imagined myself kissing Mr. Glass and being kissed in return.

As if he'd read my thoughts, his fingers touched mine. He caressed my palm and stroked upward to the underside of my wrist. He traced my throbbing vein and tugged aside the lace cuff of the dress. His finger continued up, up, until it touched the point of the knife.

He didn't flinch, didn't reel back in surprise. He knew it had been there the entire time. He continued to watch me with those deep, dark pools.

I did not pull away, despite my brain screaming at me to run. My heart protested, too, by slamming into my ribs. I couldn't move. Dared not. Running would invite him to catch me, and what he might do to me if he did scared me as much as it thrilled me.

"Careful, Miss Steele." The thick, velvety tone held more humor than threat, yet it did nothing to settle my nerves. "It's hot in here. Don't get burned." He backed away, leaving the knife concealed up my sleeve, then turned. Clearly he wasn't concerned that I'd throw the blade into his back. "Teacups are in that cupboard there," he said, walking out. "Don't stay up too late. I want an early start in the morning."

He was gone as suddenly as he'd appeared. I had to sit down on the stool by the stove or risk falling down, my legs were so weak. My chest heaved to gasp in air, as if I'd run all the way from Oxford Street again. Finally, after a few minutes, the fog receded from my head and I was able to think again and not simply *feel*. But all I could think was that my reaction to him had been sheer madness. Never had I been reduced to a trembling ball of nerves over a man.

Never had I felt so alive in the presence of one, either, or so desirable.

That last thought shocked me to the core and had me racing out of the kitchen again before he came back. I ran up to my room, shut and locked the door, and slipped the knife under my pillow.

I didn't trust him before and I certainly couldn't now. He must know that I suspected him but, perhaps worse than that, he'd proved to both himself and to me that he had the power to turn me into a brainless twit who fell far too easily under his thrall.

Even if he wasn't an outlaw, he was still very dangerous.

**

I awoke feeling more determined than ever to collect the reward for Mr. Glass's arrest. Proving he was the Dark Rider would not only make me richer to the tune of two thousand American dollars, it would prove that I wasn't going to be manipulated. He was employing me as his guide, but that was all. I wasn't going to fall for his charm then protect him from the authorities. I was going to point them in his direction.

All I needed now was proof that he was the outlaw mentioned in the newspaper. No matter how much I needed the reward money, I couldn't send the wrong man to the gallows.

Mr. Glass seemed distracted by the thoroughly uninteresting scenery outside the carriage window this morning. We were heading back to Westminster, to finish questioning the watchmakers we didn't get to the day before, and we'd not yet exchanged more than polite greetings. It made the slow drive through traffic unnerving. I wanted to break the ice, but I didn't know how. I was still reeling from our kitchen encounter, and my brain wasn't yet functioning properly. It was most disconcerting, and I didn't like it.

"The weather appears to have closed in," I said. When in doubt, discuss the weather, so my mother always said. "We shouldn't complain after our run of pleasant days, but it's a shame nevertheless."

His gaze swept up and down the street before he finally tore it away. He sat back, a frown on his brow. "I'm sorry, Miss Steele, I'm a little distracted this morning."

"Any particular reason?"

He suddenly grinned. It was a breathtaking sight. "The possibility of an attack by knife is on my mind."

"If that were the case, then your attention should be on the inside of the coach rather than outside it."

"Indeed." His eyes glittered with amusement. Clearly he didn't think me a threat.

"I hope you understand that I wasn't going to use it on you, specifically."

"Then who, specifically, were you going to use it on?"

"Anyone who tried to come into my room. I am a woman alone in a house with strangers, three of whom are men and one woman who doesn't seem to like me very much. I'm sorry if that offends your sense of honor, but I'm simply being cautious."

The smile disappeared from his face. I was sorry to see it go. "I understand completely. You are a woman alone in the world, thrust into a household full of people you hardly know. I'm not offended, I'm an admirer. You're remarkable."

He ought to have stopped after the first sentence. The rest of his praise was a little too thick to be believable. Coupled with a gentle smile that didn't seem quite genuine, it was all too much. I'd had enough. I wanted him to know I could see through his act, both last night's and today's, if only it would make him stop the ridiculous charade. "Please, Mr. Glass, such overly effusive praise isn't necessary."

"I wouldn't call it overly." He leaned forward and clasped my hand in both of his. "Miss Steele, I am sincere."

I snatched my hand away. "Stop it," I snapped. "I'm not sure if you're attempting to seduce me or merely befriend me, but let's be clear. I am not a simpering female who falls for pretty words, flashy smiles and heated gazes."

To my surprise, he started laughing, but there was a hard edge to it. "Is that so. Then how *did* Hardacre win you over?"

I bristled. My relationship with Eddie was none of his affair and it was the height of rudeness to bring it up. Yet I felt compelled to answer. I'd wanted Mr. Glass to shed his false gentlemanly manner, and now that he had, I must bear the consequences. "I considered my options thoroughly before accepting his hand. Eddie was always pleasant and agreeable. Unfortunately, he was a far better actor than you. I couldn't see past his words, smiles and gazes until it was too late. Or perhaps I've learned a few things about men since then and am wiser now."

"Or you're just a terrible judge of character. You were wrong about him, so perhaps you're wrong about me, too. It's a shame, but you'll never know if I genuinely want to be your friend." He sighed theatrically and returned to gazing through the window. "Pity."

Ugh. The man was worse than I thought.

The rest of the drive seemed to take hours, but a quick check of the watch I kept in my reticule showed that it had only been fifteen minutes when Cyclops stopped the coach outside Underwood Watches And Clocks. I remained in the coach since Mr. Underwood knew me.

Mr. Glass didn't remain inside for long, and returned to the coach after only a few minutes. He paused before climbing into the cabin, his gaze on something behind us. I turned to look out the rear window but there was only a hansom cab pulling away without a passenger.

"What is it?" Cyclops called down from his perch.

"Nothing," Mr. Glass said. "Drive on." He climbed in and settled on the seat across from me.

"Any luck?" I asked, the first words either of us had spoken to the other since our frosty discussion. Hopefully it would put an end to the silence.

"None," he said with a sigh. "Mr. Underwood is about the right age, but he's not Chronos. His nose is too large, for starters."

"Did he know anyone who might fit the description?"

"No, but I got the feeling he was lying."

"Why would he lie?"

His gaze flicked to me then outside. He stroked the bottom edge of the window with his finger. "The trick is, how to get him to tell us what he knows."

"Are you quite sure he was lying?"

"Yes." His finger stilled. "Do you know anything about him that we could use as leverage?"

"Leverage? Do you mean to blackmail him?"

I got the feeling he was trying very hard not to roll his eyes. "No, I mean leverage. Blackmail is far more sinister. I don't wish to harm him."

"Just use him."

"Access his information."

"Information he doesn't want to give you."

"Do you, or do you not, know anything about Mr. Underwood that we can use to...encourage him to tell us what he knows?" His tone was far more forceful and less patient than any he'd used with me before. I felt as if I needed to reward him for being himself around me.

"I don't, but I know someone else who may know the fellow Mr. Underwood is referring to."

"Do you think he'll reveal the information?"

"He may. Mr. Glass, is there something about your watchmaker that you're not telling me? Something that gives him a reason to remain anonymous?"

His finger resumed its slow progress along the bottom edge of the window where glass met wood. "Nothing."

"I don't believe you."

His lips flattened. I arched my brow at him in a challenge and he swore quietly. "It's not for me to divulge his reasons. They're his."

I gasped. "Is he an outlaw?"

"No. Now, no more questions, please. It's not my place to give answers. So where can we find this old watchmaker you know?"

"Across the river." I gave him directions and he opened the window and passed them on to Cyclops. Cyclops called back that he could work out the way using his map, thank you very much.

Mr. Glass returned to his seat. "What's the information that I can use as leverage?"

"It'll be better coming from me," I said. "I'll come into his shop with you."

"Is that wise, considering the reaction you received yesterday?"

"He won't try the same trick as Abercrombie."

"How do you know?"

"Because..." I *didn't* know for certain. The reaction of the other watchmakers on Oxford Street, not just Abercrombie, was unexpected and inexplicable. "He's not nasty like Abercrombie," was all I said. Although after I was through "leveraging" him, he might turn against me.

It took some time to get through the traffic, cross the bridge over the river, and reach Clapham. Cyclops didn't get lost once and pulled up outside Mr. Lawson's shop on High Street. Mr. Glass alighted first and held out his hand to assist me down the coach steps. We'd hardly spoken on the journey, so I made a point of thanking him to break the silence.

I entered first and crossed to the counter where Mr. Lawson sat hunched on a stool, tinkering with a watch. He glanced over his spectacles at me and dropped the watch on the counter. A spring fell out.

"Miss Steele! What are you doing here?"

I picked up his watch and slotted the spring back into place. The watch resumed ticking. I held it out for him, but he simply stared at it, his mouth ajar.

"It was broken!" he cried.

"And I fixed it." I held the watch higher, but still he didn't take it. "The spring just needed to be replaced." I felt like a fool explaining it to him when he would have noticed it falling out, surely.

He shook his head. "That spring wasn't the problem. I've been working on the watch all morning and I couldn't find anything wrong with it, yet it doesn't work."

Perhaps he needed new glasses. I set the watch down on the counter. He picked it up by its chain and moved it to the side, at arm's length. Then he backed away from me.

"My God," he murmured, still staring at me as if I had two heads. "Unnatural."

I felt Mr. Glass's solid presence at my back, very close. It was reassuring, but not enough to banish my curiosity. "Mr. Lawson, why are you afraid of me?"

The old watchmaker fingered the white mustache hiding his top lip. He gave a nervous little laugh. "Afraid of you? Not at all, Miss Steele, not at all. I'm simply...overwhelmed to see you after all this time." He gaze shifted to the watch then back to me. His numerous wrinkles crunched into a deep frown. "Your father and I were hardly friends these last few years."

"No, you weren't."

"What is it you want? I can't offer you employment."

"I don't want to work for you."

He looked relieved.

"This is Mr. Glass," I said. "Mr. Glass, meet Mr. Lawson."

Mr. Glass held out his hand. Mr. Lawson didn't come closer, so Mr. Glass lowered it.

"Is this Chronos?" I asked.

Mr. Glass shook his head. He then told his brief story of the mysterious Chronos and asked Mr. Lawson if he knew of a man similar in age to himself who may have been overseas five years ago.

The more Mr. Glass spoke, the wider the watchmaker's eyes became, and they were already quite wide. I was convinced he knew the fellow Mr. Glass sought.

"Well?" I prompted. "Who is he?"

"Nobody." Mr. Lawson backed up against the wall, knocking a clock hanging there. "I know of no such man."

I looked to Mr. Glass. He nodded gravely. "You're lying to us," I said to Mr. Lawson. "You *do* know who we're seeking."

He held up his hands and once again his shoulder bumped the clock. It tilted to the right. "I don't! For goodness' sakes, Miss Steele, I'm an old man. Please leave me be."

"You're an old man who is also a liar. You stole my watch design, entered it into the guild's awards and won. *My* design, Mr. Lawson. That award should have gone to me."

Mr. Glass's hand touched my lower back. Steadying me? Reassuring me? Preparing to stop me from jumping over the counter?

"Ah. That." Mr. Lawson stroked his mustache again and gave another nervous laugh.

"Yes, that."

"Come now, Miss Steele, there's no need to be upset about something that happened several years ago."

"I am not upset!" I cleared my throat and said, more calmly, "I'm willing to overlook your theft if you—"

"Theft! I wouldn't go that far, Miss Steele. You're being quite hysterical."

I pressed my knuckles on the counter and leaned forward. He flattened himself against the wall, knocking the clock off altogether. It crashed to the floor in a cacophony of splintered wood and a single out-of-tune *cuckoo*. Mr. Lawson pushed his spectacles up his nose.

"It was theft," I growled. "The guild won't look kindly on you if they learn what you did. Their bylaws state that anyone caught cheating in an awards contest will be thrown out of the guild."

"I...I'm not so sure they would believe you, considering your history with them. It might be seen as sour grapes."

That was the point I hadn't been so confident about, but I'd come this far. I could bluff my way to the end. "It would throw enough doubt in their minds that they would watch you very closely, Mr. Lawson. Now, I'm willing to leave the issue alone, as my father and I chose to do, if you tell us what you know about the fellow Mr. Glass is seeking."

He licked his top lip, dampening his mustache ends that he then proceeded to stroke.

"Come now, Mr. Lawson. I know you know him. You're not that good a liar."

He glanced past me to Mr. Glass. "His name is Mirth. He may or may not be the man you want, but he fits your description. He used to have a shop near here until he traveled overseas some years ago."

"Five years?" Mr. Glass prompted.

Mr. Lawson shrugged. "Perhaps more, perhaps less. The years all blend together at my age."

"Do you know where he went on his travels?" I asked.

"No. He simply shut his shop one day and never re-opened it upon his return."

"The name isn't familiar to me," I said. "He was a watchmaker near here?"

He snorted and pushed his spectacles up his nose again. "You don't know every watchmaker who ever worked in London, Miss Steele."

He had a point. "Where is he now?"

"I heard he was at the Aged Christian Society on Sackville Street, but that was some time ago. He may have passed."

"Where's Sackville Street?" Mr. Glass asked.

"Off Piccadilly."

"I know it," I said.

"Thank you, Mr. Lawson," Mr. Glass said. "You've been very helpful."

"Good day to you." Mr. Lawson cleared his throat and took a step away from the wall. "Miss Steele, do I have your promise not to mention that little incident to anyone at the guild? It was some years ago, after all."

"As long as your information isn't false, I see no reason why I need to speak of it." Father had decided not to make a fuss at the time, and although it galled me that Mr. Lawson had got away with it, Father was probably right. The onus of proof was on us, and I wasn't sure I had enough evidence to convince the biased guild members. "Good day, Mr. Lawson. I do hope your cuckoo clock isn't too damaged."

I walked out with Mr. Glass. "You were excellent in there," he said, as he helped me up the coach step. He was looking tired again, although not exhausted.

"Don't start that again, Mr. Glass," I ground out. "I'm not in the mood for your false niceties."

His jaw hardened. "I wasn't being false." To Cyclops, he said, "Drive to Sackville Street, off Piccadilly." He folded up the step, climbed into the cabin, and sat opposite me. He slammed the door shut.

I thought I'd upset him. Oh well. His moods were of no interest to me. It did mean an unpleasantly awkward journey, however.

It wasn't long before I regretted my outburst. Mr. Glass had seemed sincere, and it was unfair of me to snap at him when I was angry with Mr. Lawson.

"Miss Steele," he said, tearing his gaze away from the window. "I must ask you something about that exchange with Mr. Lawson. Can I, without risk of my head being bitten off?"

I pressed my lips together to suppress my smile. "Go ahead."

"You fixed that watch for him, even though he couldn't. How can that be?"

I shrugged one shoulder. "He's old and ought to retire, perhaps. It was only a matter of re-attaching the spring."

"Mr. Lawson has decades of experience, yet you wish me to believe he missed something so simple?"

"What other explanation is there? It wasn't working; I fixed it easily when he couldn't. There's nothing more to it."

He nodded slowly without taking his gaze off me. I found it unnerving so concentrated on the streets passing us by outside. After several turns, I realized we weren't heading in the right direction. I opened the window and shouted as much up to Cyclops.

He leaned over and looked back so that he could see me then touched the side of his nose as if to keep a secret. I closed the window again.

"What did he say?" Mr. Glass asked, rubbing his temples.

"That he knows what he's doing."

When we pulled into Park Street, Mr. Glass shoved open the door and leapt out before the coach had come to a complete stop outside his house. "What the devil are you doing?" he roared at Cyclops.

"Bringing you home to rest," Cyclops said. "And keep it down. You're scaring the horse."

The front door of number sixteen burst open just as I stepped out of the coach. A woman in her fifties stood on the threshold, an angry scowl on her face as she took in both myself and Mr. Glass. Dressed in black lace from head to toe, she looked like a cobweb in mourning.

"Matt!" Willie called out from behind her. "Better come inside real quick before she causes a scene."

"You!" The woman pointed at Mr. Glass before he had a chance to move. "Squatter! Intruder! Get out of my house or I'll have you arrested."

CHAPTER 7

"Vagabond!" The woman cried in a shrill voice. "House thief!" She advanced down the steps, still pointing her finger at Mr. Glass. Her hand shook, and next to him, she looked tiny and fragile, yet she faced up to him as if she were a warrior. I admired her immensely.

I remained on the pavement, waiting to see Mr. Glass's response. Cyclops didn't move the coach onward, and Duke now joined Willie at the door. Unlike her, his gaze was on Mr. Glass, not the woman. He looked concerned.

A quick glance at Mr. Glass proved why. The telltale signs of exhaustion tugged at his eyes and mouth. "You're mistaken, madam," he said. "I own this house."

He *owned* it? I'd thought he'd simply leased it. How did an American come to own a house in one of London's best areas?

"You cannot own this house," the woman said with a haughty sniff. "My nephew does."

Willie's eyes widened so far they were in danger of popping out of her head.

"Coyote's balls," Duke muttered.

Mr. Glass blinked several times before finally clearing his throat. "Then you must be Miss Letitia Glass." He bowed. "I am Matthew Glass. Your nephew."

The woman stumbled backward, only to trip up the stair. Willie and Duke caught her and righted her. She hardly seemed aware of her near-accident or the people behind her, despite another colorful phrase spilling from Duke's lips.

"No," she muttered. "No, no, no. You cannot be Matthew. He is in America, doing...American things. He would write to notify me of his arrival." She leaned forward, squinted hard at him, then leaned back and continued her scrutiny, as if the distance would help her see better.

"Why would I write when I've never written before?" Mr. Glass said. "Aunt Letitia—"

"Don't call me that," she snapped. She reached out and caught his chin. He could have avoided her grip but he bore her inspection as she turned his head from side to side. "Hmmm. You do have some of the Glass bearing, and you're as handsome as your father. But you cannot be Matthew. He is only thirty. You look much older."

"He's been ill," Willie said.

Mr. Glass gave his cousin a sharp glare as Letitia Glass let him go. "I am unconvinced. Prove to me that you are Matthew and I'll allow you to stay here."

"You'll *allow* me?"

"Yes. I'll allow you, Mr. Whoever-You-Are. The more I see of you, the more I doubt you are my nephew. My dearest brother would not bring his son up to be impertinent to his aunt. Harry had manners."

At mention of his father, Mr. Glass lowered his head. He heaved a sigh.

"*You* prove who you are," Duke said before Mr. Glass could respond.

The tiny woman turned to him. "Everyone knows me." She waved a hand at the neighboring window. The curtain moved and the face that had been watching disappeared. "I am well known in London. I was—am—a dear friend to the queen." She touched the gray curls at the nape of her neck, poking out from beneath the cloud of black veil surrounding her hat. "I've been painted by masters, courted by foreign princes, and dined in palaces. A white knight even slayed a dragon for me, once."

Stunned silence followed her odd pronouncement as we all stared at her. A light rain began to fall and the curtain of the neighbor's house parted again. Letitia Glass stood in the center of us with an outwardly thrust chin, a straight back, and a glint in her eye that I now suspected was madness.

"Miss Glass," I said, gently. "My name is India Steele and I'm pleased to make your acquaintance. Please, come inside out of the rain. We'll have a cup of tea and see if we can sort out this misunderstanding. I give my word that no one will harm you."

She took in my face, my clothes, the reticule dangling from my wrist. "You do seem like a good, respectable *English* girl." She shot Willie a barbed glance.

Willie opened her mouth to say something, but Mr. Glass shook his head and she shut it again.

Miss Letitia Glass stepped back onto the porch and, after a brief hesitation, took Duke's offered arm.

"No one will harm her?" Mr. Glass murmured in my ear. His hand on my elbow gripped hard. "You think me capable of hurting elderly ladies?"

"Mr. Glass..." I stopped myself from telling him I didn't trust him and instead said, "It reassured her, did it not? Is there anything you can show her to prove who you are?"

"Is that for her benefit or yours?" He let me go and indicated I should step inside ahead of him.

"I never doubted you were Matthew Glass," I said, passing him. "Until now."

Mr. Glass didn't join us, and Duke disappeared after depositing Miss Glass on the drawing room sofa. I sat beside her, hoping my presence would give her some sense of comfort, although she didn't look in need of it. She sat as if she ought to be just there, her black skirts taking up much of the sofa. She touched a polished black stone, set in gold, clasped to her dress at the base of her throat, and wrinkled her nose.

"This room is stale," she announced. "You ought to open it up."

"There ain't no point," Willie said. "We'll be gone soon, and it's always raining here anyways or the air's sooty."

"Miss Glass," I said, "tell me about your nephew, Matthew." I wanted to learn as much about him as possible before he returned. That's if the fellow who'd employed me was in fact her nephew.

"Ask him yourself," Willie cut in.

"Would he answer me?"

She merely shrugged.

"My brother is so dear to me," Miss Glass said wistfully. Her eyes turned cloudy and I doubted whether she saw her surroundings at all. "He's so lively and jolly, and terribly kind. He excels at everything he puts his hand to. So clever and amiable. Everyone adores him and wants to be his friend. Except Papa, of course." Her mouth twisted into a frown. "And Richard."

"Er, Miss Glass." I glanced at Willie. She shrugged back. "I was asking after Matthew Glass, your nephew, not your brother."

"Your brother is dead." Willie raised her voice, as if Miss Glass were deaf.

"Willie!" I hissed.

Miss Glass stirred and shifted on the sofa. "Yes. Of course he is. I know that." She lowered her head but not before I saw tears spring to her eyes.

"What do you know about Matthew?" I tried again.

"Nothing," Miss Glass said. "I've never met him. Harry wrote to me when his wife bore a son. That was thirty years ago, but it feels like yesterday. I was happy for him. For them both, although I never met her, of course. Her people were poor American folk, you see, and not at all suitable for a Glass. But Harry, being Harry, married her anyway. He always was the romantic one." She sighed.

Willie bristled. "Poor American folk?" she echoed.

"Quite the wrong sort," Miss Glass told her. "All very...rough, so one of Harry's early letters said." She sighed again. "He wrote often after he announced Matthew's birth, but Richard hid the letters from me. The housekeeper told me about them, but she didn't dare take them like I asked."

"Who is Richard?" I ventured.

"My brother and the current Baron of Rycroft."

"Baron!" both Willie and I blurted out.

"A proper baron or is that just what folk like to call him?" Willie asked.

"Why would anyone call him a baron if he is not one?" Miss Glass laughed like a young girl. "Silly Americans," she said to me, as if sharing a private joke with another Englishwoman.

I was still too stunned to respond, however. Mr. Glass was the nephew of a baron! But he was far too foreign. And although he could act the gentleman well enough, there was nothing noble about him. Surely there was a mistake and he wasn't the Matthew Glass related to this woman.

That would make him a liar, and a squatter, as she'd called him. It wasn't much of a stretch from there to outlaw. Dread settled into my bones. If this woman could prove he wasn't Matthew Glass then she could be in danger from him.

Duke entered carrying a tray. I poured the tea because Willie was busy telling Duke what Miss Glass had said. I used both hands, the one steadying the other.

"Did you know?" Willie pestered Duke.

He shook his head. "You didn't? But you're his cousin."

"Cousin?" Miss Glass *humphed*. "What did I tell you, Miss Steele? My brother married into a rough American family, and there's the proof." She accepted the cup and bestowed a genteel smile upon me, as if she hadn't just insulted Willie.

Willie advanced on her, hands on her hips, her nostrils flaring like a raging bull's. She didn't speak for an entire twenty seconds, simply breathed heavily and glared daggers at Miss Glass. "You take that back!" she finally said.

"Why should she?" Duke grunted. "She's right."

Willie marched back to him and punched him so hard in the shoulder that he was forced back a step. She stormed out of the drawing room to the sound of his chuckles. "We beat you in the war!" she shouted back.

"We've been at war with America?" Miss Glass asked, a hand to her chest. "Dear me, how dreadful."

"I think she's referring to the War of Independence over a hundred years ago," I said, trying not to smile in relief. Willie, at least, wasn't a threat—at present.

Miss Glass sipped her tea. "Where is he?" she asked, looking past Duke to the door. "Where is the fellow claiming to be my nephew? I want another look at him."

"Keep your hair on," Duke said. " He'll be back soon."

Miss Glass patted her gray curls.

Mr. Glass strode into the drawing room, and Miss Glass immediately sat up straighter. She couldn't take her eyes off him, nor he her. He looked healthier again, the signs of illness and exhaustion gone. He dragged a chair over to sit near her and handed her a tintype photograph. He held another back.

"This is me with my parents," he said quietly. "I was about three years of age."

He watched Miss Glass's reaction intently. Her eyes shone with unshed tears as she traced the man in the photograph with her thumb. It must be her brother then. He looked remarkably like Mr. Glass did now, only with a mustache and hair parted at the side. He stood a little behind the seated woman with hooped skirts. She was very pretty, with slender features and large eyes. She held the hand of the little boy scowling at the camera. He looked like he resented having to stand still for so long.

"And this is me with my parents just before they fell ill. I was fifteen."

The couple's appearance had hardly changed. Her gown was dark instead of light, the skirts not quite so broad, and she wore a bonnet over her hair. The man's hairline had begun to recede a little, but he was still very handsome. The boy had grown up and now stood behind his mother's other side. He was taller than his father, with wide shoulders, and he no longer scowled at the camera but looked directly into it with calm countenance. His face may have been more youthful, but it was unmistakably the man sitting opposite, and he was most assuredly the son of the man in both photographs. It was a wonder Miss Glass hadn't noticed the striking familiarity immediately upon seeing him. Then again, she was touched in the head.

She sniffed loudly. Mr. Glass handed her his handkerchief and she dabbed at her eyes. "Harry," she whispered, stroking the tintype again. "My dearest Harry."

Mr. Glass watched her, his elbows on his knees, his throat moving with his swallow. "Aunt Letitia?" he murmured.

She wiped her cheek with the handkerchief and handed back the photographs. She clasped both his hands. "Matthew," she whispered. "We have so much to discuss. We must be quick."

"Quick? Why?"

She flapped the hand that held the handkerchief. "Is it true your parents died from an illness?"

He nodded. "Both died with weeks of the other."

"Then what did you do?"

He leaned back in the chair and studied each of the tintypes. "Returned to my mother's family in California. Until I was old enough to leave," he added with chilling bite.

I sat on the edge of my seat, waiting for him to dole out more pieces of the puzzle that could help me solve the mystery of Mr. Glass.

"Why did you come to England after all this time?" she asked. "Harry vowed never to return."

"I'm looking for someone." His gaze flicked to me them back to his aunt. It was the first time he'd acknowledged my presence since walking into the drawing room.

"I see. Well, I am glad you came." She wrung his hand in both of hers. "Are you married?"

He pulled free. "No."

"Promised to anyone?"

"No."

"Excellent! We must find you a bride now that you're home. A good English girl, someone from our set." She clicked her tongue. "If only I knew who the right girls are nowadays."

"Aunt, please, I'm not looking for a bride. Just a watchmaker." Again, he glanced at me. He must want to get away to speak with the watchmaker known as Mirth. "Nor am I here for long. I leave on Tuesday."

"Tuesday! But that is too soon."

He stood. She tried to clasp his hand but he moved away. He couldn't have failed to notice the attempt, however. He held himself rigidly as he went to stand by the mantel, as far away from us as possible while remaining in the room.

"I hope you are well, Aunt."

"Fit as a fiddle. But Matthew—"

"And my Uncle Richard?"

She clicked her tongue. "Still alive, more's the pity."

"Does he take care of your needs?" Mr. Glass asked.

"I am adequately fed and housed, like one of his horses, if that's what you mean." She clasped her hands on her lap, her proud chin once more tilted at an imperial angle. This was a woman aware of her elevated position in the world. The madness was nowhere to be seen.

"Does he know I'm in England?" Mr. Glass asked.

"Yes."

"Did he have me followed?"

"Followed? Why would he follow you?"

"I don't know the answer to that, but I do know that I'm being followed."

So that was why he constantly looked out the coach window this morning.

"When?" Duke sounded worried.

Mr. Glass dismissed his question with a shake of his head. Duke's lips flattened, and I thought he'd argue but Miss Glass started talking again.

"Richard heard that Harry's house was occupied," she said, indicating the room we sat in. So the house had belonged to Mr. Glass's father, not the Rycroft estate. That explained why Mr. Matthew Glass had inherited it. "I don't know who alerted him. Perhaps one of the neighbors."

"Most likely. I've seen them watching me, but none have greeted us."

"I overheard Richard telling Beatrice that someone was occupying the house. He didn't inform me directly."

"Beatrice?"

"His wife."

Mr. Glass nodded slowly. "Was my name mentioned?"

"No, just that the house was occupied and he would look into it."

"He hasn't been here," Mr. Glass said. "Nobody from the family has, until you."

"It was only this morning that I overheard Richard and Beatrice discussing it. I came as soon as I could get away. I couldn't bear the thought of squatters in my Harry's house."

"Good of you to be concerned." I couldn't be sure from his tone if he was being sincere or not.

"I was very concerned. I doubted Richard would lift a finger to check. As soon as I escaped, I came here."

We all leaned forward, brows raised. "Escaped?" Mr. Glass said. "From Uncle Richard?"

"No, from Beatrice. I asked her to take me shopping. I'm not allowed out on my own, you see."

"Why not?"

"I buy things, then Richard gets angry that I've spent too much money, even though it's *my* money to spend. I have an allowance. Oh, and I talk to people." She grinned, as if it were the naughtiest thing to do and she only did it to annoy her brother.

"You're not allowed to talk to people?" I asked, when Mr. Glass said nothing. He looked contemplative.

"Richard only allows me to receive callers in his presence or Beatrice's. He doesn't want me telling them what a cruel man he is to me. Appearances are important to him. More important than me."

"Aunt Letitia, he can't possibly be as bad as that," Mr. Glass said.

"Are you calling me a liar?"

He sucked in a sharp breath. "Not at all. I know my father didn't get along with his father, and Richard usually took their father's side, but—"

"Usually?" She sniffed. "It was every time. Richard knew what side his bread was buttered on. No spine, that's always been his problem. Harry, however, had more bottle than anyone I've ever met. That was *his* problem, you see." The anger and vigor drained out of her as she spoke, and the wistful gaze returned to her eyes. I half expected her to mention white knights and dragons again. "Harry was selfless and brave, with a kind heart. He told our father when he was being unfair to our farmers and staff, and Father hated him for it. He hated him for being generous, hated him for being better at everything, and hated him for speaking out. He and Richard despised Harry for being himself."

I watched Mr. Glass from beneath my lashes. He went utterly still and didn't speak a word. After a moment, he swallowed heavily and blinked rapidly. I wasn't quite sure if it was a show of emotion or not.

"Does he beat you?" Duke asked Miss Glass.

We all looked at him.

"Does your brother beat you, ma'am?" He stated it matter-of-factly, as if one asked strangers that sort of thing all the time.

Distaste rippled across Miss Glass's features. "Who're you to ask me such a question?"

"I'm Matt's friend."

"I thought you were the butler."

Duke narrowed his eyes at Mr. Glass. "I need a drink. Want one?"

Mr. Glass waved him off, and Duke left the drawing room. A rather awkward silence followed his departure. I waited for aunt and nephew to fall into a discussion about family members, and catch up on old times, but they did not. It would seem they needed some assistance to get to know one another.

"Why did your brother, Harry, leave England, Miss Glass?" I asked.

Her eyes misted again, and I regretted bringing it up, but I was wildly curious. I knew I shouldn't be. The family was none of my affair. Yet I waited impatiently for her answer.

Unfortunately, she suddenly stiffened. Her gaze sharpened and cleared. "Who *are* you, Miss Steele? Why are you here?"

"I'm also a friend of your nephew's," I said.

He did not counter me but amusement touched the corners of his mouth. He watched me openly, challenging me to pile more lies onto the heap. No doubt he would remind me of them later then watch me try to dig my way out.

"More acquaintances, really." I didn't want to tell her I worked for him. It would immediately lessen my status in her eyes, and she might cease talking in front of me, the hired help.

"Acquaintance?" She nodded slowly, eyeing me again, and this time I felt certain she was assessing every piece of my clothing, right down to the cotton thread. "So I see. A mistress would be better attired and wear jewelry. No Glass would be so stingy as to dress his woman in gray cotton. So what is the nature of your acquaintance with my nephew?"

"She's my assistant," Mr. Glass answered before I could think of something. "She assists me in my work."

"You work?" She looked as if she'd tasted something sour.

"Of course I work," he said. "Doesn't everyone?"

I rolled my eyes. The man had no idea. The American upper classes might work and be proud of it, but here, the best families didn't like dirtying their hands. Most lived off their landholdings or made good marriages. Of course, there were wealthy gentlemen merchants, manufacturers, bankers and the like, but few in the nobility had done a hard day of labor in their life.

"Tell her what sort of work you do, Mr. Glass." It was rather fun watching him squirm as he tried to think of something, and I found it difficult to keep my smile off my face. Clearly he deemed it necessary to lie to her.

That thought wiped my smile clean away. If he had to lie, then his work involved something secretive, like being an outlaw, perhaps.

"I manage the family affairs," he said, giving me a smug flat-lipped smile.

"What business is your family in?" I inquired.

"Stop this talk at once." Miss Glass shuddered. "Your family is here, Matthew, and *we* do not discuss such vulgar things."

"With respect, Aunt, I have family on two continents. My American family may not be as..." He drummed his fingers on the side of his teacup as he thought. "They may not be as *highly regarded* as the Glasses, but they're still family."

She picked up her cup too. "I admire your loyalty, but do try to remember that your father's family are nobility, and your mother's are riffraff."

I thought he would be offended, but he merely muttered, "I'm not that loyal," into his teacup.

"Indeed," she said, her tone dry. "Why did you never write to me? Your father did."

"You just told me his letters were kept from you, so what does it matter if I wrote or not?"

"It matters."

I nodded in agreement.

He scowled at me then turned back to his aunt. "With respect, I don't know you. Writing to someone I've never met felt odd."

"That doesn't excuse it."

He looked uncomfortable, and I felt a little sympathy for him, although I couldn't think why he deserved it. "Now that you've met, I'm sure writing to one another will be easier," I said.

"I promise to write when I'm back home," Mr. Glass assured his aunt.

She looked pained. "We've only just met and already you're talking about leaving me."

"This was only ever going to be a fleeting visit."

"Yes, but now that you're here, why not stay longer? I can introduce you to all my friends and acquaintances. The queen! You must meet the queen, and the prince consort, too. Such a happy couple."

Oh dear. The prince consort had died years ago. Miss Glass's madness was a fickle affliction, sometimes making her seem perfectly normal, until she uttered something outrageous.

Mr. Glass knew it too. His shoulders rounded, as if the weight of her madness was a personal burden he had to carry. And yet he also seemed to want to have little to do with her. He hadn't written, for one thing, and hadn't asked her to stay for lunch. It was terribly impolite of him, and I decided to rectify it immediately.

"Miss Glass, would you join us for lunch today? Cyclops can return you to your brother's house afterward."

"No!" She set the teacup down with a clatter. Then, as if her own vehemence surprised her, she pressed a hand to her stomach, and said, "I'd rather not return to Richard's home."

Mr. Glass and I exchanged glances. "At all?" he asked her.

"At all. I thought perhaps that now you're here—"

"No."

Her eyes filled with tears, and she dipped her head to hide them. I scowled at Mr. Glass, but he merely turned his head away. Heartless man. I touched Miss Glass's hand. "Your nephew would happily welcome you into his household, but I'm afraid he's leaving in less than a week," I reminded her.

She *humph*ed. "We shall see."

I did like her conviction, but it saddened me that she wanted to stay with Mr. Glass so much. Her situation with her brother mustn't be a happy one if she was so eager to live with a nephew she hardly knew and his rough friends and family. I squeezed her hand and she surprised me by squeezing it back.

A commotion outside drew everyone's attention. Mr. Glass was at the door in four long strides, but he fell back as a woman breezed into the drawing room. She was tall and slender, with skin so pale the veins in her throat stood out. I guessed her to be younger than Miss Glass, but it was difficult to determine her exact age. The skin around her eyes and forehead was pulled back by the tight arrangement of her hair beneath her turban. The smoothness contrasted the deep grooves drooping from each corner of her mouth to her chin.

Her hazel eyes flashed in Miss Glass's direction. She didn't seem to notice anyone else as she strode up to the elderly woman on the sofa. Miss Glass shrank back and leaned toward me.

"What is the meaning of this?" Mr. Glass growled. "Who are you?"

The woman didn't turn around. She held out her hand to Miss Glass. "I knew you'd be here! Come, Letitia. Leave this place at once."

"I'd rather stay." Miss Glass picked up her teacup, only to have her arm wrenched by the newcomer. Tea spilled and I caught the cup before it tumbled to the floor. "Beatrice!" Miss Glass gasped.

So this was her sister-in-law, Lady Rycroft. She certainly wasn't behaving in a very ladylike manner.

Lady Rycroft's grip must have been hard, because she marched Miss Glass toward the door. "Richard will be furious when I tell him you ran away from me," she spat. "I knew the shopping expedition was a ruse. I told him so, but he wouldn't listen to me."

Mr. Glass stepped in the way, blocking the exit. He could look quite formidable when he wanted to, and I felt relieved to see him finally take some interest in his aunt's welfare. "Unhand her," he snarled.

"I beg your pardon!" Lady Rycroft may have been tall for a woman, but she only came up to his chin, even when she straightened her spine. "I am Lady Rycroft and your aunt. You will treat me with the respect I deserve."

So she knew who he was, then. I tried to think of something diplomatic to ease the tensions, but I could think of nothing. Behind Mr. Glass, Duke and Willie gathered close to hear the exchange.

"You can be sure that I will," he said. "When you've shown me you deserve my respect. You come into my house without greeting and drag out one of my guests against her will. I think I'm entitled to tell you to unhand her."

"I will not! You don't know how she is. She needs her rest at home. Her head is soft, you see—"

"My head is perfectly all right, thank you!" Miss Glass sniffed in her sister-in-law's direction.

"Unhand her and she will return home of her own free will," Mr. Glass said. "After lunch."

"No!" Miss Glass cried. I almost shouted at him too. How could he be so cruel? She clearly didn't want to return to her brother's house.

"Can't she stay here for a few days while you're in London?" I dared venture. "Then she could return." Or he could find other arrangements for her in the meantime.

I expected him to admonish me for my impertinence, but he merely looked away, although not before I saw a shadow pass over his eyes.

"He won't leave England." Honestly, Miss Glass's determination that he would remain wasn't helping the situation.

"I've made my decision," he said. "You may stay for luncheon, Aunt Letitia, but no longer. I'm a busy man, and I don't have time for callers." He spun on his heel and stalked out the door. "Duke, see Lady Rycroft out."

"You must return her yourself," Lady Rycroft said to his back. "She cannot be trusted with one of your men. She's very cunning."

"Very well," he said in low tones that only just reached us. "It's about time I met my uncle anyway."

"He looks forward to meeting you."

"I doubt it."

Lady Rycroft let her sister-in-law go and, head high, eased past the others, careful not to brush up against any of them. I expected Miss Glass to break down in hysteria or run after her nephew to plead with him, but she merely gathered her skirts and smiled at me.

"Will you be joining us for luncheon, Miss Steele?" she asked as if nothing were amiss. "I would very much like your company."

CHAPTER 8

I discovered over luncheon that Lord and Lady Rycroft had three daughters. They weren't in need of a governess at present, but I decided to present myself to them and offer my services to any of their friends. When I asked Mr. Glass if I could come with him to return his aunt to her home, he promptly started an argument.

"A governess?" he said as he handed my hat to me at the door. "Why do you want to be a governess?"

"Because none of the watchmakers in London will employ me as their assistant." After our recent visits, I was beginning to see that the situation was even more hopeless than I had first thought. "A governess's position might suit me just as well. I'm educated, and I can play the piano and sew as well as any woman."

"I don't doubt it."

"Then why are you being resistant to the idea?"

He wedged his hat under his arm without a care for its shape and opened the front door. Cyclops waited with the horse and carriage. "I'm not resistant, I simply don't think anyone will employ you," Mr. Glass said.

"Oh dear," his aunt muttered.

"Why not?" I asked hotly.

His aunt *tsk tsk*ed and shook her head at him as she passed. He scowled back at her. He'd been doing a great deal of scowling ever since she arrived. He hadn't joined us over luncheon, preferring to eat alone in his rooms. I wondered if he'd been resting or using his special watch again.

"Aunt Letitia, you explain it to her," he said.

"Good lord, no," she tossed over her shoulder. "You made your bed, now you must lie in it."

He jerked his head toward the carriage, but I didn't move from the doorway. "Go on then, Mr. Glass. Tell me why you think I'd make a terrible governess."

"I didn't say you'd be terrible. I think you'd make an excellent governess. But I doubt anyone will employ you."

"Because I have no experience?" I stood in the doorway only inches from him, suddenly feeling small, stupid and pathetic. My conviction rapidly drained away. I was a fool. He was right. No one would employ me as a governess without references. I lowered my head. "I'll stay here," I mumbled.

I stepped back inside, but he caught my chin. I was so shocked that I lifted my gaze to his. He seemed equally shocked by his action and quickly let me go. He tucked his hands behind his back.

"I'm sorry," he murmured. "I shouldn't have said anything. Come with us, Miss Steele. Hopefully you'll prove me wrong." He offered me a smile and his elbow.

I took it and descended the steps. He helped Miss Glass into the coach, and then me, and climbed in after us. I still felt a little bruised by his lack of confidence in my employability, but he had offered me an olive branch and it would be rude of me not to accept it.

"How does one gain experience as a governess in the first place if one doesn't have experience?" I said to no one in particular.

"It's not your lack of experience that will hold you back, Miss Steele," Miss Glass said. "It's your pretty face, lovely figure, and your forthright manner."

Mr. Glass turned to look out the window, as if he hadn't heard a thing his aunt said when she was sitting right beside him. I was too stunned to say anything.

"I'm sorry to dash your hopes," Miss Glass went on, "but you needed to be told. We women can sometimes be unfair to each other, and it would take a kind-hearted woman, sure of her own appeal and the love of her husband, to take you on in such an elevated position. Perhaps as a maid, but not a governess. Believe me, none of Beatrice's circle fit that description. A gaggle of preening geese, the lot of them."

"Thank you, Miss Glass," I said, unable to think of anything else. She had given me a compliment, and my mother had always told me to be gracious, even when the compliment was unintended or made from politeness.

"So you ought to thank me," she said with a smug curve of her lips. "The daughters of Beatrice's friends are all as awful as their mothers. Trying to educate them will send any sane woman to the madhouse."

I smiled, but there was no humor in it. My hopes of working as a governess had almost disappeared entirely. I shouldn't have come. I should have stayed home to find evidence linking Mr. Glass to the outlaw in the papers. The reward money was looking more and more appealing.

Lord Rycroft's house faced Belgrave Square. It was not unlike Mr. Glass's Mayfair house, in that it was tall and part of a series of townhouses that stretched from one end of the street to the other. Miss Glass informed us on the short journey that the Rycroft estate in the countryside was somewhat neglected, since Beatrice preferred the city and all the social opportunities London offered.

"Your father would be disappointed," she said, eyeing her nephew. "He loved Rycroft. I always thought it a shame he wasn't the oldest son. He appreciated it more."

"Yet he would have hated the responsibility," Mr. Glass said coolly. "And resented having to remain in the same place for long."

Miss Glass sighed. "Very true."

Stiff-backed footmen greeted us with blank stares. They performed their duties of door-opening and hat-taking with mechanical formality. I wanted to pinch one to see if he reacted.

"Finally," Lady Rycroft said with a pointed glance at the gilt and jet clock on the mantel in the drawing room. It was fifteen minutes fast. I wondered if she knew. "I've had to postpone my afternoon engagements to wait for you, Letitia."

"You didn't need to wait," Miss Glass said, taking a seat and indicating that I should too. I did and checked the time on the watch I'd tucked into my waistcoat pocket. The mantel one was definitely fifteen minutes ahead.

"Richard wouldn't allow me to leave until you returned," Lady Rycroft said. "He's punishing *me* for *your* little morning escapade."

"Is he here?" Mr. Glass cut in, taking up a position by the white marble mantel, his elbow near the clock. I tore my gaze away from the timepiece, only to find it kept wandering back.

"One of the footmen is notifying him of your presence."

The conversation stalled as we all waited for Lord Rycroft's entrance. I clasped my hands in my lap, twisting my fingers around one another, but it was impossible. The clock called me as loudly as any trumpet.

"Forgive me, Lady Rycroft, but have you noticed that your clock is fast?"

Mr. Glass and Miss Glass looked at the clock. Lady Rycroft looked at me.

"Who *are* you, and why are you here?" she asked, as if seeing me for the first time.

"My name is India Steele."

Before I could go on, Mr. Glass spoke. "Miss Steele is my assistant."

Lady Rycroft's eyebrows almost disappeared into her turban. Her face flushed and she picked up a fan from the table and fanned herself.

"I'm helping him search for someone," I said quickly with a glare at Mr. Glass. He wasn't smiling but somehow he managed to look amused. "After his return to America, I'll be in need of other work. If you know of anyone requiring a governess, then I would appreciate it if you could pass on my details. I have an excellent grasp of most subjects, particularly mathematics and engineering." At her look of horror, I added, "And the gentler arts, too, of course. I can be found at Mr. Glass's residence in Mayfair for a few days more."

Her gaze fell to my chest then lifted to my face. The grooves drooping from her mouth deepened. "Nobody I know needs a governess at present."

My hopes fell, although they weren't as dashed as they would have been if Miss Glass hadn't forewarned me in the carriage. I thanked Lady Rycroft and willed my face to not turn red as I felt Mr. and Miss Glass watching me.

Fortunately, Lord Rycroft entered at that moment too. Mr. Glass stood straighter, and Miss Glass shrank into the sofa, as if she were trying to make herself invisible. He didn't see her, however. He only had eyes for his nephew.

Lord Rycroft was a less appealing version of Mr. Glass, and it wasn't simply the age difference that accounted for it. The older man did sport some gray through his thick black hair, but that was his only distinguishing feature. He was shorter yet just as broad in chest and shoulder, which made him stocky. He may once have had the sharply angular cheeks of Mr. Glass but it was impossible to tell beneath the layers of sagging fat. Muddy eyes took in every inch of his nephew, slowly, as if measuring him against the memory of his dead brother and perhaps against himself. Lord Rycroft's stature straightened with every passing moment, and his chest expanded. I pressed my lips together to stop myself smiling at his attempts to make himself more impressive. He ought not bother. Mr. Glass wasn't easily matched by anyone, let alone a short, fat man twice his age.

"Good afternoon, Uncle," Mr. Glass said, holding out his hand.

Lord Rycroft ignored it. "What brings you to London?" He had a ropey voice, as if it struggled to travel through his thick throat.

Mr. Glass pulled back his hand. "I'm looking for someone. It's a private matter."

"How long are you staying?"

"Until Tuesday."

"See that you don't stay longer."

Mr. Glass's eyes narrowed. "I'll stay as long as I like."

"Let me make myself clear, you are not welcome here. Your father chose to leave his family, his home and responsibilities, and run away. He then disgraced us further by marrying a foreign girl of ill-repute." He poked a thick finger at Mr. Glass's chest. "And you are the embodiment of that disgrace. We want nothing to do with you."

Mr. Glass's face darkened. His eyes turned the color of pitch. My blood chilled as Mr. Glass went very still. I suddenly felt afraid for Lord Rycroft.

"I know who your mother's family are and what they've done," he went on, oblivious to the fuse he'd set alight. "My investigators sent me newspaper clippings and reports of their crimes."

Crimes! My gasp echoed in the ensuing silence. I was the only one who showed surprise, however. Mr. Glass swallowed but did not take his gaze off his uncle. Nor did he deny the accusation. So it was true.

I pressed my hand to my rolling stomach. It wasn't until that moment that I realized the stupidity of what I'd done. I was living with a criminal. I'd never quite believed that Mr. Glass was the Dark Rider—until now.

"Let's be clear," Lord Rycroft went on, "the estate cannot be handed over to the likes of you. It must be against the law, somehow, or what's the good of laws in the first place? I have my lawyers working on it. "

The hard planes of Mr. Glass's face slackened. He blinked. "Hand over? *I* am your heir? But you have three daughters."

"Of course you're the heir. Stupid as well, I see."

"It's true," Miss Glass chimed in quickly. "The estate is entailed, Matthew. None of your female cousins will get their greedy little hands on it because you are the sole male heir, and males inherit." At his continuing stunned look, she added, "Didn't Harry tell you?"

"No," he murmured.

Lady Rycroft sniffed into a handkerchief. "The thought of my dear girls being tossed out of their home! It breaks my heart."

I willed Mr. Glass to speak, but he didn't. He glanced at me, then quickly down at the floor, off to the side, everywhere but the faces watching him. I twisted my fingers tighter in my lap.

Lord Rycroft's grunt filled the room. "You're not welcome here. Good day." He turned to go. "Letitia, to your room. You're forbidden to leave for a week. Go!" he shouted when she didn't move.

Both she and Lady Rycroft flinched. Then she lifted her chin. "I wish to stay with Matthew."

"Go. To. Your. Room!" Lord Rycroft roared. His face blotched, his mouth frothed. "I will not tolerate any more of your mad ramblings and wanderings! Christ, woman, you're the bane of my existence."

Miss Glass's eyes filled with tears, but she continued to hold her chin high, even though it wobbled. "I wish to live with Matthew."

"I'm not staying in London," Mr. Glass said automatically.

But his aunt didn't seem to hear him. "I refuse to sleep here another night."

"I'll have you taken to the asylum if you continue to defy me!" Lord Rycroft shouted. "You're a mad old bat, and the sight of you sickens me. It's no wonder Harry left you behind. He couldn't stand your company either!"

Finally Miss Glass's face crumpled and her tears spilled. The proud dame seemed to age ten years as her shoulders stooped and trembled with silent crying. I went to her and took her hand in mine. She rallied a little and stopped crying.

Lord Rycroft looked at me as if he'd only just noticed me. I lifted my chin as I'd seen Miss Glass do, daring him to throw me out. "Take your doxy with you, Glass, and leave."

"I'm not a doxy, and you are certainly not a gentleman." I didn't know what I was saying. Perhaps I was afflicted with madness too. I just knew I couldn't leave Miss Glass with this bully. "I'm not leaving without Miss Glass."

"Nor am I." Mr. Glass held out his hand to his aunt.

She beamed up at him through her tears. I might have smiled at him too, but he wasn't looking my way, although he did stand very close to me.

Lord Rycroft glanced between his sister and nephew. He shook his head and grunted. "If you leave, Letitia, do not come back. Ever. Go to America with him. I don't care. Just get out of my sight."

"Gladly." Miss Glass took Mr. Glass's hand and tucked mine into her side. "Come, Miss Steele. We have a house to air out." She turned to her sister-in-law, sitting on the sofa with a stunned expression on her tight face. "Have my things sent to Matthew's house by the end of the day. All of them. I'll be counting every last trinket."

She marched out, taking me with her.

But Mr. Glass didn't follow. "I believe you have several letters belonging to Aunt Letitia, written by my father," he said to Lord Rycroft. "Include them in her belongings."

Lord Rycroft bristled. "You do not give me orders in my own home!"

Mr. Glass bared his teeth. "Then come outside, *Uncle*, and I will order you there." Before anyone could fully digest his words, he grasped Lord Rycroft's arm, twisted it behind his back, and hustled him toward the drawing room door. The footman standing there came to life, proving he wasn't an automaton after all. He gasped and his eyes bulged, but he did not move to assist his master as Mr. Glass marched his uncle into the entrance hall, as if he were ejecting a drunkard from a tavern.

I picked up my skirts and ran after them, not wanting to miss a single moment. Behind me, Lady Rycroft ordered Miss Glass to remain behind, but light footsteps followed nevertheless.

"What are you doing? Let me go!" Lord Rycroft struggled to pull himself free of Mr. Glass's grip.

"Not until you promise to send the letters. Every last one of them." Mr. Glass shoved him forward, and Lord Rycroft stumbled. He would have fallen if Mr. Glass hadn't still been holding his arm.

"Very well," Rycroft grumbled. "I don't care about the bloody letters anymore. Harry's dead. His letters have no meaning now."

I thought Mr. Glass would punch him, but instead he let his uncle go. He tugged on his sleeves and collar to straighten them, then held his elbow out to Miss Glass. She took it with a smile. He offered me his other arm, but I shook my head. A small triangular dent appeared between his brows.

"You've turned out to be even more of a disappointment than your father," Lord Rycroft said as we exited. "Hardly surprising considering the type of blood running through your veins.

"Pay him no mind," Miss Glass said, patting her nephew's arm. "He's simply jealous of Harry. Always has been and always will be."

The door slammed behind us.

Mr. Glass helped his aunt into the coach. I stood on the pavement and glanced up at Cyclops. His one eye watched me closely. How much of that exchange had he seen and heard?

"Everything all right, miss?" he asked.

I nodded and smiled, yet I didn't climb into the carriage. Mr. Glass held his hand out to me. "Miss Steele?"

I stared at his outstretched hand. It withered and closed upon my scrutiny. He dropped it to his side.

"You have something to say?" he said to me.

My things were at his house. All my worldly possessions were in one of his rooms. I could forgo the clothing, but not my tools or the daguerreotype of my parents. Surely he wouldn't harm me. I was no threat to him. Indeed, I was helping him. If he'd wanted to attack me, he could have done so last night in the kitchen. I made up my mind to go with him and do my best to simply perform the duty he asked of me. I abandoned the idea of notifying the police and collecting the reward. I valued my life more than money.

"No." I held out my hand for him and he took it. "I have nothing to say."

His fingers momentarily pressed mine, then he let me go. As he folded up the step, I could swear I heard him sigh.

***

Willie was not pleased to have another Englishwoman in the house. "You're a damn fool, Matt!" She paced across the entrance hall tiles and back again to wag her finger at her cousin. Some of her hair had come loose from its knot and she looked like a madwoman. I resolved to steer clear of her. Of the lot of them.

Miss Glass had no such qualms. She patted her nephew's cheek. "But a sweet fool. I knew you would be. You're your father's son, and so like my own dear mama too."

Willie snorted. Duke jabbed her in the ribs with his elbow and hissed at her to be quiet. She jabbed him back.

"She was always rescuing poor helpless creatures," Miss Glass went on.

"Helpless?" Willie echoed. "Ha!"

Miss Glass ignored her. "She used to wander in the woods on the estate, singing and talking to the birds."

"She sounds more like *you*," Willie grumbled, which she followed up with an "Ouch," when Duke once again elbowed her.

I did have to agree with her. The late Dowager Lady Rycroft sounded as mad as her daughter. But there was no harm in Miss Glass. Looking at her now, with a dreamy emptiness in her eyes, it was impossible to reconcile her with the woman we'd met on the doorstep, accusing Mr. Glass of house stealing. First appearances were definitely deceiving in some cases. Her nephew had something in common with her there, but little else.

"Willie, see that my aunt is made comfortable while Duke prepares a room for her," he said.

"Me?" Willie placed her hands on her hips. "Why me? Why can't she?" She nodded at me.

"Miss Steele is coming with me. We've got a lead on Chronos."

Willie's anger immediately dissolved. "Then what are you waiting for? Go!" She shooed us both, but I stood my ground.

"You don't need me," I told Mr. Glass. "Cyclops can find the Aged Christian Society on his own, and you don't need me to talk to Mr. Mirth."

He searched my face, and that small triangular dent at the bridge of his nose appeared again. "I would like the company."

"I'm sure my company's far too dull for someone like you." I turned to Duke. "I'll assist you with Miss Glass's room."

Duke and I headed up the stairs. The front door didn't close until we were on the first floor landing.

Miss Glass's room was situated next to mine. I opened the window to allow some of the crisp afternoon air in and to blow out the stale. Duke opened wardrobe doors to do the same, then we both searched high and low for linen.

"Must be downstairs," he said, giving up.

"I'll get it. I need to stretch my legs."

"Servant door's in the corridor wall opposite."

I found the hidden door easily enough and made my way quickly downstairs. The service area ran the length of the house below street level. The kitchen was the largest room, with a pantry and scullery off it. Signs of the evening meal preparations covered the central table, but the small dining and sitting rooms looked untouched, as did the butler's and housekeeper's offices. I found the linen press, but the sheets were stored at the top. I stepped on a lower shelf, but my weight tipped the entire cupboard forward.

I jumped down and managed to keep the whole thing from toppling on me, but a flat box slid off the very top and crashed to the floor. It missed me by mere inches.

I righted the press and bent to pick up the box. No, not a box, a case with brass clasps that had sprung open. The case's contents spilled onto the floor. I bent to gather up the sheets of paper, but froze.

A picture of a bushy browed man stared back at me, his face a map of scars. He looked about thirty or so, but it was difficult to tell from the picture. The word WANTED in bold, blocky type labeled the fellow an American outlaw. He was worth five hundred dollars, dead or alive. But it wasn't the amount or the face that had my heart stopping. It was the name.

Bill Johnson. Johnson was Willie's name. This man was a member of Mr. Glass's family. According to the poster, Bill Johnson was wanted for robbing a general store.

Each of the twelve sheets of paper was a poster showing different outlaws wanted for crimes committed in various American states and territories. Three bore the name Johnson. One was the Dark Rider, the man from the newspaper article I'd read. The sketch was the same. His face wasn't clearly shown thanks to the beard and hat. According to the poster, he was considered extremely dangerous.

My hands shook as I replaced the papers back in the case. I stood on a chair to return it to the top of the cupboard, then hurried back up the stairs with my arms full of clean linen.

Duke and I finished making up the bedroom, and I joined Miss Glass in the drawing room while he disappeared into the kitchen to prepare dinner. Miss Glass dozed by the window so I sat and read quietly. Or tried to. It wasn't easy with my mind wandering back to those posters of outlaws with their grizzly faces and cold eyes. And then there was the Dark Rider, the man no one had seen properly. His value had been the highest of the lot.

Mr. Glass returned earlier than I expected. When I heard the front door, I sat forward on the chair, my heart in my throat; not from apprehension at seeing him again but because I was eager to find out what he'd learned from Mr. Mirth. That surprised me. I ought to be more afraid of him.

Nobody met him at the door and he came immediately to the drawing room. He glanced at his aunt's sleeping form then at me. I arched my brows and he shook his head. At my frown, he indicated I should follow him back out to the entrance hall. I hesitated then went after him.

Duke and Willie emerged from the rear of the house so I hung back near the staircase. "Well?" Willie asked. "What did Mirth say?"

"He wasn't there," Mr. Glass said heavily.

"Not there?" Duke said. "Where is he?"

"He left a few days ago. He simply walked out of the facility and nobody knows where he went."

"He left!" Willie shouted.

Mr. Glass shushed her with a glance back at the drawing room.

Willie made a rude gesture in the same direction. "He can't just leave. Isn't that the point of that place? The inmates are too old to care for themselves?"

"They're not inmates," Mr. Glass said. "It's a charitable institution for the aged, and there's no obligation for anyone to remain. If the patient feels well enough to leave, or a family member collects them, they can go."

"God damn," Willie muttered. "I hate this country."

"It's hardly England's fault," Mr. Glass told her.

Willie folded her arms and turned away. Her spine curved and she lowered her head.

"Don't you go all teary on me." Mr. Glass rested a hand on her shoulder.

She shook it off then suddenly turned and threw herself into his arms. Fortunately he was strong enough to catch her. If it had been me, I would have landed on my rear beneath her.

He held her a moment, until she composed herself and stepped back. "Enough of this sentimental claptrap," she declared. "We'll find this Mirth fellow." She suddenly looked at me. Despite her watery eyes, the gaze was as sharp as a blade. "She'll find him." She marched over to me and stabbed a finger into my shoulder. "You'd better, Miss Steele. If you don't, I'll...make you regret it."

They were just words. Easy enough to say, difficult to believe. But Willie's anger wasn't something I wanted to stoke.

"Willie," Mr. Glass chided.

"Goddamn it, woman!" Duke marched over and grabbed Willie by the elbow. "You're a damn fool. Threatening her won't help."

"Paying her isn't doing anything!" Willie pulled free then ran up the stairs, taking two at a time.

Duke shook his head and left too. Mr. Glass gave me a flat smile. "My apologies for my cousin's behavior. She can get emotional at times."

"Over a watchmaker, no less."

"It's a special watch."

"So you keep saying." I waited for him to tell me about his special rejuvenating watch, but he didn't. "Will we resume our search this afternoon then?"

He leaned back against the newel post. "It's late. We'll resume tomorrow." His gaze wandered past my shoulder.

"Harry, dearest, you're back," Miss Glass said. "How was your journey?"

Mr. Glass sighed. "I'm Matthew, not Harry. Have you settled in, Aunt?"

"I'm quite settled, thank you. I do think I'm going to like it here, despite your strange cousin and that other gruff fellow. At least I have Miss Steele as a companion."

"Good," he said, once again glancing at me. "But it's only for a few days. I'll be returning to America on Tuesday."

She waved her hand and headed up the stairs. "Come, Miss Steele, and play the piano for me. This house needs music."

I went to follow her, but Mr. Glass stopped me with a hand on my arm. "She likes you, Miss Steele," he murmured, his face close to mine. "Try to make her see that this arrangement is only temporary."

"I'll do my best. Perhaps it will help if she knew what was to become of her after you leave. Her brother has forbidden her to return to his house."

"She's not going back there," he growled low. "Not while I live."

I nodded in agreement. "But she does need to go somewhere."

***

A loud bang woke me up. It was very dark, and I could only make out outlines of the furniture in my room. Someone shouted from the depths of the house, too far away to make out their words. I jumped out of bed, hitting my knee on the nightstand, and fumbled for the candlestick and matches.

Another bang echoed through the house, shaking the walls and setting my heart pounding. It wasn't just any bang; it was a gunshot.

Then Miss Glass screamed.

CHAPTER 9

I abandoned my attempts to light the candle and ran from the room. My shoulder smacked into the doorframe, but I ignored the pain and raced to Miss Glass's room. The house was filled with shouts and footsteps, and the sound of my own heartbeat echoed in my ears.

"Miss Glass!" I didn't wait for a response, just pushed open her bedroom door.

She screamed again, but quieted when I assured her it was only me. I could just make out her shape sitting up in bed, the covers pulled to her chin. "Miss Steele! Thank goodness. What was that noise?"

"A gunshot, I think." I sat on the bed and clasped her shoulders. She shook violently. "Are you all right?"

"I...I think so?"

"Aunt Letitia!" Mr. Glass burst into the room. Even in the dark, he filled the space with his presence. "Miss Steele? I heard screaming."

"That was me," Miss Glass said, crisply. "Matthew, someone is shooting inside the house!"

He crouched by the bed near where I sat. He wore only trousers, and was entirely naked from the waist up. I swallowed and tried not to stare, but I failed miserably. Even in the dark, I could see the straps of muscle across his shoulders and down his arms. Muscles like that didn't appear on the bodies of idle gentlemen. They came from hard work. Or fighting. I tried to lean forward to see his chest.

He caught me and righted me. "Miss Steele? What's wrong?" His hands explored my arms, up to my shoulders and neck. They were warm and strong as they searched me for injuries. "Are you hurt?"

I drew in a breath to steady my jangling nerves. "I, er, that is, we're unharmed. What's happening?"

"I don't yet know." He let me go, stood, and strode out the door, leaving me with a heart beating harder than ever and nerves stretched to their limit. My skin felt warm where he'd touched me.

I stood too.

"Don't go out there." Miss Glass caught my hand. "Wait for Matthew to return."

The shouting had ended, and calm voices filtered to us through the still house. "The danger, if there was one, seems to have passed. I'll return in a moment."

I lit a candle and headed downstairs. Raised voices filtered up from the service rooms, so I made my way to the kitchen. Willie's voice reached me before I saw her. "*You* didn't lock up. It ain't my fault."

"I left the door open for you!" Duke snapped. "Did you take a key? No, you did not," he answered for her. "If you hadn't gone out, Willie, this wouldn't have happened."

"If I hadn't shot at him, you would all be dead in your beds! I scared him off, good and proper."

"You almost committed murder on English soil," Mr. Glass growled.

"What was I supposed to do? Wait for him to shoot me first?"

"Was he armed?" Cyclops asked.

"How should I know?" Willie said with a pout in her voice. "It was dark."

Nobody had a response to that, and I deemed it a good time to make my presence known. "Is anyone hurt?" I asked, stepping into the kitchen. A hissing gas lamp on the table illuminated their faces and the gun in Willie's hand. It also illuminated Mr. Glass's chest. I kept my gaze averted with some difficulty.

"We're all unharmed," he said.

"How long have you been standing there?" Willie asked.

"Long enough to hear there was an intruder," I said. "What did he want?"

I counted three whole seconds before anyone responded. "Money, perhaps," Mr. Glass said. "Silver."

"I didn't stop to chat with him." Willie thrust the gun into the waistband of her trousers. The flap of her jacket hid it from view. Did she go out with the gun every night? Did she wear it during the day around the house?

I swallowed heavily. "Did you hit him?"

"Would have, if it weren't so dark."

"And he wasn't so fast," Duke sneered. "Or it wasn't a Thursday in London and you hadn't eaten beef for dinner. You missed, One Shot Willie. You've lost your touch."

"Shut your mouth," Willie snapped. "You're lucky I came home when I did."

I shivered, suddenly aware that I was standing in the kitchen in nothing more than a nightgown. "Surely not. Burglary is one thing, but murder is entirely another. He wouldn't have harmed any of us."

The heavy silence blanketed us until Cyclops lifted it with a hearty, "I'm going back to bed." Like Mr. Glass, he wore no shirt. It wasn't until he walked off that I saw the scars crossing his back. There was at least a dozen, all old. "Goodnight, Miss Steele. Hope you can sleep after this ruckus."

"Goodnight, Cyclops."

"We should all return to bed," Mr. Glass said, dragging his hand through his hair and down the back of his neck. "Duke, make sure *all* the doors are secure now."

Duke didn't respond. He was too busy staring at my chest. It would seem I wasn't the only one who'd become aware that I wore only a nightgown. Thank goodness the lamp didn't cast enough light to reach my hot face or show the outline of my figure through the thin cotton. At least, I hoped not.

Willie smacked Duke's arm. He cleared his throat. "Right. Doors and locks. Doing it now."

He hurried off, taking the lamp with him, leaving my candle as our only light.

"Goodnight, Willie," Mr. Glass said.

"I'm not leaving you here alone with her," Willie said, folding her arms.

"Miss Steele is perfectly safe with me."

"It's not her I'm worried about."

He gave her a little shove and a stern, "Goodnight, Willie."

She grunted and stormed off.

"I ought to return to bed too," I said, edging away. "I'll look in on your aunt as I pass."

"Take her a cup of chocolate." He plucked a copper pot off its hook and disappeared into the pantry. He reappeared moments later with the pot half full of milk and a jar of honey in hand. He set them down and fetched a bag of sugar, chocolate and implements.

143

"You know how to make it?" I asked.

He laughed. It was so odd hearing the sound after such a trying day and evening. "Of course. I'll make you some."

I settled on the stool by the table and tried not to watch him as he stoked the fire in the stove to life, but I gave up. It was impossible. He was right there in front of me. No woman could look away when she was presented with such a fine masculine specimen. I'd never seen so many muscles before. Never seen a half naked man before. It was quite an, er, education. He was completely unconcerned about the damage his lack of attire could do to my virtue. Perhaps Americans weren't as troubled by propriety as we British. If that were the case, there was no need to feel guilty for staring.

"I want to apologize for my cousin's behavior," he said dripping a dollop of honey into the milk. "Again."

"She's very loyal to you."

He spooned in some sugar and stirred the contents. "Willie's got a good heart. It's difficult to find beneath all those prickles, but it's there. We've been through a lot together, and she worries about me as much as I worry about her."

"Why does she need to worry about you? You seem quite capable of taking care of yourself." All those muscles explained how he'd fought off those three brutes. Clearly he knew how to use them effectively. "Aside from your occasional bouts of illness, that is."

His stirring slowed, his attention focused on the task. When the milk began to simmer, he shaved off flakes of chocolate into the pot with a knife and whisked it into a froth.

I fetched cups and a chocolate pot from a shelf. He poured the chocolate into two cups and the pot. The pot and a spare cup he set aside, and handed one of the full cups to me. He indicated I should sit opposite on the stool. I did and looked up. His cheeks flushed and his gaze plunged to his cup.

I crossed my arms over my chest, hoping I didn't push up my bust more. "I know why you asked me to remain."

"I very much doubt that you do, Miss Steele." He swallowed loudly and rubbed a hand over his face. I suspected he was tired, but at least he didn't look exhausted to the point of illness.

"Then why?"

He set his cup down on the table and placed his palms flat on either side of it. He drew in a deep breath and let it out slowly. "I asked you to stay back because I need to talk to you." Finally, he would explain about his mysterious illness and the watch! "I think it's best if you leave tomorrow."

"Pardon?"

"I'm severing our arrangement."

No. He wouldn't. Surely he knew how much I needed employment, and somewhere to live for a few days. Surely he saw that I had nothing and nowhere to go. "But...you can't! You've paid me in advance."

"Keep the money. But you can't stay here. It's too dangerous."

My heart sank to the pit of my stomach. "Because of one intruder?"

He continued to avoid looking at me.

"It wasn't merely a burglar, was it?" I prompted.

"You can go back to the Masons," he said quickly. "Or secure new lodgings tomorrow. You'll find other employment soon enough too, I'm certain of it. You're a remarkable woman and—"

I stood abruptly. The stool's feet scraped on the flagstone floor. He finally met my gaze, but I found I could no longer meet his. It was all I could do to hold myself together and not burst into tears at the hopelessness of it all, at the heavy weight once again settling on my shoulders, trying to push me down into the floor.

He stood too. "Say something, Miss Steele. You can shout if you like. In fact, I wish you would."

"What of your aunt?"

He blinked. "You have no home to go to, yet you're worried about Aunt Letitia?"

"I am employable, Mr. Glass. I haven't had much luck yet, but it will turn soon. There must be a shopkeeper in London in need of an assistant. But your aunt is vulnerable. I doubt she can look after herself properly. I wouldn't want her to return to her brother's house when you leave."

"She won't."

"Does she have other relatives? Friends?"

"None that I know of." He pressed his knuckles on the table and lowered his head between his shoulders. I waited, but I wasn't really sure what for. I knew I ought to take Miss Glass her chocolate, but something kept me rooted to the spot. "Damn it!" he finally growled. "You can't stay here, Miss Steele. Don't you understand? It's enough that I have the welfare of Cyclops, Willie and Duke on my hands. They can at least defend themselves."

"Tell me about the intruder."

"It's better for you if you don't know too much."

"You're deciding what's best for me now?"

"I'm deciding what's safest for you, yes."

"I do wish you wouldn't treat me like a child or a simpleton. I'm neither."

"I'm very aware of that." His dark lashes lifted, casting shadows over his eyes as he watched me for a long time.

I bore it with what I hoped was defiance, while everything inside me wanted to shrivel up. I was about to be cast out on my own—again—without employment or accommodation. Living with outlaws suddenly seemed the lesser of two evils. I wanted to stay, very much. "Please don't do this," I said simply.

"Damn," he said on a sigh. "You're very persuasive."

I was?

"Do you still sleep with that knife?" he asked.

"Yes."

"Continue to do so. You can stay until Tuesday. My aunt too. I'll consider what to do with her in the meantime." He picked up our empty cups and stalked into the scullery. "Goodnight, Miss Steele."

"Goodnight, Mr. Glass." I left the kitchen with the chocolate pot and cup. My heart was still hammering by the time I reached Miss Glass's room.

***

Mr. Glass, Duke, Willie and Cyclops went out after breakfast, and it had nothing to do with finding Mr. Mirth, so I was informed. They wouldn't tell me where they were going, but I suspected it concerned the intruder Willie had shot at.

I spent the morning getting to know Miss Glass better as two charwomen worked in the other rooms. Indeed, I found her eager to discuss her family, and it took little prompting from me to discover her father had been just as horrid as her older brother. The free-spirited and kind-hearted Harry, the youngest of three siblings, had left the country as soon as he reached his majority.

"He asked me to go with him," she said with a sad smile. "He pleaded with me, in fact. Mama had passed by that time, and Harry was everything to me. I gave it some serious thought, but decided to remain here. Having his spinster sister trail along would have stifled him. He needed to be free more than he needed to breathe. Father and Richard had been so cruel, always telling him he was worthless. As the younger brother, he inherited nothing and had to find his own way in the world. Father wanted him to become a lawyer, but working in an office would have slowly killed Harry's spirit. So he escaped and never came back."

"Was your father angry?"

"Terribly. He flew into a rage after he discovered Harry had left. I was the only one he told, you see, and I kept the secret until after his ship departed."

"Where did Harry go?"

"Everywhere. He traveled to exotic lands—Egypt, Turkey, Russia, all over the Orient, Canada and America. He had a small annuity from our mother that funded his travels. She left him this house too, but he never let it out. He may have worked, but his letters never mentioned such things."

Perhaps because he knew his sister thought "such things" vulgar. "He met his wife in America?"

"Charlotte." She folded her hands over her lap where one of Harry's letters lay open. They'd been delivered to the house, along with her belongings, the previous evening. "He adored her. I could tell from his writing that he thought the world of her. But he never wrote about her family and friends. It seems Richard had one of those Pinkerton detectives find out more, but he didn't confide what he'd learned to me. All I knew was that he considered her beneath us."

I didn't remind her that Lord Rycroft accused Charlotte's family of being criminals or mention that my own investigation confirmed it. Nor did I tell her that both Harry and Matthew had probably joined in with the Johnsons' criminal ways. How else could Harry and Charlotte have funded their travels? How else could they have afforded a good education for

Matthew? For he was certainly a well-bred, intelligent man.

"Matthew was born nine months after they married." She picked up the letter in her lap and smiled as she scanned the page. "This one was sent from Zurich." She pointed to another, folded on the table. "That one from Venice. They went everywhere. Matthew was a well-traveled little boy."

"Until he returned to America when he was fifteen."

Her face darkened. Her lashes lowered. "I wish I'd seen Harry one last time before he died. I wish I'd known Charlotte, and met Matthew when he was a boy. He's a fine man, isn't he, Miss Steele? A handsome, strong man."

"He's certainly that."

"Kind too. So like his father." She sighed and closed her eyes. I thought she'd fallen asleep, but she opened them again with a start. "Ring for tea, please, Beatrice."

"I'm India," I said gently. "Not Beatrice."

"Yes, of course you are. Beatrice has a face like a sour hound, but you're so pretty, Miss Steele."

"Please, call me India. I'll fetch some tea."

"Matthew ought to engage servants," she said, unfolding another letter.

"He says he's not staying long, so servants aren't required. He uses charwomen. They're here now."

"I wish you would stop saying he's leaving when he's not."

I pressed my lips together. Disagreeing would only upset her, and it was her nephew's place to disappoint her in this matter, not mine.

"That's one thing I will miss about Richard's home," she said, spreading the letter on her lap.

"What is?"

"My maid. I must offer her a position here."

I left to make tea. Maids were not my area of expertise.

The mail slot in the front door squeaked and a letter dropped through by the postman. It bore an American stamp, but there was no return address on the back. I deposited it on the hall table, but its presence bothered me for the rest of the morning. I handed it to Mr. Glass upon his return in the late afternoon.

I expected him to look tired and pained, since he hadn't come home for luncheon, but he seemed to be in sturdy health. He must have taken the glowing watch with him this time, as he had done that first day I'd met him at my—Eddie's—shop. Perhaps he'd been worried that I would see it on his person and left it at home when we searched for Chronos together. I was glad to see him looking healthy. Illness didn't suit him at all.

"This arrived for you," I said. "Did you have any luck?"

"With what, Miss Steele?" he asked, checking the envelope.

"With finding the intruder."

He glanced up. "What makes you think we were looking for him?"

I arched my brows.

He grunted. "All is well. Please don't alarm yourself. I won't see any harm come to you or my aunt while you're under my protection."

It was quite a noble little speech, and it rendered me senseless for a moment. It had been some time since Father had been capable of protecting me, and for the last few years, I was the one taking care of him. I wasn't sure how to react to Mr. Glass's reassurance.

"Is my aunt well?" he asked.

"She is." I cleared my throat. "You'll also find there is a new addition to the household."

"Who?"

"Her ladies' maid. Miss Glass reinstated her this afternoon. She assures me her wages will be paid from her own funds."

"Money isn't a problem," he said absently, tearing open the envelope. His face hardened as he read, then re-read, the letter. "Excuse me." He left before I could ask him about our search for Mirth.

Miss Glass had retired for an afternoon nap and I found myself at a loose end. I'd already fixed the dining room clock, so decided to inspect the others in the house. The long case clock was in good working order, so I simply dusted out the housing and moved on to the other timepieces I'd spotted in other rooms. The brass Rococo in the music room simply required winding, and the lovely four glass clock in the drawing room was in perfect working order. I pulled out its mechanisms anyway to clean them, simply for something to do and to admire such fine workmanship. Tears sprang to my eyes as I set all the pieces back into place again. I might never work with clocks and watches again, never get to admire the fine craftsmanship that went into them, or the precise cohesion of the many parts to make something both beautiful and functional. I allowed my mind to wander as I worked and simply *feel* instead.

I don't know how long I spent on that clock, but I was woken from my trance-like state by the loud whispers of Willie and Duke coming from beyond the door.

"Why can't you do as you're told for once?" Duke hissed.

"You should know me better by now." Willie sounded huffy, but not angry. "I do as I please, and what I want to do is go out tonight."

"Stay home."

"No."

"Willie…" Duke growled. "It's dangerous. He's out there."

"He's got no argument with me, and you can stop giving me orders. You ain't nothing to me." She stormed into the drawing room, only to stop short when she saw me. "How much of that did you hear?"

I glanced past her, but Duke hadn't followed. "Most of it. But don't worry. I don't care about your squabbles with Duke, or anyone else for that matter."

She came to stand beside me and inspected the clock, although I suspected she wasn't really taking much notice. "I don't like being dictated to by him. Or by any man."

"Do you mean to say we actually agree on something?"

She smirked. "I know why I think like that, but why do you? I thought you liked your pa."

"I did. My former fiancé, however, is another matter. If I learned one thing from my time with Eddie, it's that I didn't like the person I became when I was with him."

She sat down and rested her elbows on her knees. "Go on."

"I know now that I wasn't myself when I was engaged to Eddie. I was trying to be an ideal version of womanhood to make him like me. I haven't had all that much luck with men, you see, and Eddie made me feel special. I didn't want to lose him because I voiced an opinion he didn't agree with." I didn't know why I wanted Willie to understand something so personal about myself, something I had only just begun to realize. Perhaps because we were both women around the same age, or perhaps because I knew she would applaud me rather than condemn me. I may be considered forthright but she was ten times more so. Besides, simply saying the words out loud was cathartic.

"You stopped being yourself, you mean," she said quietly.

I nodded. "I thought it would help keep Eddie. I was wrong. Not only did I lose him anyway, I almost lost myself too. *That* was much worse."

She leaned back and crossed one leg over the other. She regarded me with a frown on her brow but a smile on her lips. "I hate men too."

"I don't hate men. Just Eddie. My attitude toward them is different now, though. I won't go throwing myself at the next man who shows some interest in me." Not that I expected any interest now.

"You don't know men like I do, Miss Steele."

"Call me India."

"You don't know men, India." Her smile vanished altogether and the frown took over her entire face, tugging at her mouth, shadowing her eyes. "I pray you never do."

I wanted to reach out and touch her hand in sympathy, but I suspected she wouldn't like me to, so I simply nodded.

"Excepting Matt, of course. He's a good man, despite..." She waved a hand, as if I should know what she meant.

I waited, but she didn't elaborate. "And Duke and Cyclops?"

She merely lifted one shoulder. "I don't know them like I know Matt."

It would have been the perfect time to ask her for information about him, but I was worried it might be too soon and she'd push me away again. I liked that she was no longer resentful of me.

"Come with me tonight, India," she said suddenly. "Let me show you what a woman can do when she has a mind to do it."

"Go where?"

"There's a gathering of card players above a shop in Jermyn Street."

"A gambling den?"

"I'll teach you to play like a man and how not to be one of them silly, simpering females."

"I don't think I'm either silly or simpering, thank you."

She rolled her eyes. "You'll see how men treat you different when they know you're not helpless. Come with me. I would like some company."

"Why not take Duke with you?"

She pulled a face. "Good company. Well? Are you brave enough?"

I laughed. "I won't fall for your baiting. Let me think about it. I'll give you my answer later."

She left and I finished putting the clock back together, my mind on Willie's offer. Going to a gambling den wasn't something I would ever have contemplated until now. But I could do it. What was to stop me? Surely she wouldn't go if there was a chance of encountering danger. It sounded like a thrilling idea and not at all something the old me would have done. I had always done the proper thing, but now I felt like I'd woken up from a fog. I wanted to try new things.

Yet years of cautious behavior and a gentle upbringing made me hesitate. I warred with myself for the rest of the afternoon. I was only distracted by the deep rumbling of Mr. Glass's voice as I checked the clock on the half table near the door to his rooms.

"According to Jem's letter," he said to someone with him, "Sheriff Payne knows we're here."

Duke and Willie both swore. "How did he find out?" Duke asked.

"If my little brother told him, I'll gut him," Willie snarled.

"Jem doesn't say how the sheriff found out," Mr. Glass said, "only that he came to the house and demanded to know when we'd left."

"It won't be Jem's fault," came Cyclops's resonant voice. "It's more likely someone who wants Matt out of the way."

"That narrows it down." Willie's voice dripped with sarcasm.

"Someone who also knows the sheriff wants me, dead or alive," Matt said.

Wanted, dead or alive. Those were the words on the poster of the Dark Rider. I pressed a hand to my stomach and tried to catch my breath but my corset was too tight. I felt sick. A *sheriff* was after Matt. Then he *must* be the Dark Rider.

"He don't want you alive, Matt," Duke said heavily. "In a coffin is the only way Sheriff Payne will take you home."

They fell silent and I crept away from the door, abandoning the clock. I ran to my rooms and locked the door behind me.

CHAPTER 10

I didn't come out of my room until the dinner gong sounded. Not joining the others would have seemed suspicious, so I decided to act as normally as possible but I found it difficult to look anyone in the eye.

Fortunately Willie and Cyclops were distracted by Miss Glass's grand entrance alongside me. She'd decided to dress in a gown more suited to dinner with royalty. The silver thread through the dark gray silk shone in the candlelight, and the pearls at her throat and in her hair only drove home to me that I was in the presence of aristocracy. Me, a humble watchmaker's daughter.

"Miss Steele?" Mr. Glass's firm hand on my elbow caught me by surprise. "May I escort you to your seat?"

"Thank you."

He folded my fingers over his arm and trapped them there with his own hand. "Are you unwell?"

"No."

He bent his head toward mine. He smelled like spices and lavender, an intriguing combination that set my heart racing. "You look a little pale and you've been in your room most of the afternoon."

"Sometimes I like to be alone."

"So you weren't avoiding me?"

My heart rose to my throat. "Why would I avoid you?"

He pulled out the chair for me. "Because you believe me to be insincere. I would hazard a guess that you think me ungentlemanly too."

His hand felt heavy on mine but not unpleasantly so. "You *are* a gentleman, Mr. Glass. Your grandfather was a baron, no less."

"I hope I'm more gentlemanly than he was." One side of his mouth kicked up. "And please, don't hold my connections against me. I can't choose my family, but I do choose my friends very carefully." His breath ruffled my hair near my ear. "I hope you will be one of them."

Heat crept up my throat and touched my cheeks. His smile widened. He *knew* what affect his charm had on me, and that unsettled me more. "Mr. Glass, in all honesty, I don't know what to make of you. My thoughts swing from one direction to the other every hour of the day, even when you're not present."

He suddenly grinned. "I'm glad to know that you think of me that often."

I sucked in a steadying breath. Despite my determination to remain calm, it sounded ragged. "Mr. Glass, are you flirting with me?"

"Is that a crime?"

"Some would say it is, since you plan on leaving England in a few days' time. Besides, haven't we already established that you're insincere?"

The muscles in his arm tightened. He let me go. "My apologies, Miss Steele. I don't know what I was thinking." He strode off to the other side of the table and didn't look at me again.

By the end of dinner I felt hot and my nerves frayed, and I didn't know why. He'd done exactly what I'd wanted and ended his flirtations, as a decent man—a *gentleman*—ought to have done. So why did part of me wish he hadn't?

I couldn't sit still afterward in the library as I tried to read by the lamplight, so when Willie found me and asked if I was going to join her for cards, I agreed without hesitation. I needed to *do* something. A small voice told me I was being reckless, but I ignored it. I *wanted* to be reckless tonight. Hopefully a little adventure would put an end to my restlessness.

"India is coming out with me," Willie announced to Mr. Glass after his aunt retired to her room.

He lowered his brandy glass very slowly and deliberately. "India? What happened to Miss Steele?"

"She said I could call her India, so I will." Willie crossed her arms over her chest.

"I did," I said, although they seemed to have forgotten I was there. We three were alone in the drawing room where Willie and I found Mr. Glass reading the newspaper. Duke and Cyclops were nowhere to be seen.

"Miss Steele, would you mind stepping outside for a moment? I need to speak with Willie alone."

I agreed, since I planned on listening in anyway. He shot me a hard smile then shut the door on me. I placed my ear to it and listened to Mr. Glass rant at his cousin.

"You are *not* taking her with you," he growled.

"She's quite capable of making up her own mind," Willie retorted. "We're both grown women."

"Grown women are as capable of getting themselves into trouble as girls."

"We're neither of us silly, Matt. If we sense danger, we'll leave."

A moment's silence followed in which I thought she'd won the argument already. Then he said, "I forbid it. She's not like you. She's not...worldly."

"She damn well is, and if you can't see it then you're not looking hard enough."

"Worldly isn't the right word." A floorboard creaked and footsteps tapped before the floor creaked again. He paced across the room. "You're going into a room full of men. Men who will be drinking and flush with money."

"Not after I fleece them."

"Willie! Listen to me. Miss Steele is an innocent."

"No, Matt, she isn't."

"She is, damn it!" His vehemence surprised and confused me. Why was he being so fierce with Willie over this? "She presents herself as confident and resilient, but she's not. She's vulnerable and too trusting. You and I both know those are the qualities of an easy target."

I stumbled away from the door, tears stinging my eyes. I wasn't sure what hurt more, that he thought I was weak and pathetic or that he pitied me.

Perhaps he was right and I *was* the woman he described. I had trusted him in the beginning, after all. But I no longer wanted to be that person. I didn't want to be taken advantage of ever again. Eddie had taught me the error of blind trust. Nor would I be spoken about in such a manner. Mr. Glass didn't know me.

I burst through the doors and stormed up to him. "You are very much mistaken, Mr. Glass. I am not easy, nor am I a target, as you put it."

He caught my arm as I moved away, pinning me against him. We were so close he must be able to feel my heart beating through his body. His dark eyes swirled like thunderous skies as they held me as thoroughly as his grip. "You shouldn't listen at doors, Miss Steele. It's not polite."

"I think we are well past being polite to one another, don't you?"

"Yes," he murmured. He lowered his face until it was only inches above mine. My heart almost jumped out of my chest. "Politeness be damned."

Willie cleared her throat. Next thing I knew, she'd grasped my hand and I was being dragged out of the drawing room. "Don't wait up," she called out to her cousin. "You need your rest."

I glanced back at him. He stood as rigid as a statue, his severe gaze on me as if he could will me to remain behind with just his glare alone. I smiled and waved at him.

"Be home by one," he snapped.

"Two," Willie said, already halfway out.

"*One.*"

"Yes, Pa," Willie mocked. To me, she said, "We'll stay out 'til three, eh?"

***

"Watch and listen, but don't talk," said Willie as we approached a boot maker's shop on Jermyn Street. "Don't utter a sound, frown, smile, or try to signal me in any way, even if you think I have the winning or losing hand."

"How do I know what a winning or losing hand is?"

"Don't roll your eyes, raise your brows, or chew your lip or the inside of your cheek."

"May I breathe?"

"If you must, but not huffily."

My gaze slid to her, but it was difficult to see if she was being serious in the glow cast by the streetlamps. While the lighting here was better than most streets, it still wasn't enough to cut through the thickening fog. I pulled my coat closed at my throat, but the chill settled into my bones anyway.

It hadn't been a long walk from Park Street and the area was the best in London, but I jumped at every sound. The rumble of passing carriages and *tap tap* of footsteps were eerily disembodied in the dense air, like ghostly beings passing by. Willie seemed perfectly composed as she led the way to the Jermyn Street shops.

"Do you need new boots?" I asked as she knocked on the door of the boot maker's shop.

"This is the place," she announced.

"It doesn't look like a gambling hell. It looks like an ordinary shop."

"That's because it is, during the day. At night, the proprietor operates tables upstairs."

A thick-necked man with a small mouth opened the door, nodded at Willie then stared at me. I smiled and bobbed a curtsy. He continued to stare.

With a click of her tongue, Willie said, "Anyone would think you ain't never seen a woman before, Pinch."

"Not here, I ain't," he said.

"Oi!"

"You don't count."

She wove around the displays of shoes and boots to a door at the rear of the shop where the scent of leather was stronger. She pulled on a shiny brass bell and a clang responded from somewhere upstairs before another fellow opened the door. I turned back to see the first porter still staring at us. I hazarded a smile and, to my surprise, he smiled back.

The second porter didn't acknowledge us in any way. He was even burlier than the previous man. His jacket stretched over shoulders as large as boulders, and even his eyelids were thick with muscle. He took my presence in his stride and stepped aside so we could pass and climb the staircase, at the top of which was another door, reinforced with iron panels. A small lamp hung from a hook beside it, barely illuminating the top step. I had to feel my way up and take care not to trip. Masculine voices filtered out to us from the room beyond, mostly quiet but twice cut through by a raucous laugh. I pressed my hand to my roiling stomach. It was too late to back down now. Willie was unlikely to walk home with me and the thought of traipsing through the dark streets alone made me feel even sicker.

"Where did you learn about this place?" I whispered as Willie knocked.

"If you splash your money around at the hotels near the railway stations, someone flash will approach and tell you about a nice, friendly place where you can drink with his friends and enjoy a quiet game of dice or cards."

"You mean they go looking for likely gamblers?"

"They do. I made sure to find the ones where poker is played. It weren't easy. Poker's not well known here in England."

"What's poker?"

"A card game."

"Are you good at it?"

Her white teeth flashed in the dimness.

A narrow rectangular panel in the door slid open and a pair of eyes peered at us. They widened ever so slightly upon seeing me, before the panel slammed shut. The door opened and a tall, slender fellow, dressed like a gentleman, greeted us. He nodded at Willie and she nodded back. We handed him our coats and hats.

"Will you introduce me to your friend, Miss Johnson?" he inquired.

"Miss Steele, this is Mr. Unger," she said as she looked past him.

He bowed to me. "Welcome, Miss Steele. Have you come to play?"

"Observe only," I said. "Are you the proprietor of this establishment?"

"No." He didn't elaborate and merely stepped aside so we could pass.

Smoke rose in slender columns from a dozen cigars. It clung to the beams, disturbed only by the occasional draft. Gentlemen sat at tables, their concentration on the rolling dice or cards in their hands. Chairs clustered around some of the tables in the windowless room, and a door on the far side led to a second room. The fireplace was unlit, but the air felt cloying. Men dressed in crimson waistcoats and crisp white shirts stood at each table and seemed to be in charge of the play. The one at the hazard table held a hooked stick.

Willie headed to a table of card players to the left and took a spare seat, but it was several seconds before the hum of voices quieted. One by one, all the men turned to me until eighteen pairs of eyes focused entirely on my person. Clearly women dressed as women were an oddity in their den. I bobbed an awkward curtsy and hurried after Willie. She chuckled and shook her head at me. The fellow in charge of her table found me a chair and the portly middle-aged gentleman next to her made space for me to squeeze in.

"Good evening, miss," he said with a gap-toothed smile. "It's not often we're graced with such gentle company."

Willie muttered something under her breath that I didn't quite catch.

"I'm here in an observational capacity only," I assured him.

"Like our other new friend tonight." He pointed his cigar at the gentleman sitting directly opposite me. "Seems poker is becoming all the rage in London now. I can see why. Jolly good game." His rolling laugh filled the room. It must have been his laughter that I'd heard from outside. No one else seemed in such a jovial mood, most likely because he had the largest stack of money in front of him.

The other observer nodded at me with a friendly smile and I nodded back, then we both concentrated on the game.

"Five card cowboy stud," said the dealer to Willie as he dealt.

The man next to me leaned closer. "What do you know about this great American game, Miss...?"

"Steele," I said. "I know nothing about it."

"Name's Travers." He placed a monocle into his eye socket and studied his cards then turned his scrutiny onto me. He scanned me from head to toe, then shifted his chair even closer. He smelled like cigars and brandy. "You don't sound American."

"I'm English."

"Aha. A pretty young English rose. Perfect."

Clearly the lighting wasn't very good if he thought me pretty and young. "Thank you," I said, nevertheless.

"Has your friend taught you to play?" he asked, nodding at Willie.

"No. We've only just met."

He squinted at me through his monocle. "You're not a hustler, are you?"

"A what?"

"A confidence man, or woman, who pretends not to know the rules then fleeces everyone at the table."

"I assure you, I don't know how to play poker. Whist is more my game."

He chuckled and the monocle fell onto the table. He returned it and studied his cards again before plucking a single coin off his pile and placing it beside the others.

"She fleeced me last night," he said with a nod at Willie, "but I think I know her ways now."

Willie smirked. "Then I wish you luck, my lord."

Lord? I stared at Travers, but he was engrossed in the game and paid me no mind. I caught the gaze of the newcomer opposite and he shrugged. His bright blue eyes sparkled with intelligence.

I watched several rounds and thought I'd worked out which combination of cards constituted a winning hand. Then everything I'd learned was thrown upside down when the lord beside me won with nothing more than a pair of eights. Willie watched him rake in his winnings with a scowl on her face.

"Why did he win?" I whispered. "You had a pair of threes and sixes."

"He was bluffing. I folded too early." She picked up one of her coins and rubbed its surface with her thumb as if she were trying to remove the queen's face. She seemed in no mood to answer any more of my questions.

Lord Travers draped his arm across the back of my chair and leaned so close to me I could hear his moist smile. "My dear girls, why not call it a night? This is no place for lovely roses. We thorns might prick you." His guffaw had heads at the other tables turning.

"Speaking of pricks," one gentleman muttered loud enough for everyone to hear.

A sprinkle of laughter filled the room, led by Travers himself.

He won the next two rounds, much to Willie's annoyance. She tossed her cards into the middle of the table and sat back in the chair, arms folded over her chest. She was down to her last five shillings.

"Your friend doesn't like to lose," Travers said in my ear.

I swayed away from him. "I'm quite sure nobody likes to lose."

Willie's flinty glare slid toward him. She hunched over the table and scooped her coins toward her like a protective mother cat. Lord Travers chuckled. His fingers skimmed my shoulder up to the bare skin above my collar. I shivered and recoiled.

"Would you care for a drink, ladies?" asked the blue-eyed gentleman who'd suddenly appeared between Willie and me. He addressed me, but his hard gaze fell upon Travers at my other side. "Why not join me in the refreshments room, miss? All this poker is making my head spin."

"Thank you." I put out my hand. "I think I will."

He led me away from the table. Willie didn't seem to notice that I'd left, and even Travers didn't seem to care all that much. He simply returned his monocle to his eye and studied the new hand he'd been dealt.

The gentleman steered me to the adjoining room where sandwiches and little cakes were set out on the table. A long white tablecloth edged with lace draped to the lushly carpeted floor. Decanters and glasses stood ready on a sideboard, their crystal facets glinting in the candlelight cast by the overhead chandelier.

"Brandy?" he asked. "Wine? Sherry?"

"Brandy. Thank you for your gallant rescue, sir. I appreciate it."

He smiled at me over his shoulder. Although he wasn't a strikingly handsome man, he had a friendly smile and clear blue eyes. I guessed him to be in his mid-thirties, going by the lines fanning out from the corners of his eyes and stretching across his forehead. "I'm at your service. Miss Steele, was it?"

I nodded and joined him at the sideboard.

"My name is Dorchester." He poured two brandies from a decanter and handed one of the tumblers to me. "To your health, Miss Steele."

I sipped and eyed him over the rim of the glass. "Have you learned anything tonight, Mr. Dorchester?"

"I've learned not to play poker with Lord Travers."

"He does seem to win a lot." And have roaming hands.

"Your friend is an interesting character. Did I catch an accent?"

"Willie's American."

He made a face.

"You don't like Americans?" I asked.

"I've only met two, and they were somewhat brash, boastful fellows. They lacked polish and sophistication, if you know what I mean."

I simply smiled. While Willie and Duke certainly fit that description, Mr. Glass didn't, and I wasn't yet sure what to make of Cyclops. "What brings you to this gambling house?"

"Gambling." He grinned. "I'd heard about this new game of poker and decided to see what it was all about. I admit that I enjoy the thrill of winning, but I'm cautious too. I never wager more than I can afford to lose."

"Hence the evening spent observing rather than participating?"

"Indeed. And you, Miss Steele? Are you planning on returning to try your hand at poker another night?"

"I don't gamble." I had nothing to wager with, but even then I couldn't see the appeal.

"Perhaps you'll simply come and keep your American friend company again. It would make the evening more interesting if you were here." He smiled again.

Heat crept up my face. I sipped to hide it. "Are you from London, Mr. Dorchester?"

He shook his head. "I studied here in my youth, but reside in Manchester. I'm in manufacturing."

"Oh? Your accent sounds pure London to me." And upper class at that.

"So I've been told. I must have picked it up years ago." He sipped. "So tell me how a nice English girl winds up at a gambling den with an American woman who dresses like a man."

I laughed. "It's a long story."

"I have all night."

"Don't you want to return to the poker table?"

"Not when there is a more interesting option." Those lovely blue eyes fixed on me, and my face flamed.

I searched for something to say, but could only smile pathetically and sip my brandy. I was saved from responding by two men who joined us at the sideboard. They sported the cocky swagger of youth dipped in privilege and money. One poured drinks and the other, more portly fellow, helped himself to the cakes. The one with the drinks leaned back against the sideboard and downed the contents of one of the glasses.

"What's your name?" he asked me.

"Miss Steele," I said.

His pale gray gaze slipped over me, lingering on my chest, my throat, my mouth. His top lip curled into an indolent smile. "I'll double whatever he's paying," he said with a jerk of his head at Mr. Dorchester.

I blinked. "Pardon?"

He rolled his eyes. "Don't pretend innocence, Miss Steele. It's not going to earn you anything more with us."

Us? I glanced at his companion. He sneered, but thanks to the dusting of sugar on his lips, it didn't seem quite as sinister as his friend's. Even so, I knew what these men wanted and what they thought I was selling. I backed away.

"You're mistaken, sir," I said with as much courage as I could muster. "I'm not what you think I am."

"Course you are. Why else would you be here?"

Why indeed?

Mr. Dorchester stepped between the gentleman and me. He was shorter by a full head, but strongly built, where the other man was slender and wiry. "Kindly leave Miss Steele alone."

"I'm not paying a penny more," the gentleman snarled. "Your doxy isn't worth the double I'm offering."

Before my gasp had left my lips, Mr. Dorchester grabbed the man's coat at his chest and lifted him clear off his feet. The fellow swung his fist but missed. Mr. Dorchester threw him bodily against the wall. A moment later, Unger rushed in, and at least a half dozen gamblers crowded in the doorway behind him. More than one sniggered at the dazed looking fellow on the floor.

"India?" I could hear Willie before I could see her. She managed to push through the small crowd and rushed up to me. She clasped my forearms and searched my face. "What happened? Are you all right?"

"Quite, thank you." My hands shook and my heart pounded, but I wouldn't admit that to Willie. I was unharmed, after all, and the danger was over now.

She blew out a long breath and checked me over once again. "Thank God. Matt would haul me over hot coals if something happened to you."

Mr. Dorchester looked up sharply then away. He scratched his jaw but stopped suddenly and dropped his hand to his side. It was as if he didn't know what to do with it, or with himself, now that all eyes were on us both.

Willie eyed the fellow slumped groggily on the floor. "What happened?"

"Mr. Dorchester defended my honor against that man," I said.

Willie grunted. "Your honor?"

Mr. Dorchester straightened his tie. "It's impolite to call a lady a doxy."

"A doxy!" Willie hooted with laughter and kicked the shoe of the fellow on the floor. "Are you blind, sir? She's tied up tighter than a miser's purse strings. Wait'll I tell Duke and Cyclops. They'll laugh 'till their sides split."

I thrust my hand onto my hip. "And Mr. Glass? Will you tell *him*?"

Her grin faded. "Best not to tell him, unless you don't want to come here again."

At that moment, I didn't care if I never set foot in this gambling house or any other again. I'd wanted to be a little reckless and experience something I'd never done before, but staying in with a good book now seemed more appealing.

"This is why you should forbid women," one of the gamblers said to Mr. Unger. "They cause trouble."

"I'll have to ask you to leave, sir," said Mr. Unger to Mr. Dorchester. "No fisticuffs. House rules."

Mr. Dorchester held up his hands. "I understand."

"He was protecting me," I protested. "You should ask that fellow to leave. *He* started the trouble."

"Lord Dennison and Mr. Fryer-Smythe are regulars here." He nodded at the friend who'd set aside his cake to help his companion to his feet. "They've caused no problems prior."

"It's quite all right, Miss Steele," said Mr. Dorchester. "I don't think poker is for me, and there are other gambling dens in the city willing to take my money."

"But it's not fair!" I said. "You don't deserve this treatment."

He took my hand between both of his. "I'm tired anyway. May I be so bold as to suggest you leave now too, for your own safety?"

"Not yet," Willie said before I could respond. Her mouth set into a determined line. "I need to win back what I lost first."

"Or lose more!" called Lord Travers from the other room.

"Mr. Dorchester is right," I said. "We should go."

Willie seemed not to hear me. She marched back to the gambling room and resumed her seat at the poker table. She tapped her finger on the surface. "Deal."

"Would you like me to escort you home?" Mr. Dorchester asked as the others returned to their seats.

While the offer was tempting, I refused. I didn't know him well enough to walk alone with him in the dark. "I'll wait for Willie."

"Very well. But do be careful, Miss Steele. I'd hate to think of anything happening to you." He bowed. "It's been a pleasure making your acquaintance. I hope we meet again." He collected his hat, coat and gloves and spoke quietly to Mr. Unger, perhaps seeking assurance from him that I wouldn't come to any harm. Mr. Unger glanced at me then nodded, and Mr. Dorchester left.

I was sorry to see him go; not because I missed his company, but because it meant I ought to remain in the gambling room and not retire to the refreshment room. The fellow who'd called me a doxy—Lord Dennison—had fully recovered. He sauntered out too, a glass in hand, and leaned a hip against the roulette table. His cold eyes watched me and his lips twisted. I shivered again.

Lord Travers patted the empty chair beside him. "Come sit by me, Miss Steele. I'll keep you warm."

"I prefer to stand," I said and moved to the hearth behind Willie's chair.

They played a few rounds, with either Lord Travers or Willie winning most hands, even when they lacked good cards. I couldn't tell when either of them was bluffing, but Lord Travers seemed to have Willie's measure. He also had more winning card combinations.

I grew bored so picked up the carriage clock on the mantel. It was running perfectly well, but I removed its casing and inspected its mechanisms anyway. I ran my thumb over the wheels, feeling comfort in the familiar parts and their small yet precise movements. The metal warmed to my touch. I would have taken it apart and put it back together again for something to do, but I didn't have my tools with me. I replaced the back casing and returned it to the mantel.

After half an hour, the other two players on the poker table retired, having lost everything, and Lord Travers possessed most of the money. Willie was down to her last coins, and I found myself hoping she would lose so we could go home. According to the clock, it was half-two. I wanted to go to bed. My heart sank when I saw the three tens in her hand. A winning hand now would keep her here longer.

She pondered her cards for some time then pushed all of her coins forward.

Lord Travers matched her wager without hesitation, and added an entire stack more. Willie couldn't possibly meet it.

She lifted her brows at Mr. Unger who'd come to watch.

He shook his head. "I'm sorry, Miss Johnson, but the bank only lends money to patrons well known to us. If you return to America, we have no way to get our funds back."

She swore under her breath.

Lord Travers chuckled. "Surely you have something of value that you can wager, Miss Johnson." He licked his fleshy lips, wetting them even more. "Or your friend does."

Surely he didn't mean *me*? I recoiled. "Willie, it's time to go."

But I may as well have not been present. She didn't seem to hear me. She passed her hand over her chin, down her neck, and let it rest on her décolletage.

Lord Travers leered at me. The gamblers at the other tables had all stopped and now watched us with interest. The fellow who'd called me a doxy ambled over and leaned down to Travers' level to whisper in his ear. Travers snickered and licked his lips again.

"Come now, Miss Johnson," he said, "where's that American pluck you displayed the past few nights. You're not a coward, are you?"

Willie bristled. "Of course not."

I pressed Willie's shoulder. "You don't have any more money," I hissed. "Let's go."

"I have this." She pulled out a chain from beneath her shirt, at the end of which dangled a gold locket the size of a farthing. "My grandmother gave it to me before she died. It was her wedding present from my grandfather. It's all I have of them."

Travers looked disappointed. "Sure you want to wager it?"

Willie hesitated then nodded. She held it out for Travers to inspect.

He weighed it in his palm before opening it and inspecting the miniatures inside. "A handsome couple. I accept."

"Willie, is that wise?" I whispered. "What if you lose it?"

"I won't lose."

Lord Travers placed the locket with Willie's coins and rested his hand on the seat next to his thigh. "We'll see, shall we?" He returned both hands to his cards, fanning them out on the table. "Full house."

I'd not seen that combination of cards all night, but I knew it must be good. Willie's white face confirmed it. She looked like she would faint as she stared hard at her own cards, perhaps willing them to be better.

With a click of her tongue, she threw her cards on the table. She stood, shoving back her chair. "You cheated!"

Lord Travers laughed as he scooped his winnings toward him. Willie's locket glinted in the light. "Now, now, Miss Johnson. Don't be a sore loser."

"You cheated!" she shouted again. "You had a card under your leg. I saw you remove it and add it to your hand!"

Travers slipped the locket into his dinner jacket pocket. "What rot. Did I cheat, gentlemen?"

The other gamblers shook their heads.

"Stand up!" Willie growled. "You must have placed the card you removed from your original hand somewhere. Let's see under your fat ass."

"Willie!" I tugged on her arm, but she shook me off. "Please let's go."

"Listen to your friend, Miss Johnson." Travers collected the cards on the table and shuffled them. "Be a good girl and go home before you say something you regret." He stopped shuffling and eyed me. "Unless you're willing to wager something else."

I straightened. "That's quite enough of that. You may be a lord, but your behavior is deplorable. As is yours, sir," I spat at Lord Dennison.

Travers laughed around the cigar in his mouth, sending ash onto his lap. "Hear that, Dennison? The little chit thinks she can lecture *us*. She deserves a good spanking to be put back in her place."

I gasped and looked to Mr. Unger for assistance, but he merely shrugged an apology. I would get no help from him. Travers was worth too much to his business to risk offending him. And Mr. Dorchester, my only champion, was gone.

I grabbed Willie's arm. "Let's go. Now!"

But she didn't move. She bared her teeth and pointed her finger at Travers. "You're a low down dirty cheat and I will prove it. Stand up!"

Travers sprawled in his chair and grinned around his cigar. "Make me, little girl."

"Oh, I will, with the help of my friend, Mr. Colt." Willie jerked her coat aside and pulled out the gun tucked into the waistband of her trousers.

Several men fell back, bumping into one another in their haste to remove themselves from the vicinity, but none left the room. All were glued to the scene.

"Willie, no!" I cried. "Don't!"

But I might as well not have spoken. "Stand up, Travers," she said.

He placed his hand on the seat near his thigh again. "It's 'my lord' to you, miss, and no, I will not."

"For God's sake, move!" I shouted at him. "She *will* use it."

"I'm not afraid of a girl," Travers said with a chuckle.

Willie squeezed the trigger.

Nothing happened. She frowned and inspected the cylinder. She spun it round and round. It was empty. "Damn him!"

My heart sank. Mr. Glass must have removed the bullets after the shooting episode of the previous night. I wanted to swear as loudly as Willie. While I didn't want her to shoot anyone, we now had no weapons to defend ourselves. And the men knew it. They advanced.

Lord Dennison and his friend, Smythe-something-or-other, grinned like madmen and approached with slow, predatory steps. Dennison rubbed his crotch. Travers sat back and watched, smiling with those fishy, wet lips of his.

"That's it, gentlemen," he said, chomping down on his cigar. "Teach 'em how to respect us."

"On your knees," Dennison ordered, pointing at me. He fumbled with the opening of his trousers and his tongue darted out to lick his top lip.

His companion wiped beads of sweat from his brow. His breathing became ragged. I glanced at the men behind them, but none came to our aid. All watched with keen interest. This nightmare couldn't be happening. Surely I would wake up soon. My weak knees were very real, however, and so were the men leering at us with lust in their eyes.

I touched Willie's hand. Her fingers curled around mine and gripped hard. My heart plunged to my toes. I'd hoped she had something up her sleeve, but it would seem the gun had been her only security guard. Without it, she was as vulnerable as me. We were two women up against more than a dozen men, and she was as terrified as me. We didn't stand a chance.

CHAPTER 11

"How is your aim?" I whispered to Willie.

"Why?" she whispered back, her voice shaky.

Dennison wiped the back of his hand across his mouth, smearing saliva across his cheek. He grinned, a distorted stretch of thin lips.

"Get on with it, man," Travers urged him. "I want to keep playing."

"Throw the gun," I whispered to Willie.

I thought she'd protest, but she wasted no time hurling her weapon at Dennison.

He ducked, lost his balance, and fell to his side. The gun clattered to the floor, where it skidded under a table. Willie swore. Travers roared with laughter.

"Stupid whore!" Dennison shouted. "You missed."

He lurched to his feet. There wasn't a moment to lose. I reached behind me and snatched the carriage clock off the mantel. It felt solid, reassuring. The gold plating heated my skin and glowed in the candlelight. I threw it at Dennison's head. He saw it coming and ducked again, but the clock suddenly dropped too. It hit him square on the forehead. He fell back, unconscious.

"Bloody good arm," Travers said with admiration as he surveyed Dennison's prone form.

"Run!" I shouted.

Willie and I ran for the unattended door. Mr. Unger didn't try to stop us. Thankfully, no one did. Willie pulled open the door. I glanced back to see a collection of gentlemen gathered around Dennison, helping him to sit up. Blood trickled from his head wound, but he was alive, thank goodness.

A bell clanged and the porter at the base of the stairs opened the door there. Mr. Glass strolled through, holding a lantern.

"Matt!" Willie cried.

He lifted the lantern high. It illuminated the hard planes of his face and the black pools of his eyes. "Finally," he ground out. "I've been looking—"

"Yes, yes." Willie rushed down the stairs and met him half way. "Make yourself useful and fetch my revolver for me. It's up there, under a table."

Mr. Glass looked to me and then back to his cousin. His face darkened. "Why is your revolver not with you?"

"There's no time to explain." She shoved him. "Go!"

"No," I said as Mr. Glass climbed the stairs toward me. "Leave the gun." I glanced behind me, but the doorway was unattended. No one chased us.

I tried to push past Mr. Glass, but he caught my arm. "What is going on?" His voice sounded strained, tight, and a little tired.

"Matt will be fine," Willie assured me. "No one will try anything with him, and if they do, he'll just throw a punch or two. Won't you, Matt?"

Mr. Glass went very still. He stood two steps below me, bringing our faces level. His chest rose and fell with his heavy breathing, and his gaze bored into mine, as if he could dig out answers. I swallowed and considered heading back into the gambling room. It could be safer.

"Stay here," he growled. "I want an explanation upon my return."

He let me go and pushed past me. He only got as far as the doorway, however. Mr. Unger stood there with Willie's gun. He handed it to Mr. Glass.

"Do not return, Miss Johnson," he said to Willie. "This establishment can't afford to attract unwanted attention." To me, he said, "You should have stayed home, miss. Places like this are not for gently bred women." He slammed the door in Mr. Glass's face.

Matt whirled around. The lantern light swung in an arc, and the handle squeaked with the violent movement. "Get out. Now. Both of you."

The porter held the door open for us. We hurried through the boot maker's shop, where the other porter let us out to the street. Cyclops leaned against the carriage but straightened upon seeing us.

"That was fast," he said.

"We were on our way out when Mr. Glass arrived," I told him.

Cyclops lowered the step, and held the door open for me, but moved to the driver's seat when Mr. Glass ordered him to prepare to leave immediately. Willie followed me inside, and Mr. Glass came in behind her and suspended the lantern from the hook by the door.

He thumped the ceiling and Cyclops drove off. He sat on the seat opposite Willie and me as the coach rolled away from the curb. "Explain."

Willie *humphed* and held out her hand. "Give me my Colt."

"Not until I get a satisfactory explanation."

"You explain," Willie spat. "Why did you remove the bullets?"

"To avoid you winding up on a murder charge."

"You left me unarmed!"

"If you stayed in at night, you wouldn't need to be armed."

She crossed her arms and turned away from him. "You should have told me about the bullets," she mumbled at the wall.

Mr. Glass set his hat on the seat beside him and scrubbed his hand through his hair. "You're right. I shouldn't have left you vulnerable. But my opinion still stands—if you'd stayed away from the gambling houses, you wouldn't require a gun." He handed back the weapon.

"And my bullets?"

"Are at the house. I'll return them to you only if you promise not to gamble again."

"Ever?"

"Ever."

"Matt! I can't! I have to win back my locket."

His jaw fell open. "You lost your locket? Christ, Willie, I'm sorry." He closed his eyes briefly. "But I can't allow you to attempt to win it back. Promise me you won't gamble again."

"Promise," she mumbled.

He sighed and his expression softened. "Your opponent must have been formidable to have beaten you."

Her lower lip wobbled. "He cheated."

"I think he did too," I said.

Mr. Glass pinched the bridge of his nose. "Now I know why you were attempting to use your Colt."

"Oh, that's not why," I said.

"Shhh," Willie hissed at the same time that Mr. Glass growled, "Then why?"

He glared at her. She looked out the window and sniffed. I rested a hand on her arm, but she shoved it off. "Leave me alone."

I endured her silence and Mr. Glass's glare for the rest of the short journey to his house.

Once inside, Duke greeted us with an equally formidable scowl. Willie tried to push past him, but he blocked her path.

"Move," she snapped. "I'm in no mood for your lectures."

"I don't care! You were supposed to be home hours ago."

"I've been out later than this before."

"Not with her, you haven't."

Willie turned her thunderous look onto me. I hardly thought it fair to blame me when she'd invited me to go with her. I thought it wise to keep quiet on the matter, however. Her mood was black enough, and there was no telling if she had another stash of bullets for that gun.

"Selfish, that's what you are," Duke went on.

Willie lips flattened, but Duke gave her no opportunity to cut in.

"Yes, you are. You're a selfish woman and it's time you were told. Matt does everything for you—"

"Enough, Duke," Mr. Glass chided. "Willie, go to bed. We'll talk in the morning."

"See!" Duke waved a hand at Mr. Glass. "See what you've done."

Willie and I both turned to face him. He scowled at Duke, but in the better light of the overhead chandelier, I could now see the gray pall of his jaw, the dark smudges beneath his eyes.

"You didn't rest, did you?" Willie said quietly.

He didn't answer.

She blinked rapidly and folded her arms across her body, as if warding off a chill. "Did you at least use the—" He cut her off with a shake of his head and a glance at me.

Her chin wobbled and her face crumpled. She threw herself at him and he caught her, staggering a little under her weight. "I'm sorry, Matt. I'm so sorry. I'll never take India to play poker again."

I stamped a hand on my hip.

"She wasn't even that good a distraction," she went on.

"Is that why you invited me along?" I asked, as Mr. Glass held her at arm's length.

"A good question," he growled.

She wiped her nose on her sleeve. "I thought Lord Travers would find her...interesting. Unfortunately he was too engrossed in the game to pay her more than cursory attention."

"You *used* me!"

Willie merely shrugged. "I think I'll go to bed now. Matt, you must too. There's no point in staying up longer. Understand?" Her gaze flicked to me then back to him. Clearly she didn't want me detailing the evening's events to him.

He kissed her cheek. "Goodnight, Willie," he said on an exasperated sigh.

"Why are you being so nice to her?" Duke said once she'd gone. "After your ranting and raving for the last hour, I thought you'd be sending her to her room for a week."

"I have no authority to send her anywhere," Mr. Glass said. "She can do as she pleases. Besides, she's suffered enough tonight. She lost her locket."

"Hell." Duke's tapped his head back and shook it at the ceiling. "She'll want to win it back."

"I made her promise not to try."

"You think that'll stop her?"

"She's never broken a promise to me before."

Duke sighed. "You have more faith in her than I do."

"Therein lies your problem, Duke."

Duke grunted. "I'll wager you had quite a dull night, Miss Steele. Willie's not good company when she's got the gambling fever."

"Dull is certainly not a word I would use to describe our evening. It was anything but."

"Care to explain why Willie's Colt was under the table?" Mr. Glass asked. "And why you were both fleeing when I met you?"

"Fleeing?" Duke echoed.

"I also heard a thud," Mr. Glass said.

"That was the sound of Lord Dennison falling to the floor," I said.

Mr. Glass raised his brows. Duke gawped. "Why'd he hit the floor?" Duke asked.

"A clock hit him in the head."

Mr. Glass and Duke exchanged mysterious glances. "How?" Mr. Glass pressed.

"I threw it."

"Why?"

"He was paying me some unwanted attention. I suspect he was also drunk."

"Bloody hell." Mr. Glass searched my face, his eyes sharper than they'd been since entering the house. "Miss Steele, tell me honestly. Are you unharmed?"

"I am."

He blew out a measured breath then shot a glare up the staircase in the direction Willie had gone.

"Don't blame her," I said. "It's not her fault. The blame rests entirely on the shoulders of Lord Dennison and his friend. They're not gentlemen at all. I've known vagrants with better manners."

Mr. Glass bowed his head but not before he closed his eyes. He really ought to be in bed, or using his special watch. Perhaps both.

"Let's return to the clock," Duke said with earnest. "So you threw it and it hit that fellow?"

"Yes."

"Did it feel...odd to you?"

"In what way?"

"Did it sort of...fly of its own accord?"

"No." I laughed. "I threw it."

"Did it feel warm to touch? Did it glow?"

"That's enough, Duke," Mr. Glass said. "Miss Steele is tired and your questions are confusing her."

"But—"

Mr. Glass laid a hand on Duke's arm. They exchanged no words, but an understanding seemed to pass between them.

Duke sighed. "Goodnight, Miss Steele."

I watched him go, trying to fathom what he meant by his questions, and how he'd known the clock had felt warm. Was it special, like Mr. Glass's watch? If so, how and why? What metal had the watchmaker used? I'd never seen the likes of it.

Mr. Glass seemed determined that I not be given any answers to my questions. That only made me more curious. They were all hiding a secret. If it didn't have anything to do with timepieces, I probably wouldn't have cared so much, but since a watch was involved, and now a clock, I wanted to know quite badly. But I would get nothing from him.

"Do you require hot chocolate?" Mr. Glass's rich, melodic voice rumbled across the space between us.

"No, thank you. I'm all right."

His searching gaze studied every inch of my face. "Are you sure?"

I nodded. Something Duke had said occurred to me. "Why were you ranting and raving earlier?"

Several heartbeats passed before he responded. "Because you didn't return."

"But Willie says she's been out later than this and you've never worried so much."

"Willie dresses like a man and acts like a man. That keeps her safe. You, however, cannot hide your womanliness. Or your vulnerability. Is it so terrible that I was worried about you?"

My heart skipped to a mad tune in my chest. It was deeply satisfying to know he'd been concerned for my wellbeing, and yet it didn't quite make sense. We hardly knew one another. Perhaps he was presenting a façade again, but for what end, I couldn't fathom.

I began unbuttoning my coat, only to freeze when Mr. Glass slipped in behind me. His fingers brushed my neck above my collar and settled on my shoulders. He did not remove my coat but bent his head to mine.

"You haven't answered me," he murmured.

"I...I..." What was his question again?

"Cat got your tongue, Miss Steele?" His breath fanned my hair at the nape of my neck. If I leaned back, just a little, would he move away? Or would he allow me to rest against his chest?

"I can assure you I won't be gambling again," I said, my voice breathy.

He drew the coat off my shoulders and down my arms, slowly. "Good." His voice vibrated through my body. "I'm glad to hear it."

"Why?" I simply *had* to know or be eaten up with curiosity. If he was only pretending to flirt with me, I wanted to catch him out. I didn't want to be made a fool of again. "What does it matter to you?"

He slipped the coat over my hands, but did not remove it entirely. I was trapped by my own clothing, yet I felt no panic and no vulnerability. This man wouldn't harm me. Why I felt so certain of that, I didn't know. While my head was telling me to run to my room, every other piece of me wanted to remain.

"You're living under my roof, for the time being," he murmured. "It's my duty to protect every member of this household. Including you, Miss Steele."

"It's not necessary." I hardly knew what I was saying anymore. My mind was filled with a fog that made it difficult to think beyond the present, heady moment. "Does a landlord care what his lodger does in the evenings?"

"You are not my lodger."

"Employee then. Until Tuesday, that is."

He drew in a sharp breath. Then he stepped away, taking my coat with him. He folded it over his arm, smoothing it with his hand. "Thank you for the reminder."

"Reminder?" I shook my head. "Had you forgotten already?"

He grunted a laugh. "In a way."

"Mr. Glass, are you feeling all right? May I get you something from the kitchen? Or perhaps you ought to go directly to bed. Pass me the coat. I'll hang it up." I was very aware that I was rambling yet I couldn't stop. "You do look very tired."

His jaw hardened. "Thank you for your concern, but I'm fine. I'm capable of hanging up the coat myself. Goodnight, Miss Steele."

I sighed. I still wasn't sure if what had passed between us was real or not, but I missed it now it was gone. "Goodnight, Mr. Glass."

***

"I ought to be doing something," I told Mr. Glass over breakfast when he declared that I wasn't required that day. "You're paying me to help you find Chronos,

186

but sitting here while you go out is a waste of time. Surely there's something I can do."

"I'm not looking for Chronos today," he said yet again as he buttered his toast. "And you can't search for him without me. Only I know what he looks like."

Cyclops and Duke busied themselves at the sideboard, piling toast, bacon and eggs onto their plates, but I got the distinct impression they were listening intently to our exchange. Neither Willie nor Miss Glass had ventured down from their rooms yet.

"I can ask after Mirth," I said. "Someone may know where he's gone, who his friends are, *et cetera*."

He bit off the corner of his toast and didn't answer me until he'd swallowed. It gave me time to study him. While he looked less tired, the shadow of illness still clung to him. He required more sleep. "Someone may," he said, "but they're unlikely to give the information to you. We've seen how the watchmakers of London react to you. I don't want a repeat of your encounter with Abercrombie."

That encounter was still troubling me, too, as was Mr. Glass's reaction to it. Whatever he'd said to Abercrombie the next day had appeared to put an end to the accusation. The police hadn't come looking for me. I wouldn't risk going to see Abercrombie, however, and asking him why he'd been so cruel. Not until I knew for certain that he wasn't going to call for the constables at the first sight of me.

"I think I'll visit the Masons," I said. "Mr. Mason may know about the Mirth fellow."

"Very well. Enjoy your day out."

"Thank you." I sipped my tea. "I thought the search for Chronos was vitally important."

"It is."

"Then why are you not spending today looking for him? You're running out of time."

"A damned good question," Duke growled as he sat beside me. "Forget about...the intruder, Matt. Your other business is more pressing."

"I beg to differ," Mr. Glass said.

"Cyclops, you tell him."

Cyclops sat too. His pile of bacon toppled, sending the topmost piece onto the table. He stabbed it with a fork and stuffed it into his mouth as if he'd been starved of bacon for years. After he swallowed, he dabbed his mouth delicately with a napkin. "Matt is right," he said. "We need to find...the intruder."

"But—"

"But you're also right," Cyclops went on. "We need to find Chronos."

"Thank you for your insightful observation," Mr. Glass said wryly.

"Including today, and not counting Tuesday as we leave in the morning, we have three days. The question is, can we find both men in that time?" He picked up his teacup and swallowed the contents in one gulp.

"No, we cannot," Duke said. "We've made almost no progress in the hunt for Chronos. That must be our priority. The other thing can wait until—" His gaze flicked to me. "Until after your watch is fixed."

"It can't wait," Mr. Glass growled. "The intruder must be stopped before he returns."

"Why would he return here?" I picked up the knife and leaned forward. "You know him, don't you?"

He nodded. "It's someone we've crossed paths with in America."

"Who?"

"That's a private matter."

I sliced the top off my boiled egg with a single strike of my knife. The force caused it to miss my plate and land on the table. Mr. Glass reached across the table, picked it up and placed it on my plate. He smiled. I scowled back.

"Mr. Glass," I said. "Who *are* you?"

"I don't understand the question."

"Let me rephrase that." I picked up my spoon and dipped it into my egg, but did not eat. "What do you do in America? What is your business?"

He sipped his tea slowly. Duke and Cyclops stopped eating to watch their friend. They seemed as curious as to how he'd answer as I was. "Let's not discuss such vulgar things, as Aunt would put it," he finally said. "I don't want to bore you, Miss Steele."

"I wouldn't find the opportunity to get to know you better boring," I said, hoping to bait him into telling me *something*.

His lips parted. Then they kicked up on one side.

"If you insist on finding the intruder first and not the watchmaker, then so be it," Duke said quickly before Mr. Glass could speak. "But I'd like it noted that I'm unhappy with the order of your priorities."

"Noted." Mr. Glass fetched the teapot from the sideboard. He refilled my empty cup. There was no more discussion of his business affairs or of the intruder. Of course, if he were an outlaw, he wouldn't tell me outright, yet I was surprised he didn't lie either. "Miss Steele, may I ask you some questions about last night?"

"Of course," I said, hoping he wouldn't ask for specifics about the attack on Lord Dennison. I didn't want to relive the moments leading up to the clash. The thought of what could have happened made me feel even sicker today. I set aside my egg, no longer hungry, and placed my hand to my stomach.

"Miss Steele, is everything—?"

"Mr. Glass! The tea!"

He'd been refilling his teacup, but his gaze had been on me, not on his task. Tea spilled over the rim onto the saucer. He returned the teapot to the sideboard and picked up an empty cup. He tipped the spilled tea on the saucer into it and some of the excess from his own cup.

"Your questions, Mr. Glass?" I prompted.

"Yes. Last night." He cleared his throat and sat. "The man who won Willie's locket, Lord Travers. What was he like?"

"Portly, middle-aged. He liked cigars and he laughed a lot, but it had a somewhat arrogant edge to it. I also believe he cheated."

"If we were in America, I'd call him out," Duke snarled. "If a mob didn't attack him first. We don't stand for cheats, Miss Steele."

"We English don't, either." Except Mr. Unger, the dealers and other gamblers hadn't challenged Lord Travers. Were they afraid of him? Was he too valuable to the house? Or was it a case of Britain versus America? "Usually, anyway."

"How was his accent?" Mr. Glass asked.

I shrugged. "Plummy, as with all toffs. Why?"

"Did the others seem to know him?"

"Yes. Why, Mr. Glass?"

"He played poker extremely well if he beat Willie. It's an American game, and he went from losing to her on previous nights to winning last night."

"You think he's actually an experienced American poker player disguising himself as an Englishman in order to dupe people into betting against him? That's quite an accusation."

"Aye," Cyclops muttered.

"Perhaps he's a fast learner," Duke said.

"Perhaps," Mr. Glass said, thoughtful. "But I think it's something to consider."

I shook my head. "I disagree."

"Do you now?" he drawled.

"Yes," I said primly. "If he is an American pretending to be an Englishman for the sakes of fleecing unsuspecting gamblers, why would he choose to be a lord? It only draws more attention to himself, when he'd want to avoid notice. Besides, it's likely he'd run into other lords at gambling houses, and surely they must all know each other, if only by name."

"A good point," Cyclops said with a challenging lift of his one good eyebrow.

"It would seem my theory doesn't hold water," Mr. Glass said on a sigh.

"What theory is that?" I asked. "Why did you think Lord Travers might be American?"

"That is my affair."

"Oh? Do you think the explanation would bore me?" I asked, throwing his words back in his face. "Or are you hiding something?"

"We all have our secrets," he said quietly. "Even you."

I met his dark gaze with what I hoped was a fierce one of my own.

"Tell her," Cyclops said suddenly. "Tell her what you do, what you've done. I don't see no reason not to."

Mr. Glass's gaze slid to his friend and darkened. His nostrils flared. "My business is mine alone. If I wish to keep it to myself, that is my affair."

"But—"

"Don't, Cyclops." Mr. Glass's hand curled into a fist on the table. He held himself rigid as he continued to glare at his friend.

Cyclops was the first to look away. "You're making a mistake."

Mr. Glass got up and walked out. I waited, hoping Cyclops would go against his friend's wishes and tell me anyway, but he didn't. He and Duke finished their breakfast in silence. I gathered up a plate of eggs and bacon and took it up to Miss Glass's rooms.

I read the morning newspaper to her as she ate, then carried the tray and dishes downstairs afterward. I took the service stairs and met Miss Glass's maid, Polly Picket, on her way up, a shawl over her arm. She stepped aside to allow me to pass and bobbed a curtsy.

"May I take the tray for you, miss?" she asked.

"No, thank you. And please, Polly, there's no need to curtsy every time you see me." Although I'd been introduced to her as Mr. Glass's employee, she'd treated me as a member of the family ever since. I suppose the rules in this household were unclear, to her and to me, and she thought it safer to be submissive to all of us.

She continued on her way up and I continued on my way down. Mr. Glass's deep voice rumbled from the direction of the kitchen, but I couldn't quite make out the words. As I drew closer, I heard Cyclops's even deeper voice respond quite clearly.

"Better for her that she doesn't know what you are? Or better for you?" he asked.

I stilled, hardly daring to breathe. It sounded like Cyclops was rebuking Mr. Glass for not answering my question about his business affairs over breakfast. I shouldn't eavesdrop—

Bollocks. Yes, I should. If I wanted to learn more about the people I was living with, I had to resort to underhanded methods. I inched closer.

"It's not *what* I am," Mr. Glass said, "but what I've done. I don't want her to know." This last was added quietly. I had to strain to hear him. "Answering her question would have inevitably led to...that."

"Why don't you want her to know?"

"Why do you think?" he snarled. "Aunt Letitia too. Don't tell either of them."

"It happened years ago. It's in the past, buried and forgotten."

"Then why does it follow me everywhere, even here and now?"

Their silence was punctured only by the sound of liquid being poured. I was about to walk into the kitchen, when Mr. Glass spoke again.

"She's keeping a secret too. The watchmakers are wary of her. She must know why."

Now *that* I resented. I didn't have a clue why they shunned me.

But it was time I found out.

CHAPTER 12

I headed out at the same time as Mr. Glass, accepting a ride in his carriage to the Masons' St. Martin's Lane shop and house. Mr. Glass paid me little attention. His nose was glued to the windows, watching for signs of someone following us, I suspected. If he spotted anyone, he didn't say so to me or Duke who rode with us. Willie hadn't risen by the time we departed, so he'd left her home.

"Enjoy your day, Miss Steele," Cyclops called down as I alighted from the carriage.

I clamped a hand to my hat to stop it falling off as I peered up at him. "You too, Cyclops."

Mr. Glass tugged on his hat brim. "I'll see you for dinner."

The coach rumbled away. It hadn't even reached the corner when Catherine burst out of the house like an excited puppy. She threw her arms around me, almost knocking me over.

"India! It's so good to see you." She clasped my hand and dragged me toward the door. "I've been dying to tell you something."

"What?"

She pushed the door closed and took both my hands in hers. Her grin split her flushed face. "You'll never believe it, but John Wilcox has come calling."

"Who?"

"John Wilcox! The manager from the steelworks factory."

"I remember him now." I'd run occasional errands to the steelworks factory when I'd needed supplies over and above our regular delivery. "Do you mean to say he's calling here with a view to courting you?"

"Yes! Isn't it thrilling?"

Clearly she thought it thrilling, since she couldn't stand still. Her fingers kneaded mine and she bounced on her toes. I wasn't as thrilled as her. John Wilcox was in his thirties and rather dour in nature. I couldn't imagine him keeping up with such an energetic person as Catherine. I hoped he didn't stifle her. Of course, it may not get to that stage. Surely she'd tire of him first.

"India?" Mrs. Mason emerged from the kitchen, wringing her hands in her apron. "I didn't know you were stopping by today."

"My visit wasn't planned," I said, smiling.

"Well. You're welcome, of course. I've just baked fresh butter biscuits." She returned to the kitchen, leaving me staring at her back. She'd never been an enthusiastic person, like Catherine, but she'd always been welcoming. While she wasn't rude this time, she wasn't keen to see me either. Something had changed. Perhaps her husband had finally confided in her about whatever it was that troubled him—whatever was troubling all the watchmakers.

"He's quite distinguished, don't you think?" Catherine said, once again taking my hand and pulling me after her. We didn't head to the kitchen, however, but to the sitting room.

"Ye-es," I said. "I suppose he does look distinguished." If a little thick in the middle and around the jaw. And in the head.

"And he says I'm the most agreeable young woman he's ever met. He smiled as he said it. Most flirtatious."

"Agreeable? That's what he gave as his main reason for courting you?"

"I know! It's quite a compliment, isn't it? And we're not courting *yet*, India. Steady on. He has only said that he'll call on me."

"Catherine, do promise you'll be careful. Don't jump at the first proposal you get." Unlike me. "I'm sure there'll be others."

"Don't be silly. Why do I need to be careful? India, he's a *manager*. They earn much more than ordinary shopkeepers, so Gareth said."

"I do hope that's not your primary consideration for encouraging him," I said. "Your brother doesn't know the particulars of Mr. Wilcox's situation. Besides, some shopkeepers do very well."

Catherine flounced into a chair by the unlit fireplace. "Why won't you be pleased for me?"

I crouched in front of her and took her hand in mine. "Catherine, you are a lively, friendly, beautiful girl, and I'm sure Mr. Wilcox is the first beau of many for you. I just don't want you to rush into anything, like I did."

"Mr. Wilcox isn't like Eddie, India. He's honest and solid. He's a good man."

"And Eddie is the dried turd on a sheep's behind."

She snickered. "Yes, but don't let Mama hear you say it."

I grinned and stood. "Speaking of your mother," I whispered, "she seems upset with me. Both your parents do. Have I done something wrong?"

"I'm not sure," she whispered back, glancing at the door. "She did mention that she's disappointed in your choice to live with Mr. Glass."

"I'm his lodger."

"She thinks you've lost your moral compass since your father died." She frowned. "Or that it's no longer pointing north. Something like that." She waved her hand. "I overheard Papa tell her that he's worried about your influence on me."

As had I. The Masons had never been worried before Father died. Why had everything suddenly changed? It was disconcerting, to say the least. The Masons were good people and my friends. Without them... I didn't want to think about the loneliness the loss of their friendship would bring. "Do your parents think I'm going to corrupt you?"

"I don't know."

"Would you like to come and live in Mr. Glass's harem with me?" I teased, trying to make light when all I felt was heavy.

She giggled again. "You're so wicked, India. If only everyone knew you like I did, you'd have a dozen beaus knocking on your door. You ought to allow men to see you as you are and not be so stern with them."

I blinked down at her, the wind well and truly knocked out of my sails. "Stern? Is that how others see me?"

She bit her lip and lifted one shoulder. "If my brothers can be taken as a good representation of the masculine gender, yes. Sorry," she squeaked. "I've upset you."

"No." I laughed as I sat on the chair. "Not at all. Don't take offence on your brothers' accounts, but they don't appeal to me either. Perhaps my sternness is a way of keeping men like them at a distance." I laughed again, but her words struck a chord. It wasn't the first time she'd called me prickly, nor was she the only person to have done so. Perhaps there was some truth to it. Perhaps I only had myself to blame for being a spinster.

If they thought me prickly, what would they think of Willie? I was a sweet angel compared to her. That thought lifted my mood somewhat.

Mrs. Mason entered carrying a tray with teapot, cups and warm butter biscuits. "I thought you would have been too busy to make calls," she said, setting the tray down.

"Not too busy to see old friends," I said. "Good friends."

She smoothed down her apron, her lips flattening. "Yes. Well."

"I'll pour," I said. "Please sit down, Mrs. Mason. Have tea with us."

"Very well. Has Catherine told you about Mr. Wilcox?"

I nodded. "I'm pleased for her."

"India has cautioned me from rushing into anything," Catherine said. "As you have, Mama."

"You always were a cautious, considerate girl, India. A steadying influence on our Catherine, that's what you were."

Were? I tried to catch her attention, but she wasn't looking at me. She didn't meet my gaze as we sipped our tea and ate biscuits like three ladies without a care in the world. But the tense undercurrent wasn't lost on me—or on Catherine, I suspected. She became extra bubbly, filling in the conversational gaps with gossip she'd heard from other families in the watch and clock business. I let her continue in the hope she'd mention something about why I was no longer welcomed by people I'd known for years. Finally my patience was rewarded when she mentioned Mr. Lawson, the watchmaker I'd forced to tell us about Mirth. Catherine's pretty face crumpled into a frown when she spoke about his new apprentice.

"What is it?" I asked. "Is there something the matter with the apprentice?"

"It's not him." She glanced at her mother. "It's nothing."

"It can't be nothing," I said, wishing I hadn't invited Mrs. Mason to join us for tea. "Is something wrong with Mr. Lawson? Is he ill?"

"Oh, India, he's being beastly about you." Catherine never was very good at keeping secrets from me.

"Catherine," her mother said stiffly, "you shouldn't tattle."

"But India ought to know what people are saying about her. You said so to Papa yourself."

Mrs. Mason's face colored. "You shouldn't listen at doors."

"I wasn't," Catherine muttered. "I heard you through the wall."

"What are people saying about me? Go on," I said when she hesitated. "I can take a little criticism on the chin."

She drew in a deep breath and let it out slowly. "Mr. Lawson is saying that you've become wicked since your father passed."

"Wicked? Because I'm living in Mr. Glass's house?"

Mrs. Mason sipped her tea loudly. It would seem she wasn't going to disagree with me. Perhaps because she wasn't prepared to offer me a bed here.

Catherine winced. "I suppose so. Eddie has chosen not to defend your honor, too. Can you believe it? What a horrid man he turned out to be, and yet he was so nice in the beginning. So, your Mr. Glass, is he as lovely as he seems?"

"He's...quite well mannered." Except when he was stroking the underside of my bare breast after opening my corset. And when he was flirting with me for reasons I couldn't fathom. "He's been kind to me. His aunt too, and his cousin, Willemina." It was worth reminding them about the females living in Mr. Glass's household. I may not have been able to stop the gossip, but I could reassure my friends. "Neither Eddie's nor Mr. Lawson's opinions matter to me now. Did Mr. Lawson tell you that I called on him recently as part of our search for Mr. Glass's mysterious watchmaker?"

"No, but perhaps he told Papa. They were alone for some time last night in the workshop." Catherine's gaze slid to her mother's. She bit her lip then sipped her tea.

I forged on. "Apparently Mr. Lawson knew the whereabouts of a Mr. Mirth, a watchmaker who closed his shop some years ago and traveled overseas. Do you know Mirth, Mrs. Mason?"

She frowned into her teacup. "The name does ring some bells, but I can't picture him. He couldn't have been one of our close circle or I would know."

I believed her. She wasn't a liar. "Hopefully he'll turn up," I said. "Mr. Glass is quite keen to find him."

"Your Mr. Glass if a very determined man," Catherine said with a sly smile. "What will he do if he can't find Mirth?"

"Continue to question the other London watchmakers I suppose, although he has to speak to them on his own while I remain in the carriage." Although I looked at Catherine, I watched her mother out of the corner of my eye. She held herself quite still. "Many of them seem wary of me."

"Wary?" Catherine repeated. "How so?"

"Almost as if they're afraid of me. It's quite odd."

"Why would they be afraid of you? Do you think it's because Mr. Abercrombie has accused you of stealing?"

"I don't think so. Mr. Abercrombie's accusation seemed to be a product of his wariness, not the other way round. Speaking of which, have he or the police come here asking after me?"

"No," Catherine said. "I do hope that means he retracted the accusation. Horrid man. I never liked him."

"He has retracted it," Mrs. Mason said. "So your father told me last night."

"He has?" I felt faint with relief. "Thank goodness." So Mr. Glass *had* taken care of it, like he'd promised. It only remained to be discovered *how* he managed to get Abercrombie to do an about-face. "Do you know why he changed his mind, Mrs. Mason?"

"No."

Her coolness toward me was beginning to grate on my nerves as well as worry me. I decided to confront her on it. "I do hope you don't believe the rumors Mr. Lawson, Eddie and the others are spreading about Mr. Glass and me. I can assure you, our arrangement is decent and correct." I just thought of something that might get her to think differently. "He's the nephew of Lord Rycroft."

"He's a lord!" Catherine half rose out of her seat in excitement.

"No, just a mister. His uncle is the current baron."

Both Mrs. Mason and Catherine pressed their hands to their chests, as if trying to still rapid heartbeats. "He's a gentleman of quality then," Mrs. Mason said, her face lifting. "How kind that he's taken you in, India."

My smile tightened. "Very kind."

"Don't allow your head to be turned, though," she warned. "Nobility is all well and good, but he's a man underneath it all. Mark my words, India, high born men are not very different from low born men when it comes to it."

"Mama! You're frightening her."

I laughed. "Not at all. Thank you for your concern, Mrs. Mason, but I am in no danger from Mr. Glass." It was time to change the subject. Being lectured wasn't something I was used to, or liked. Father had never been one to do so after my mother died. "Mr. Glass had other errands to run today, but we hope to resume our search for Mirth and the watchmaker tomorrow and discover if they are one and the same."

"On a Sunday?" Mrs. Mason said. "The shops will be closed, and I don't recommend you visit anyone at home."

"Why not?" Most watchmakers lived above their shops or nearby. I knew where to find many of their homes.

"I don't think it's a good idea."

"Mr. Glass leaves on Tuesday, so we need to use all the time left to us."

"Tuesday? Good."

"Why?" both Catherine and I asked.

Mrs. Mason shrugged and glanced at the door. She looked like she wanted to escape but didn't want to leave either. Perhaps she didn't want to leave me alone with Catherine. She was afraid of me too.

The notion opened a well inside me that filled with an ache. "Mrs. Mason," I ventured, "why have you changed toward me? What have I done to deserve this...coolness I'm confronted with at every turn?" I managed to keep the wobble out of my voice until the end.

"Nothing," Catherine said brightly. "No one is cool toward you. Are they, Mama?"

But Mrs. Mason didn't answer. She set down her cup and buried her hands in her apron.

"Mama?" Catherine shifted forward on her seat and glanced nervously at me.

"Mrs. Mason?" I prompted. "Please."

"I don't know anything," she said, sounding wretched. She was an honest, good woman with a kind heart. So what was stopping her from being open with me? "Mr. Mason was urged not to help you find the watchmaker, that's all. Not that he can! He doesn't know of anyone fitting the fellow's description, and nor do I."

"But you were warned, nevertheless," I said, sitting back heavily. "By whom?"

Catherine gasped. "That's why Papa has received so many callers of late. Several guild members have visited him in the last two days," she told me. "We never usually see them, as Papa isn't particularly friendly with them, so it's been quite noticeable."

"Some of the more senior members have paid calls," Mrs. Mason clarified.

"Led by Abercrombie," I muttered.

"He hasn't been here himself," she said.

But he was most likely behind the visits. "Why does he dislike me so much?"

Catherine set her cup down and crouched before me. Her sweet face was full of earnestness. "I've never liked him. He's an upstart and a...a toad, and he thinks women are beneath him. He's afraid of your skill as a watchmaker, that's my theory. Afraid of seeing a woman surpass him." She looked to her mother. "Do you agree, Mama?"

"I do," she said with an emphatic nod and a sigh of relief. Why would she be relieved by such an explanation?

Unless it wasn't the entire explanation, yet it meant not having to give me the other, more troubling one.

Part of me wanted to push her to tell me, but I suppressed the urge. I didn't want to place her in an awkward position.

"My presence here is making things difficult for you," I said, rising. "I'll leave."

"No, please stay longer," Catherine urged.

Her mother, however, rose too. "It was lovely seeing you again, India. Do take care." She set about gathering the dishes, ignoring her daughter's narrow-eyed glare.

I took Catherine's hand and led her to the front door. "You've been very kind, Catherine, but I won't visit for some time. I don't want to trouble your parents any more than I have."

"Don't mind Mama." She lowered her voice. "Mr. Abercrombie and the guild frighten her. She's not strong like you or me."

"And your father? Do they frighten him too?"

"He must do as they say or risk censure."

"Yes, of course. You're right." It was selfish of me not to think about the predicament the Masons were in. Whatever reason they had for being wary of me, explaining might get them into further trouble with the guild. Trouble they could ill afford with an organization that held such power over their livelihood. I needed to find another way to find the answers. I had an idea. "I wish I could give Mr. Abercrombie and the other Court members a piece of my mind. Do you know when they next meet?"

Her eyes bulged. "You're not considering going, are you?"

"Why not?"

"Because...it's madness! They'll all be against you, and...and it would be awful."

"On the contrary. I might finally get some answers. Besides, what can they do to me now? They've kept me from becoming a member, warned their members not to employ me, and almost had me arrested for a crime I didn't commit. They've used their power to rob me of my home and my livelihood. As I see it, I have nothing more to lose. They cannot possibly take anything else from me, as I have nothing to take."

Her lower lip wobbled and she threw herself into my arms. "Oh, India, you are the bravest soul." Her voice shook and I felt a wet tear fall onto my neck. "I wish I could do more to help you, but I feel so useless."

I hugged her and patted her back. "You're doing more than enough simply by remaining my true friend. Besides, you can help me. You can tell me when the guild next meets."

She pulled away and wiped her cheeks with her thumb. For a long moment, I thought she wouldn't answer me, then she said, "I overheard Papa tell Mama it's tonight at seven o'clock."

***

I spent the afternoon looking for employment and suitable accommodation but my mind was on the task I'd set for myself that night. I would confront the guild members about their changed attitude toward me and see if the reason behind it was merely their resentment of my gender or something more. I would also ask them about Mr. Mirth. That way, Mr. Glass could come along. While I didn't think they'd use force to throw me out, it would nevertheless give me more confidence to have him at my side.

My distracted mind was probably the reason I was unsuccessful in securing new employment. I did, however, find clean and comfortable rooms to let on the second floor of a modest Bloomsbury house. The landlady was a widow of the late curator of the British Museum's medieval collection and seemed relieved to have a female applicant. I promised to deliver references before Tuesday. I didn't tell her that my employer would leave London that day and I had nothing further lined up.

It was a mere forty minute walk back to Park Street, but a sudden burst of rain forced me to make an unscheduled stop beneath the butcher's awning at the Circus end of Oxford Street. I waited with several shoppers who'd also been caught without umbrellas, much to the butcher's annoyance. He huffed and puffed in the doorway but fortunately didn't force anyone to move on.

"Miss Steele?" The voice behind me was familiar, yet I couldn't quite place it.

I turned, and drew in a sharp breath. "Mr. Dorchester! What a coincidence." The fellow from the gambling house looked fairer in daylight; his eyes bluer. They turned his rather ordinary face into something remarkable. I couldn't look away.

He smiled and doffed his hat. "It certainly is. I see you've been caught without an umbrella."

"I have, and the rain looks set in for the day."

"Then allow me." He handed me his folded umbrella.

"No, I couldn't possibly take it."

"Then may I walk you home and we can share it? It's large enough."

It wasn't far to Park Street. Besides, Mr. Dorchester was an amiable fellow and having some company might take my mind off the guild meeting.

"Thank you, I accept, as long as Park Street isn't out of your way."

"Not at all. I was on my way home anyway."

"Is that nearby?"

"This side of Piccadilly Street, so not far."

We stepped out of the milling crowd, and he put up his umbrella. Our arms touched as we walked so that neither of us got too wet.

"I must say, I'm glad to see you," he said as we passed shoppers hurrying to get out of the rain. "I was worried about you."

"Oh, thank you, but we were fine." Thanks largely to my aim.

"Nevertheless, I didn't like leaving you there, but Mr. Unger assured me you wouldn't come to harm. If he hadn't promised, I would have insisted on staying."

I didn't tell him that Mr. Unger and the other gamblers hadn't been any assistance at all when we'd been attacked. The incident was in the past, and I saw no reason to let Mr. Dorchester feel terrible for leaving us there.

"Did your friend win after I left?"

"She lost quite badly."

"That's a shame. It doesn't look like a game for the faint of heart. All that bluffing...I'm not sure I have the right countenance for it."

"And what countenance do you think is required of a good poker player?"

"The ability to lie with a straight face."

I laughed. "I quite agree. It's not a game for me. My father used to tell me that my thoughts were written all over my face."

"Your father is a wise fellow."

I didn't tell him my father should be mentioned in the past tense. I was still very aware that Mr. Dorchester was a man and I a single woman alone. Allowing him to think there was no man to care for me might give him ideas similar to those the horrible lords in the gambling house had. Although I couldn't imagine Mr. Dorchester being like them, it never hurt to be cautious.

We maneuvered around a large puddle as we crossed New Bond Street then fell into step once again.

Our pace and stride matched, but I couldn't tell if that was a deliberate effort on his part.

"Tell me about your factory, Mr. Dorchester."

He frowned. "You cannot possibly be interested in that."

"I'm sure it's very interesting."

"Thank you, but I won't bore you with the details. Tell me about yourself."

I provided him with the briefest summary, once again avoiding mentioning my father's death. "I'm staying with Willie and her friends, newly arrived from America," I told him. "But only until they leave on Tuesday."

"How does a watchmaker's daughter make friends from so far afield?"

"We met through an acquaintance." Eddie could be considered an acquaintance of both Mr. Glass's and mine, so it wasn't a lie.

We talked the entire way back to Park Street, mostly about the sights he'd seen since arriving in London a few days before. He'd combined a sightseeing journey with a visit to his lawyer's office, but was only in the city for a few more days. I told him which coffee shops had the best coffee, and where he could find the best silks as gifts for his mother and sister back home. That steered us onto the subject of his family. Unlike me, he was quite keen to talk about them. His eyes lit up even more as he did so. By the time we reached Park Street, I was regretting parting company with him.

"This is me," I said, stopping at the steps of number sixteen. I smiled up at him. "Thank you for walking with me. It was very kind of you to offer me refuge beneath your umbrella."

He chuckled softly. "The pleasure was all mine." He glanced past me to the door. "I am glad you emerged safely from that ruckus last night, Miss Steele. I was terribly worried about you after I left, asking myself if I'd done the right thing in leaving you there."

Something he said sparked a memory, but I couldn't place what it was. Perhaps it was merely the horrid memory of the night before.

"May I be so bold as to ask you something?" he said.

"Of course." My heart skipped, but I wasn't sure why. If Mr. Dorchester asked to see me again, I wasn't sure what I'd do. Did I want to see him? Did I want to get to know him further? I supposed it couldn't hurt.

"Will you be at church tomorrow?" he said.

"Yes, of course. Why?"

"Because I'd like to know which one to attend in order to see you again."

I laughed and bowed my head to hide my blush. "I believe Grosvenor Chapel is the nearest."

"Then I hope to see you in the morning." He walked me up the steps and deposited me at the door. "I'm glad I bumped into you, Miss Steele."

"So am I," I said. "I'd be thoroughly wet otherwise."

He laughed, but I winced on the inside. I'd made it sound like I'd used him for his umbrella. I had enjoyed our walk together, but not in *that* way, I realized. Not in the same way I enjoyed Mr. Glass's company. It was like comparing chocolate and apples. Both tasted good, yet one was a decadent experience to be savored, and the other something that could be found in every grocer's cart on every corner. I liked both, but I would always choose chocolate over an apple.

"I hope I haven't caused you any trouble," he said.

"Not at all."

"It's just that you have an observer." He nodded at the window. The curtain fluttered, but not before I saw Miss Glass's face disappear from sight.

I smiled. "Goodbye, Mr. Dorchester. And thank you again."

I slipped inside and shut the door. I'd barely removed one arm from my coat when Miss Glass emerged from the entrance to the sitting room.

"Who was that, dear?" she asked.

"An acquaintance by the name of Dorchester."

"I don't know any Dorchesters."

"He's from Manchester."

"Manchester!" She wrinkled her nose. "What's he doing in London?"

"Visiting."

"From Manchester?" she said, incredulous.

"It's hardly the other side of the world."

"It might as well be. Those accents." She shuddered. "It's like listening to glass break."

"His accent is quite refined. I didn't detect a hint of Mancunian."

She sniffed and I thought that the end of it, but she followed me all the way to the kitchen. I fetched bread, cheese and plum jam from the pantry and set them out on the table.

"Have you eaten?" I asked.

"Picket fixed me something earlier." She sat at the stool and watched me spread jam on a slice of bread. "He's not particularly handsome."

"Are we still discussing Mr. Dorchester?"

"He's rather short too, and he had a way of walking that I didn't like."

I pressed my lips together to suppress my smile. "Perhaps they walk differently in Manchester."

"I suppose he's in trade."

"He has a factory."

She clicked her tongue and picked at the cheese I sliced off the wedge but didn't eat it. "You can do better than an ugly factory worker from Manchester."

"You forgot his odd walking style."

"This is not a joke, India."

I set down the knife with a sigh. "I appreciate your concern, but there's no need. I'm not considering Mr. Dorchester as a suitor."

"You may not be, but *he* might be considering *you*. Sometimes men—I won't refer to him as a gentleman, since I don't know his connections—can be difficult to remove once they latch onto you. I've seen very eligible girls swept up by a romantic gesture from a man who is not at all suitable."

I was about to protest that I wasn't susceptible to romantic gestures, but past experience showed that to be false. While Eddie hadn't shouted his love for me from a rooftop, he had given me flowers and trinkets on a regular basis and been attentive from the start.

I stuffed my mouth full of bread and jam, to avoid answering, and hoped Miss Glass would leave the topic of Mr. Dorchester alone. Unfortunately, she was only getting started and proceeded to warn me about the dangers of a woman alone in the world and men of unknown connections. The only way I could see to stop her was to tell her that I'd learned my lesson from Eddie. Thankfully Willie walked in, distracting Miss Glass. I'd never been so pleased to see her, even though she wore an ominously thunderous expression.

"Bread?" I offered. "Cheese?"

"God, yes." Willie descended on the table like a hawk on a field mouse. "I'm half starved."

I handed her a slice of bread with jam and hoped it would be enough to chase her black mood away. She bit into it, tearing off a chunk with her teeth like a lion ripping apart a poor creature it had just caught.

"Don't see you down here much," she said to Miss Glass around her mouthful. Miss Glass looked horrified, which I suspected was Willie's intention. "That Polly girl not feeding you?"

"Picket takes good care of me, thank you."

"Why do you call her by her last name?"

"It's the way things are done here. I don't expect anyone from an American backwater to understand."

"Miss Glass wanted to talk to me about Mr. Dorchester," I said quickly, before Willie's temper had a chance to flare. "He escorted me home just now."

"Who?"

"The man from the poker game last night. The one who punched Lord Dennison."

"Punched!" Miss Glass's hand fluttered at her black lace collar. "I knew he was no good."

"He defended me," I said.

"Tosh. He's a Dorchester from Manchester. It even sounds ridiculous."

Willie snorted. "That it does."

I couldn't help smiling, even though I wanted to defend him. "That's not the point. He was kind to me, and I like him, but not in *that* way," I assured Miss Glass. "Nor will I be seduced by romantic gestures, if he performs any. It takes more than trinkets and promises to intrigue me now."

"Good," Miss Glass said with a satisfied nod. "I'm glad to hear it. Your mother will be pleased that I saved you from an unfavorable attachment."

My mother? Willie and I exchanged glances. She drew a little circle at her temple and rolled her eyes, then stuffed more bread into her mouth.

"Perhaps you should have a rest," I said to Miss Glass.

"I do feel a little tired." She wandered out of the kitchen, and I hoped she didn't wander out of the house altogether. When I heard her maid's voice, my concern eased. Polly would care for her.

Willie dragged over a stool and slumped onto it. She threw down her uneaten bread, smearing jam on the table. It would seem her mood hadn't been lifted by our discussion.

"You're still upset about your locket," I said, sitting too. I reached for her hand but she snatched it away.

"I went to see Travers."

Oh dear. I didn't need a crystal ball to see where this was going. "Did he speak to you?"

She nodded. "I offered to buy back the locket, but he refused."

I doubted she had any money left after the previous night, but I didn't ask where she planned on getting the funds.

"He said I could try to win it back," she went on.

"You told him no, didn't you?"

"I had to. I have nothing more to my name, and Matt, Duke and Cyclops won't lend me nothing. They hate me playing poker. They warned me this would happen." She placed her forehead in the crook of her arm on the table. "They must be patting themselves on their backs now."

"That doesn't sound like something they would do." I touched her shoulder, but she shrugged me off. "What if you offer Lord Travers double its worth, then ask Mr. Glass for a loan? I'm sure he'll help if he knows it'll get the locket back for certain."

"Travers won't accept it. He wants to play poker, and what the high and mighty lord wants, the high and mighty lord gets." She proceeded to call him a vile name that had me blushing.

I tried to think of another solution but came up with nothing. She'd brought this on herself, and I shouldn't feel sorry for her but I did. Although I couldn't see her face, I knew from her sniffing that she was crying.

"Do you think you can beat him?" I asked.

"Yes. If I'm dealt good cards and he doesn't cheat again."

I sighed. It was hopeless. "You should speak to Matt. I mean, Mr. Glass. Perhaps he can talk to Lord Travers, man-to-man. It's unfair, but Travers strikes me as a fellow who respects men and not women. Mr. Glass has a way with words and might be able to convince him to sell the locket back to you."

She sat up straight and swiped at her eyes and cheeks. "Don't tell him, India. What you're saying makes sense, and if anyone can convince Travers, it's Matt. But he's got so much on his plate right now, he doesn't need the extra burden. Nor does he have the time."

It was the least selfish display I'd seen from her, and it quite flipped my opinion. "He's quite ill, isn't he?" I asked softly. I hardly breathed as I waited for her answer.

It came in the form of a small nod, nothing more.

"What does his doctor say?" I pressed.

She hopped off the stool. "Matt wouldn't want me discussing it, so don't ask."

"But—"

"His health is not your concern." She grasped my shoulders and shook them. "Your job is to find the watchmaker. Even if Matt's caught up with other matters, you must continue with the search on your own." She shook me again, harder this time. "Promise me that you will."

"I will," I said. "I promise. There's an important guild meeting tonight. Several watchmakers will be there. Attending it will save a lot of time over seeing them individually."

She let me go. Relief flooded her face. She even smiled, sort of. It was twitchy and uncertain, but it was an improvement on her scowl. "Good."

Unfortunately, my plan to take Mr. Glass with me to the meeting didn't come to pass. He hadn't returned home by seven o'clock. Waiting longer might mean missing the meeting altogether. I would have taken Cyclops or Duke, but they were still out too. Willie would probably have come, but she was a volatile weapon that might go off at the wrong time. I would have to face the guild alone.

I wasn't looking forward to it.

CHAPTER 13

The Worshipful Company of Watchmakers met in their modern Warwick Lane hall not far from St. Paul's. The building had only been completed two years ago, and I'd never been inside. The red bricks and heavily carved arched doorway surround were clean compared to their sooty neighbors, and the colors on the coat of arms were still vibrant. The loincloth-clad Old Man Time and the robed emperor glared down at me from their position above the door, looking stern as they clutched hourglass and scepter respectively. *Tempvs Rervm Imperator*, so the motto reminded me. *Time is the ruler of all things*.

Indeed. Time had certainly ruled me of late, as it did with Mr. Glass. His hourglass was running out.

I knocked, and a middle-aged man with bushy white eyebrows opened the door. I didn't recognize him.

"Yes?" he intoned.

I barreled past him, taking him by surprise.

"Stop! This is a private hall."

"I need to speak with the Court," I tossed over my shoulder. "It will only take a moment."

I charged past the stained glass windows and the wooden paneling, wondering if any of the clocks on display belonged to my ancestors. There was no time to check the plaques. The porter was quickly bearing down on me. I pushed open the nearest door and was rewarded with some twenty heads turning my way. I'd found the court room where the members met. Meetings were only compulsory for the ten elected Court of Assistants, the men in charge of the day-to-day running of the guild, but were open to all members. Twenty was a good turnout.

"India!" Eddie pushed to his feet, a look of utter stupefaction on his face. "What are you doing? You shouldn't be here."

"That's what I tried telling her," said the porter, wheezing beside me. He tried to grab my elbow, but I stepped out of his way.

"Leave her, Mr. Carter," said Mr. Abercrombie. He sat at the head of the table, the crimson velvet and white fur master's robe draped around his shoulders, the ceremonial scepter lying on the table in front of an open ledger. All he needed was a crown and he'd resemble the emperor in the coat of arms that hung behind him. "We don't want this descending into a farce."

"So you don't want me calling the constables?" Carter asked.

Mr. Abercrombie sighed. "I don't think they'd help us."

Thank goodness for that. My greatest fear had been that he would have me arrested for the so-called theft from his shop. It would seem he'd well and truly abandoned that accusation.

"Miss Steele, I won't pretend that I'm glad to see you." He flicked his hand at Carter, and the porter exited with a bow.

I scanned the faces of the men at the table as Eddie resumed his seat. I recognized all of them. Eddie was by far the youngest. Everyone else had white, gray or balding heads. Mr. Mason wasn't present.

Mr. Abercrombie beckoned me with a crook of his finger. "Come closer, Miss Steele."

I inched forward, feeling very much like a lowly courtier who'd caught the king's disapproving eye. I stopped well back from the table, but the fellows at the nearest end shuffled their chairs farther away. I tried to recall the speech I'd rehearsed on the way over, but the beginning evaded me.

"India," Eddie said, in a voice deeper than his usual one. It sounded so ridiculously false that I almost giggled. He puffed out his chest and sat very erect in the chair, no doubt to make himself appear larger and more commanding among such important men. "What's the meaning of this?"

"Quiet, please, Mr. Hardacre," Abercrombie said with a lift of his hand. He removed his pince nez and placed it on the ledger. "Allow me to interrogate her."

Interrogate? Oh no, no, no. I hadn't come so that *he* could ask questions of *me*. "Mr. Abercrombie, I would like some answers."

"Then you shall have them."

All heads swung round to look at him. "What?" more than one of them snapped. "Don't," said others. Abercrombie held up his hand for silence. I didn't trust his sly smile, his apparent openness.

I forged on anyway. "Why are you all afraid of me?"

"Afraid of you?" He laughed. "Don't be absurd. You're just a little woman. None of us are *afraid* of you."

His laughter was eventually joined by a smattering of others, all of them half-hearted, cautious.

I abandoned that angle and picked up another. "As most of you know, my employer, Mr. Glass, is searching for a particular watchmaker, who may or may not go by the name of Mirth. Do any of you know Mr. Mirth?"

Several members looked to Abercrombie. "I know him," Abercrombie said.

I was so surprised that I stepped forward before I remembered I didn't want to get too close.

"Mirth isn't the fellow your employer seeks," he went on.

"How do you know?"

"The confusion came about because Mirth traveled overseas at the same time as Mr. Glass says his mysterious watchmaker was in America. Mirth did not travel to America, however, but to Prussia."

"How can you be sure?"

"Because he confided in me at the time. He was looking for his daughter. She'd run off with a foreigner. Sadly, he never found her, which goes some way to explaining why he never re-opened his shop. He no longer had the heart for it. I'm afraid he's been something of a lost man ever since."

It sounded plausible, but I couldn't trust him to tell me the truth. He hated me and would try to thwart me at every turn. To what end, however, I couldn't fathom. "Then why did he suddenly disappear from the Aged Christian Society house?"

He spread out his hands. "Your guess is as good as mine. I haven't seen much of him of late." He picked up his pince nez and tapped it on the ledger in front of him. "All I know is the small allowance he receives from the guild is paid into an account at the Bank of England, and will continue to be until such time as we hear of his death. We do what we can for all our members in need, past and present."

"Hear, hear," said one man, as another thumped the table in agreement.

"Do you know of anyone else who traveled overseas about five years ago?" I asked, searching their faces as I spoke, hoping to find a hint of recognition in one of them. Those that met my gaze were blank. Those that did not looked to Abercrombie.

"No," he said.

Several clocks, both within the court room and without, chimed half seven with orchestral rhythm.

I steeled myself. "I don't believe you."

A collective intake of breath echoed around the room. "Miss Steele, have you considered that the watchmaker doesn't want to be found?" Abercrombie asked.

"We've considered that he might be dead, but why wouldn't he want to be found?"

He once again set down his pince nez. "Your employer, Mr. Glass..."

"Yes?"

"What do you know about him?"

"What's your point, Mr. Abercrombie?"

Eddie shook his head and rolled his eyes. No doubt he was congratulating himself on becoming un-engaged to such a difficult woman.

"My point is," Abercrombie said, "Mr. Glass threatened me."

So he did, did he? It was difficult to keep the smile off my lips and out of my voice. "I can't pretend I'm sorry. You accused me of stealing, and whatever you all think of me, I am not a thief."

Several of them shifted uncomfortably in their seats. Eddie no longer met my gaze. Abercrombie merely lifted a hand in dismissal, as if my concerns over his accusation weren't important.

"That incident is not up for discussion," he said.

"I beg to differ. I'd very much like to know why you did it. I could have gone to prison if it hadn't been for Mr. Glass stepping in on my behalf. I am not sorry that he threatened you. Not in the least."

"It wasn't merely his threats." He waved his hand again. "But that's by the by. Water under the bridge. We should all move on."

Dear lord, hold me back from leaping across the table and strangling him. "Mr. Glass saw an injustice occur, and he stepped in to save me. I think that noble. Are you implying something else about his character?"

"I'm merely suggesting that you should be careful with whom you associate, Miss Steele. After he pressured me to drop the accusation, I decided to do some research. What I learned was that your *employer*," he said with a sneering curl of his top lip, "associates with criminals."

I already knew about his mother's family, but it was a timely reminder nevertheless.

"That's the best case scenario," Abercrombie went on.

"Best case?" I echoed.

"At worst, he is a criminal himself."

Several of the members gasped, including Eddie. I did not. From the smug look on Abercrombie's face, he knew that I'd already suspected Mr. Glass of being the Dark Rider.

"Anyone who's read the newspaper of late will be aware that the American outlaw known as the Dark Rider is here in England," he said. "It's not a big stretch to connect him to Mr. Glass. Indeed, it's not a big stretch to say that the one is also the other."

"You can't say that for certain."

Abercrombie shook his head. "You're naive for your age. Out of respect for your father, I must warn you against men like Mr. Glass."

"Do not bring my father into this," I growled.

"Calm down, India," Eddie said. "Your father was a member in good standing here. No one is deriding him."

"Do shut up, Eddie."

A couple of members smirked, but the man sitting beside Eddie turned to him and said, "Was she always this willful?"

Eddie shook his head. "If I'd known earlier, I would never have asked for her hand."

"And missed out on inheriting my shop?" I snarled.

"It was never *your* shop to begin with." Eddie's retort was met with a series of nods from the other members.

"Perhaps the watchmaker that Mr. Glass wants to find is also a criminal," Abercrombie said, stroking his oiled moustache. "That might explain why he doesn't want to be found and why no one here can identify him. The Worshipful Company of Watchmakers upholds the very highest of principles. Our members are honorable, decent men and do not associate with outlaws. Consider that, Miss Steele," he said, interrupting my protest. "Consider that the reason it's been so difficult to find the watchmaker is because he's a wanted man. Wanted men associate with other wanted men, and Mr. Glass's visit coincides neatly with that of the Dark Rider. Too neatly, an independent observer would say."

A chill trickled down my spine and raised the hairs on the back of my neck. I wanted to disagree with him, but I could not. I had no evidence of Mr. Glass's innocence and quite a pile suggesting his guilt, from the coincidence of his and the Dark Rider's arrival, to his fighting ability, connection to the Johnsons, and now his threats toward Abercrombie. I swallowed loudly.

"In memory of your father's long-standing membership in the guild," Abercrombie went on, "I will offer you some advice, Miss Steele. Sever ties with Mr. Glass. Tell him you can no longer assist him in his search. Your father would be disappointed to see that you've fallen in with a disreputable crowd."

"But...he's related to Lord Rycroft." My voice sounded weak, pathetic. I didn't believe his association with the Rycroft title mattered, considering he'd only just met them.

Abercrombie merely spread out his hands, as if to say, "So?"

Eddie shifted in his chair and leaned forward. His face brightened. He turned to Abercrombie for a moment, then to me. "Indeed, it's Mr. Glass's reputation as the Dark Rider that has us all wary of you, India." He looked to his fellow members, one pale eyebrow lifted in a hopeful tilt. Abercrombie urged him with a small nod. "We told you earlier that it's not *you* who worries us, India. That's because it's Mr. Glass."

I didn't quite believe him. Why not mention this before? Yet it was logical. Too logical. I couldn't fault it.

Eddie once again looked to Abercrombie. The master of the guild ignored him. "If you have any sense, Miss Steele," Abercromie said, "you would notify the police and have him arrested. We would do it, but it might be seen as vengeful after his recent threats toward me. If *you* were to speak to them about your suspicions, however, I'm sure you'll be taken seriously."

He gave me a flat smile that several of the other members echoed, including Eddie. The smiles were false, but that didn't lessen the impact of Abercrombie's words.

Because I knew he was right. Mr. Glass must be the Dark Rider.

***

I didn't see Mr. Glass until the following morning. He must have come home extremely late, and it showed in the deep bruising beneath his eyes, the paleness of his cheeks, and his tardiness in joining us for breakfast. He'd shaved, but not well, missing some of the dark stubble near his ears and the underside of his jaw. He hadn't bothered to put on a tie or waistcoat. Clearly his special watch wasn't enough, and he required more sleep to help battle his mysterious illness.

"Eat quickly, Matthew," Miss Glass said with a smile for her nephew. "We don't have much time."

"For what?" he asked, carrying his plate and cup to the table. He gave me a small smile, which I tried to return without letting on that my thoughts were in turmoil. I'd tossed in bed half the night thinking about all the awful things the Dark Rider had done and whether I ought to pass on my suspicions to the police.

"For church, of course," Miss Glass said. She had joined us for breakfast today, whereas she usually ate alone in her room. She seemed particularly spritely and alert. Perhaps she enjoyed church—or simply getting out of the house. I ought to walk with her later, if Mr. Glass didn't need me.

"Church? It's Sunday already?" Mr. Glass pinched the bridge of his nose and squeezed his eyes shut.

"You will go, won't you, Matthew?"

"No, he won't," Willie said. "He doesn't have the time."

"I beg your pardon, young lady." Miss Glass's lips pursed so tight they went white. "Are you a heathen?"

"I'm as godly as you, and I pray as regular as anyone. *I'll* go, but Matt's too busy."

"Nobody is too busy to worship."

"Enough," Mr. Glass said on a long sigh. "Do you wish to attend church this morning, Miss Steele?"

"Me?"

"I need you to continue our search today, but if you prefer to attend the service..."

Mr. Dorchester had hinted that he might attend church to see me, but I wasn't sure if I wanted to see him. Miss Glass may have been correct and he may be interested in being more than a friend. I wasn't prepared to take that path. "Yet," a little voice in my head said.

"Most watchmakers will be in church too, so I don't think we'll have much luck if we pay calls this morning."

Willie clicked her tongue and huffed out a breath. "We're running out of time," she muttered to the fried eggs on her plate.

Mr. Glass folded his hand over hers. "It'll be an hour and a half, at the most. And Miss Steele is correct. No one will be home this morning."

"I have news," I said. "I went to the Watchmakers' Guild meeting last night and—"

"You did *what*?" Mr. Glass's bellow made his aunt jump, and every one else look at him warily. "Why did you go without me?"

"You weren't here. I had planned—"

"Then you should not have gone at all. Going alone was dangerous, considering what Abercrombie tried to do."

I swallowed. "I was aware of that, but after due consideration, I decided he was no longer going to follow up on his accusation. Thanks to whatever it was you said—or did—to him."

He grunted. "Nevertheless, it was a risk you shouldn't have taken."

"It was a risk that paid off. I learned that the members in attendance don't know of any watchmakers who traveled overseas five years ago. That's twenty we no longer need to visit. I recognized them all and wrote their names down as soon as I returned home."

"Damn good work, India," Willie said, with more admiration in her voice than I'd ever heard when she addressed me.

Both Duke and Cyclops praised me too. Miss Glass seemed to have fallen into one of her dazes, and Mr. Glass continued to scowl at me but a little more softly.

"Not only that," I went on, "but Mr. Abercrombie informed me that he knows Mirth and believes he's not the man you seek."

"How so?"

"Mirth traveled to Prussia, not America, in search of his wayward daughter. He returned a broken man without her and had no interest in his shop anymore."

"He could be lying."

"Why would he lie?"

His gaze slid away.

"Because he doesn't like you," Duke said with a shrug.

Cyclops shifted in his seat and Duke winced then glared at him. I suspected his friend had just kicked him under the table.

"Yes," I said, deciding to tackle the issue head on. "But *why* doesn't he like me?"

"Because you're a woman," Willie said quickly. "You're cleverer than he is and you challenge the rules he lives by. You threaten the foundations of the patriarchal system he profits from."

"Patri-what?" Duke asked, screwing up his face. "Willie, you going all educated on me?"

Cyclops grinned. "She's been hiding her light from you, Duke."

"She's been hiding something. Not sure it's a light though."

"And I'm not sure that explains why Mr. Abercrombie dislikes me so intensely," I said. "But I can see that no one wishes to tell me." I pushed back my chair and made my exit. I didn't turn around, even though I could feel their gazes boring into me.

***

I nodded at Mr. Dorchester when I spotted him sitting at the back of Grosvenor Chapel as we walked past. He smiled.

"Who's that?" Mr. Glass whispered.

"An acquaintance we met at the gambling house," I said as we took our seats three pews in front of Mr. Dorchester.

Mr. Glass looked over his shoulder and nodded a greeting then turned back to me. "Was he involved in the incident that caused Willie to draw her Colt?"

"He'd left by then."

I didn't speak to Mr. Glass again until after the service as we made our way out. As we exited the narthex, he suddenly caught my elbow and steered me to the right. It wasn't until we drew clear of the crowd of parishioners that I saw Mr. Dorchester on the left, waiting.

He spotted me and waved. I waved back. "One moment," I said to Mr. Glass. Mr. Dorchester had come to Grosvenor Chapel specifically to see me. The least I could do was exchange a few pleasantries with him. It would be rude not to.

I pulled away from Mr. Glass and met Mr. Dorchester as he approached. "Good morning," I said, smiling.

"Good morning, Miss Steele." He doffed his hat. "It's lovely to see you again. I'm glad I came." His gaze rose. He nodded in greeting.

I turned to see Mr. Glass standing behind me, all dark scowl and hard features. I made the introductions.

"You play poker?" Mr. Glass asked.

"Not at all," Mr. Dorchester said on a laugh. "I went to learn what it was all about, but decided the game is not for me. It was an, er, interesting night though. Wasn't it, Miss Steele?" His cheerful manner had me wondering if he was referring to something I'd not been aware of. As far as I was concerned, nothing cheery happened that night.

Mr. Dorchester's gaze flicked from my face to that of Mr. Glass behind me. He cleared his throat more than once, and the silence stretched. It seemed rude to leave immediately, so I searched for something to say.

"It looks like being a pleasant afternoon," I began.

Mr. Dorchester smiled. "It does. Perfect for a walk around Hyde Park. Miss Steele, may I be so bold as to invite you to join me?"

I opened and shut my mouth without words coming out. Then suddenly Mr. Glass was right at my back, so close that I could feel his warmth. Fortunately he didn't answer for me. If he had, I would have been quite cross.

"I'm afraid I'm busy all afternoon," I told Mr. Dorchester. "But thank you for the invitation. It's appreciated."

He lifted his brows, not at me, but at Mr. Glass. His jaw hardened. "I see." He touched the brim of his hat. "Good day, Miss Steele. Mr. Glass." He strode off.

Mr. Glass came up beside me and offered me his elbow. "Ready?"

I hesitated. Now that the moment had arrived, I wasn't sure if leaving with him was a wise idea. We would be alone in the carriage the entire afternoon.

There would be no opportunity to go to the police and tell them my suspicions about him being the Dark Rider.

And there would be no opportunity to escape.

Duke, Willie and Miss Glass decided to walk back to the house, while Cyclops climbed onto the driver's seat. He pulled his crumpled map out and I pointed to the areas we would cover. Mr. Glass held the door open for me then shut it as he sat opposite. As the carriage lurched onward, he scanned the street out the window.

"Every time we go out, your nose is glued to the window," I said. "Are you expecting the intruder to follow us?"

I thought he wouldn't answer, or would dismiss me with a story, but he sat back with a resigned sigh. "I've had word that someone I know is looking for me."

The sheriff. I nodded quickly, but could no longer meet his gaze. Why had I not gone to the police before now, particularly after learning about the lawman who'd followed Matt here? I was a bloody fool, that's why.

"That fellow, Dorchester," he said stiffly. "What interest does he have in you?"

The question caught me off guard but not as much as his earnest, piercing stare. There wasn't a hint of tiredness in it now as he focused on me. "I know you Americans are bolder than we English, but I think even you know that your question is overstepping the boundaries of our relationship." I sounded like a prim schoolmistress, and yet I couldn't help my clipped tone. "His interest in me is none of your affair."

My admonishment had no effect on him. His gaze didn't waver, his jaw didn't soften. "It *is* my affair."

"Why?"

Finally, he blinked. He looked away and rubbed his chin. "What if he's the intruder?"

I laughed, but there was no humor in it. "Clearly you need more sleep if that's the direction your mind is wandering."

"I am simply worried about your welfare."

"Don't be. I can take care of myself where the likes of Mr. Dorchester are concerned. He's quite harmless."

His gaze snapped back to mine. "How can you be sure?"

"He's been very nice to me. He saved me from a brute the other night, if you must know. That's not the action of someone intent on doing me harm. Quite the opposite."

"What do you mean, he saved you?"

I waved his question off. "It no longer matters. Mr. Dorchester is a good man, and I think he likes me. That's all. Or are you telling me that I'm not the sort of woman who would interest a gentleman?"

"That is not what I'm saying at all," he ground out through a rigid jaw.

"Then what are you saying?"

He planted his hands on his knees and leaned forward. "I'm saying that not everyone is as they seem. You hardly know him."

My blood turned to ice in my veins. A foggy sensation descended over me, and I felt somewhat disembodied, like I wasn't in control of my mind any longer. "I hardly know *you*, either." My voice sounded hard, sharp. "And the facts I do know frighten me. Yet you dare to call *him* the untrustworthy one."

He straightened. "What facts?"

"The fact that your mother's family are outlaws. The fact that a sheriff is chasing you. The fact that you arrived in England at the same time as the Dark Rider." Each sentence was like a punch, pushing him a little further toward the back of the seat. "The fact that your special watch temporarily reinvigorates you by injecting a...substance into your veins that makes them glow."

His hands gripped the seat edge on either side of him. The knuckles turned white. "You are an observant woman."

I pressed a hand to my stomach and waited for him to refute my facts. He did not. Not even one. He turned to look out the window and declined to speak to me for the remainder of the journey.

We ended our search well before the sun set. Mr. Glass was too tired to continue, despite using his watch to re-energize himself a little after we paused for lunch at an inn in Hampstead. He pretended he needed to speak to Cyclops in the yard, but I knew he'd gone to use his watch in private. Why else would he close the carriage curtains?

We had no success. Some of the watchmakers we visited weren't home, and those that were treated us with reservation. We were not offered tea, and children and wives were ordered to leave our presence. One watchmaker shut the door upon spying me approaching. I remained in the carriage after that and allowed Mr. Glass to do all the talking.

We returned to the house and he went immediately to his rooms. Willie and Duke must have noticed the carriage roll up. They greeted us at the door, hope lifting their faces. Their expressions soon fell when they saw Mr. Glass's stooped shoulders and heavy eyelids. He didn't exchange a single word with them and headed straight for the stairs. Every step seemed to take enormous effort, as if he could barely put one foot in front of the other. We watched him until he disappeared.

"It's hopeless, isn't it?" Willie looked to Duke, tears in her eyes.

"There's always hope." He turned to look at me and frowned. I waited, but he said nothing, he simply looked.

"Do you think...?" Willie asked him.

"I don't know," he said.

"Ask her."

"Ask me what?" I looked from one to the other, but it was as if I wasn't there anymore. Unspoken words seemed to pass between them, and I hadn't a clue as to their nature. I cleared my throat.

"He'll be furious if we do," Duke cautioned.

"Only if she doesn't know," Willie said. "If she does know, then no harm done. In fact, if she does know then it could change everything. She could cure him."

"What?" I blurted out, half laughing.

"But if she does know, wouldn't she have said something already?" Duke said. "That's what he says."

I stamped my hands on my hips. "Will you tell me what you're talking about!"

"I'm asking her," Willie declared.

Duke clicked his tongue and shook his head. "I don't think—"

"India, are you magical?"

CHAPTER 14

Magical? Had Willie lost her mind? Duke too?

"I don't know what stories your government tells you in America, but magic doesn't exist," I said. "Not here and not there." I laughed and waited for them to join in. They didn't. "It's the stuff of children's fantasies," I added, sobering.

The hope glinting in their eyes vanished. Willie looked as if she were trying not to cry. "Do you, or do you not, possess magic?" she said again in a thin, strained voice.

"Going by her shocked expression, she doesn't." Duke sighed. "Forget we said anything, Miss Steele. And don't tell Mr. Glass about this discussion. He'd have our heads."

"But Matt said it's warmer when she's near, like it's responding to her."

She believed his watch reacted to my presence too? And I'd thought Miss Glass was the mad one.

"Don't," Duke warned. "Enough now. He was mistaken."

"He's never mistaken." Willie's face crumpled. "About anything. Ever." She turned and ran up the stairs, taking two at a time.

I stared after her. I didn't know for how long. Time slowed. The air thickened. My breaths sounded labored and my blood felt sluggish.

Magic.

The word rattled around in my head. I grappled for some clear thoughts, but they were like ribbons tossed by the breeze. I would grasp the end of one, only to have it ripped from my fingers before I could gather it all.

The hand on my arm brought me out of my trance. "Miss Steele?" Duke said gently. "Are you all right?"

I nodded numbly. "Duke...what did Willie mean when she asked about Mr. Glass's watch responding to me?"

"So you've felt it?" His fingers tightened. "It does speak to you?"

"No. So...what is it? How does it work? Why does it glow like that and make his veins glow too?"

If he said magic, then I'd...what? Pack my things and leave?

"So you've seen it," he said. "You've seen it work on him."

I nodded. "But how does that watch help Mr. Glass feel better? I don't understand."

"It doesn't," he said heavily. "That's the problem. It used to, and now it's broken."

"Broken?"

"It used to make him feel better for longer. He could go days without needing to use it again. Now it's only a few hours."

"I see."

"Do you?"

I shook my head.

He sighed. "Thought not." He glanced up the staircase. "Best forget this conversation ever happened, Miss Steele. Best not mention it to Matt. He won't like that we told you about magic."

"Why not?" Because he didn't want me to know he was as mad as them? As mad as his aunt?

"Because it's a secret."

"From me?"

"From everyone."

***

It was clear from the expressions at the breakfast table that they held little hope of finding the watchmaker on the final day of the search. Even Miss Glass seemed forlorn, and she wasn't aware of what was at stake. Perhaps she was simply anxious because she knew her nephew was leaving the following day; although she continued to deny it. When she caught Duke and Cyclops discussing departure plans, she scolded them for wasting time on "nonsense."

As we were about to leave, Willie signaled me to speak with her in private. If she started spouting about magic again, I would walk away. I refused to be taken for a fool. After spending many hours lying in bed thinking about what she and Duke had said, I'd managed to see through the veils they'd been trying to cast over my eyes. What I saw was just as worrying, however, as Mr. Glass being the Dark Rider.

He must be an opium addict. Or if not opium, some other potent substance that made his veins glow. The watch was a clever device that hid the substance in liquid form. It likely also hid a tiny syringe that he used to inject the liquid into himself as he held the watch in his palm. Whether it was also a functioning timepiece remained to be seen.

Clearly the device had stopped working properly and so he needed the original maker to fix it. I'd never seen such a watch before, so it most likely required special care. I hadn't yet worked out why he couldn't inject the substance into himself without using the watch, but there must be a reason.

I did not plan to tell any of them that I knew their secret.

I did plan on telling the police that I'd found the Dark Rider. Just as soon as I could get away.

"You must do your absolute best to find the watchmaker today," Willie told me. She took my hands and wrung them so hard I had to ask her to let go. "You know how important this is. You *know*."

I didn't tell her that it was almost hopeless. Or that the police would be stopping them from leaving tomorrow.

Perhaps.

Oh, I didn't know what to do! Perhaps I ought to remain silent. No one had harmed me. Indeed, Mr. Glass had saved me from Abercrombie and the thugs and seen that I was well cared for. To betray his trust would be cruel. Besides, if they left tomorrow, they would no longer be England's problem. As far as I could see, they'd done nothing illegal here anyway.

He tried to engage me in conversation in the carriage, but I wasn't keen to talk. I was in turmoil. Not only about telling the police but also about his addiction. Should I try to help him? Could it explain his outlaw ways? If he was desperate for opium and couldn't afford it, then he would need to steal to pay for it. Perhaps if his addiction went away, there would be no need for criminal activity.

"You're very quiet today," he said.

"Am I?"

He smiled crookedly. "Thinking about how much you'll miss me when I'm gone?"

I rolled my eyes. "Thinking about where I'll live and what I'll do." Which only reminded me that I hadn't asked him for a reference yet.

I was about to when he said, "Perhaps we'll need to postpone our journey. Even if we do find the watchmaker, there's no need to hurry back. I like it here. London intrigues me. And, to be honest, there's not much to keep me in America."

"Your friends and Willie will be disappointed."

"They don't have to stay."

"Disappointed to leave you behind, I mean. They're very fond of you."

"And I them."

"If you stay, you will require my assistance." It wasn't a question, for I knew the answer before he spoke.

He nodded. "I would like you to help me. Would you, on the same terms?"

My gaze slid to the window. "I don't know. I...I don't know what to think anymore. About anything."

He leaned forward and rested his hand on mine. It was probably meant to be a reassuring gesture, but it made my heart skip to a more erratic beat. "I'm sorry I'm not the easiest of men at times."

I blinked at him. He did not remove his hand, nor did I want him to. "You have nothing to apologize for." Not to me. He'd been the perfect gentleman at all times. Hot tears rushed to my eyes and I had to once again look out the window so he couldn't see.

His thumb stroked mine, gentle and insistent. My breath hitched at the intimacy of it. I shouldn't want him to touch me like that. Not this...outlaw, this addict. But I couldn't bring myself to tell him to stop. I simply sat there and allowed him to do it.

"India," he said, his voice low and rough. "May I call you that?"

I nodded.

He let me go, but only to touch my chin and gently force me to look at him. "Then you must call me Matt or Matthew from now on."

I nodded again.

"I know we're not friends," he said. "Not really. But...I feel a connection to you, and I hope you feel the same with me."

I sucked on the inside of my cheek. I nodded again, unable to speak, and not daring to disagree. Not wanting to.

"Good. Then...I need to say something to you." He let my chin go and rested his hand on his knee. His lowered his head and shook it slightly. After a moment, he looked up. "Why is a remarkable woman like you not married?"

That wasn't what he wanted to say. For starters, it had been a question and yet he'd said he wanted to *say* something to me. So what had been on his mind? Was he going to tell me a magical watch was keeping him alive? That he was addicted to opium? Or that he was an outlaw?

The carriage slowed and he leaned back. He wasn't even interested in my answer.

The first watchmaker on the list was a Mr. Ingham, a short, round man with a bald head and a pair of spectacles perched on the end of his nose. He took one look at me and inched away from the counter. I stood to one side as Mr. Glass—Matt—spoke to him about Chronos.

As Mr. Ingham told him he didn't know anyone fitting that description, my gaze fell on the newspaper spread out on the counter nearby. The main article was about the Dark Rider again; the police believed he was here in London, based on information received from their American counterparts.

As Matt turned to go, Mr. Ingham glanced at me then down at the paper and up at me again. He scooped it up. "Good day, Miss Steele."

"Good day, Mr. Ingham," I said and followed Matt out of the shop.

We accomplished a great deal, visiting many shops and only stopping for a quick bite to eat and for Matt to use his watch while I powdered my nose in a Wandsworth inn. We did not have any luck, however, and headed back to Mayfair in a thoughtfully grim mood.

"That's all the watchmakers I know in the city," I said. "There are others, of course, but I've never met them. Even if you do remain in London to continue your search, you don't require my services anymore. I can't help you."

He'd closed his eyes upon settling in the carriage, and now he raised his eyelids slowly, half way. The effect lent him a lazy, dissolute air. "I beg to differ. You're familiar with London. I'll need a guide."

"Cyclops knows where we haven't been. He can drive you without my guidance."

He closed his eyes again and I thought he'd fallen asleep, when his eyes suddenly reopened. He grinned. It was so unexpected that I couldn't help smiling back at seeing the change in him. "I've got it! You can be my aunt's companion."

"Me? A lady's companion?" I snorted. "Don't be ridiculous."

"Why not? You're honest." He held up a finger. "Easy to get along with." Another finger rose. "Kind." He lifted a third. "And my aunt likes you. There. It's settled. You'll live with her."

"Where? At your house, or is she moving back to Lord Rycroft's after you've gone?"

He rubbed his forehead. "It looks like I'll be staying. I want you both to live with me."

I didn't say anything, and he didn't seem to require an answer. He closed his eyes again and tipped his head back. After a moment, his head tilted to the side and his breathing became even. He'd fallen asleep.

I had to shake him awake when we arrived back at the house. He didn't look at all refreshed; rather, he looked wearier than ever.

"Why didn't you use your watch again?" I asked before I realized that I'd just told him I knew what he used it for.

He eyed me closely and my heart stopped. I swallowed. Would he hate me for knowing about his addiction?

He didn't answer me, but got out and unfolded the step for me. I took his offered hand and climbed down. He did not let me go when my feet hit the pavement but tightened his grip.

"Matthew." I didn't know why I said his name. If I'd planned on asking or saying something, it immediately flew from my mind when he drew me closer.

"Yes?" he murmured.

His small finger hooked mine. We stood as close as my skirts would allow, his face only inches above me. He looked exhausted, and yet he was still so handsome. His illness didn't lessen that.

"You should go inside to rest," I said, stepping back.

He didn't let go of my finger. "India—"

"She's right," Cyclops called down from the driver's seat. "Go inside, Matt. Rest."

Matt turned his frosty glare onto his friend but let me go. As Cyclops drove the carriage off, I headed up the steps. Willie opened the door, but the hope in her eyes soon vanished.

"You look awful," she said. "You should rest."

"I know," he snapped.

Willie's chin wobbled.

Matt sighed and drew her into a hug. He kissed her forehead. "Sorry. I'm going up now."

"I'll leave some supper on your desk," she said, as he headed to the staircase with plodding footsteps.

Duke and Miss Glass emerged from the dining room. Embroidery thread looped around Duke's hands and connected to the spool Miss Glass held. At my raised brows, he said, "Tangles," with a shrug.

Someone knocked on the door, and Willie opened it. A grizzly looking man in a brown coat and skewed mustard colored tie stood on the stoop. No less than five police constables, dressed in their distinctive blue uniform and helmet, squeezed onto the porch behind him.

"Is Mr. Matthew Glass here?" demanded the man in front.

"Who's asking?" Willie said, hands on hips.

"Detective Inspector Nunce, Scotland Yard."

"There's no one here by—"

"I'm Matthew Glass," Matt said, placing a hand on Willie's shoulder.

She shoved him away. "Matt! You *know* why they're here."

"Willie, it's all right."

Nunce stepped inside without being invited. His constables followed him like a tail. "Mr. Glass, you're under arrest."

"No!" Willie cried.

One of the constables caught Matt's wrist, but he pulled free.

"What's the meaning of this?" he demanded.

"You're under arrest on suspicion of being the American outlaw known as the Dark Rider." Nunce jerked his head and two constables grabbed Matt, one taking each arm.

"There's been a mistake," Matt said, his voice calm. "I'm not an outlaw."

"Let him go!" Willie lunged at one of the constables holding Matt, only to be caught from behind by another. "Get off me!" She kicked and lashed out, but couldn't reach the man behind her. His arm locked around her waist and he dragged her out of the way. Her screeching grew louder.

"You're under arrest too," Nunce told her.

"What for?" she shouted.

"For being a member of the Dark Rider's posse."

"You're a damned idiot fool!"

"Let her go," Duke said, stepping forward. He tried to separate his hands, but only managed to get himself more tangled in the thread. "God damn it!" he shouted, resorting to brute strength and still failing.

Miss Glass dropped the spool and came to stand by me. "Stop this at once," she said with haughty crispness. "There's been a mistake. This gentleman is my nephew, and the nephew of Lord Rycroft. Release him at once."

Nunce touched his hat brim. "I cannot, ma'am. He's the Dark Rider."

"Who or what is the Dark Rider?"

"American outlaw. Don't you read the papers?"

She bristled. "Of course not. I've no interest in idle gossip."

Nunce signaled for another of his men to grab Duke. "Take him, too. He sounds American." He sized me up.

"She's English," Matt said. "A friend of my aunt's. I hardly know her."

Nunce grunted but didn't order anyone to arrest me. One of the constables took hold of Duke's arm, but Duke jerked away. The constable tackled him, and with his hands still tied, Duke couldn't defend himself. They both crashed to the floor.

"That was uncalled for," Matt growled.

Nunce merely shrugged.

"Duke!" Willie screamed. "Duke, are you hurt?"

Miss Glass's fingers gripped my arm. I closed my hand over hers, hoping to reassure her somewhat. I don't think it helped. She could most likely feel my body shaking through the connection.

"Contact Commissioner Munro," Matt instructed Nunce, struggling to pull free of the two constables who held him. "He'll set you straight."

Nunce snorted. "That's what they all say."

Willie stomped on the toe of the bobby holding her and managed to pull free. She ran to Duke, who was struggling to sit up on the floor, but was caught again by the long-limbed youth in uniform. She smashed her fist into his cheek, drawing blood, before he grasped her hands and twisted them behind her.

"You're hurting me!" she cried.

Matt lurched to his left, using his superior weight and height to force the constable on that side to stumble. The one on his other side also lost his balance, and Matt was able to pull free of them both.

But his freedom was short lived. The last of the constables threw a punch at Matt's jaw. While Matt managed to dodge it, the interruption gave the other bobbies precious seconds to recover and throw punches of their own. One hit Matt's mouth, the other his stomach. He doubled over, coughing.

Miss Glass whimpered and clutched her throat. I turned her so she wasn't facing the scene and patted her back. Yet I felt anything but soothed myself. My heart thundered and every part of me shook.

"Stop at once!" I shouted. "Inspector Nunce, control your men. You're upsetting an elderly lady with this unnecessary display."

But it was Matt who responded, not Nunce. He stopped fighting. "I'll go with you," he said. "Willie and Duke too."

"No!" Willie shouted. "Why should you go, Matt? You've done nothing wrong."

"We'll sort it out at the station. Vine Street?"

Nunce nodded. "Check they have no weapons hidden on their person," he said to his men.

His constables checked pockets, removing every item they found and placing them on the hall table. Among the handkerchiefs and coins sat Matt's special silver watch.

"Take them away," Nunce said.

Willie and Duke gasped. "Your watch!" Willie cried. "Matt!" She struggled against the constable trying to force her through the door.

"May I take my watch with me?" Matt asked Nunce.

Nunce pursed his lips, looked at the watch, looked at Matt, then said, "No. You have no need to tell the time in the holding cells."

A bead of sweat trickled down Matt's temple. His breathing turned ragged. His face was the color of cold ash. The two constables on either side of him marched him forward.

"He has to take the watch," Duke said to Nunce. "Please. It's important. He'll die without it."

Die!

Miss Glass sobbed into my shoulder. I tried patting her back harder, but it was useless. I couldn't offer support when I needed it badly myself. My gaze connected with Matt's over the top of her head. What I saw in his eyes brought burning tears to mine. His illness savaged him, yet it wasn't that which made my heart ache. It was the sorrow and disappointment I saw in his face.

He thought I'd betrayed him. He thought I'd told the police that he was the Dark Rider.

He wasn't the only one. "You did this!" Willie hissed at me.

"No," I said. "I didn't."

But she shouted over the top of me, and couldn't have heard. "You heartless witch! If he dies, I'll come looking for you. I'll cut you up—"

"Willie!" Matt's sharp voice could hardly be heard over her ranting.

Nunce and his constables marched Duke and Matt outside too, and my heart sank even further when I saw Cyclops join them, restrained by another two bobbies. Everyone seemed to be shouting. I caught snatches of pleas, begging Nunce to allow Matt to have the watch. The inspector continued to refuse.

"It's *her* fault!" Willie screamed. "You've condemned him to death, India!"

I shook my head, but they weren't looking at me and wouldn't have seen.

"If he doesn't get that watch," she continued, "his death will be on *your* conscience."

CHAPTER 15

Miss Glass and I stood clinging to one another in silent horror. Willie's words rang in my head, clanging like a bell. She thought I'd been behind the arrest. They all did, including Matt. Yet it wasn't that which made me feel sick to my core. It was Willie's desperate pleas, her wild, fanciful claims that he would die without that watch. There must be medicine inside it, not opium as I first thought.

I handed Miss Glass over to Polly, who emerged from the rear of the house with raw fear in her wide eyes. "Everything will be all right," I assured them both. My calm and confident voice seemed to rally Polly, at least. "Take Miss Glass upstairs," I told the maid. "See that she has everything she needs."

I felt anything but calm and confident. I couldn't stop shaking. *He needed the watch or he'd die.* I picked it up by its chain. A wave of heat washed over me, rushing up my arm from my hand.

I dropped the watch and jumped back. It throbbed once then stilled.

Throbbed.

Inanimate objects did not throb. They didn't grow warm. They weren't alive.

I must have been mistaken. I picked up the watch again. Once more, heat flooded me, beginning at my hand and traveling up my arm with such speed and force that my breath whooshed out in surprise.

But I didn't let go. I cradled it in my palm, its chain dangling between my fingers. The case pulsed, like a heart restarting after a stoppage, but did not do so again. It remained warm, though not hot as it had been on initial touch, and I could feel the warmth through my entire body, as if my veins carried it along with my blood. When Matt held the watch, his veins glowed, but mine did not.

It was an incredible device. I couldn't feel any medicine seeping into me, yet somehow it must be able to emit a substance. I turned it over and studied the back. There were no distinguishing features, no holes or slits for medicine to seep through.

I opened the case. My breath hitched. Not because it was filled with medicine, but because it wasn't. The watch looked like every other watch I'd ever worked on. The dial and hands were simple, plain, the Roman numerals clearly marked in bronze.

I took it up to my rooms and used my tools to open the housing at the dressing table. The mechanism consisted of wheels and screws, tiny springs, pinions, and an escapement, just like an ordinary watch. I'd worked on hundreds like it. Any watchmaker could have made it. According to the etching in the metal, it was made by A.W. Waltham, NY.

New York. It was an American watch. So why was Matt scouring London for his watchmaker? Surely he had looked inside the case and seen the maker's name.

I closed the watchcase and stared at it for a long time. Somehow this watch grew warm when I touched it, and when Matt did too. Somehow it came to life. And somehow it was responsible for keeping Matt alive.

Magic.

The word flittered through my mind like a butterfly, daintily and carefully at first, but growing louder, stronger, with each passing second. I tried to dismiss it, but couldn't.

I slipped the watch into my waistcoat pocket where it soon warmed the skin over my lower ribs. I raced downstairs and out the door.

***

Vine Street Police Station cast a long shadow in the late afternoon and presented an austere front to the world. Iron bars covered the windows at street level and a bobby stood at the door, stiff and tall. More visitors than I would have expected came and went, though there were few constables. Most would use the rear courtyard entrance after apprehending criminals, I supposed. Which barred window housed Matt and the others? Or did their holding cell not have a window?

I plucked up some courage and strode past the constable at the door. "Afternoon, miss," he said.

Inside was much like any office, only staffed with uniformed policemen. Behind the long front counter ranged several desks, and I spotted no less than four doors leading into the wings of the vast building. I inquired after Matt at the counter where the bushy-browed policeman glowered back at me.

"He's not allowed visitors," he said, returning to his paperwork.

The watch in my waistcoat pocket throbbed. "Can you give him something for me?"

"No," he said without looking up.

I blew out a breath. "I only need to see him for a moment. You can have someone accompany me to make sure I don't help him escape."

My attempt at a joke was met with a scowl. He picked up his pen and dipped it into the inkwell. The scratching on the ledger page grated on my already taut nerves.

"May I speak with Detective Inspector Nunce?" I asked.

"Regarding?"

"Regarding Mr. Matthew Glass."

"No."

"Why not?"

"Because you're going to waste his valuable time by asking him if you can visit Glass in the holding cells, and he's only going to tell you the same thing I have— no."

"You could at least look at me when you speak to me."

He lifted his gaze but not his head. "No." He returned to his ledger.

The watch in my pocket pulsed again, stronger this time. What did it expect me to do? "Please tell Inspector Nunce that I'd like to see him."

The constable sighed. "Miss, I told you, he's busy."

"It's a matter of life and death!" I punctuated the sentence with a slap of my hand on the counter. A dozen heads looked up from their paperwork.

The constable rolled his eyes and muttered what sounded like "Bloody women," under his breath.

The door nearest me burst open and Nunce himself barreled through. "Fetch a doctor!"

"Sir?" the bobby asked.

"A doctor!" Nunce pulled out a handkerchief from his pocket and dabbed his sweating brow.

My blood chilled. "Is the doctor for Mr. Glass?"

Nunce narrowed his gaze at me. "You're from Glass's house."

"I'm his aunt's companion. She's Lord Rycroft's sister."

"No need to tell me again. His friends keep on saying it, too, and I don't bloody care if he's the Prince of Wales. He's not going nowhere until he faces trial. Unless he dies, of course. It ain't looking too good for him."

Oh God. I clutched my throat, and gathered my scattered wits. "Please, Inspector, I need to see him. For his aunt's sake." I had an idea, and before he could refuse me entry, I said, "I have his medicine."

"What sort of medicine?"

"It's in this vessel." I pulled out the watch. "I know it doesn't look medicinal, but American manufacturers like to make their medicine bottles into novelties. So Mr. Glass tells me." *Please don't ask me to open it.*

"I'm not sure it'll be able to help him," Nunce said. "He's unconscious."

I covered my gasp with my hand. Tears welled in my eyes. "It's not too late. Please don't let him die, sir, when help is at hand."

He lifted the barrier. "Come through."

He had the constable check me for weapons. When he gave the all-clear, I hurried after Nunce, along lime-washed corridors and past wooden doors, all closed. Each door housed a small rectangular panel designed to slide open and allow communication between those inside and those without.

Someone thumped on one of the doors as we passed, and others called out, their voices muffled by the thick walls. Up ahead, three constables surrounded a door. One looked through the panel and was calling to the person on the other side. There was no answer.

"Still out of it, sir," the bobby said when Nunce inquired after Matt's state.

"May I administer the medicine?" I said. "I'm a trained nurse," I added as inspiration struck. "That's why I'm companion to his aunt. She requires nursing from time to time."

He hesitated.

"Come now, sir. What do you think will happen? Your constable has checked me for weapons, Mr. Glass is incapable of standing, let alone fighting, and I am a mere woman surrounded by policemen."

"Sir, it looks like he has stopped breathing," the constable at the door said.

The blood drained from my face. I bit on my lower lip but couldn't stop it wobbling.

"Open the door," Nunce said. "Let her in."

The constable seemed to take an age to find the right key hanging from the ring at his belt. Finally he placed it into the keyhole and unlocked the door. I pushed it open myself and ran to Matt, stretched out on the floor on his side. The red gash on his lip and the blue-black bruise around it stood out starkly against his deathly pale face. He was so still, I feared it was too late. Then he exhaled, albeit weakly.

I heard the policemen come in behind me, but none spoke as I pressed the watch into Matt's hand. I cradled his head and shoulders in my lap. With my back to the policemen, and his hands covered by my skirts, his exposed skin was shielded from sight.

Inch by inch, his body warmed, beginning with the hand that held the watch. I kept his fingers wrapped around it so that he didn't drop it, and watched as the glow chased away the sickly pall all the way up to his hairline.

His chest expanded. He sucked in a deep breath and spluttered. I felt the breath against my throat and smiled through my tears.

"Thank God," I whispered. I held him close, not sure if I should let him go yet. If he was still glowing, Nunce would see. Besides, it felt so good to hold him. I had never held a man like that before.

His body felt warm now, alive with his steady breathing, and no longer limp. His free hand closed over mine, so solid and wonderful. Neither of us wore gloves.

Nunce cleared his throat. "That's some strong medicine."

Matt withdrew his hands from mine and slipped the watch into his pocket while his body was still hidden from view. His veins immediately stopped glowing. He looked up at me and smiled the most dazzling smile, which tugged something deep inside me. I smiled back. He was alive. That was all that mattered.

"Give me a moment," he said to Nunce. "I've just been brought back from the dead by a beautiful angel. Forgive me if I'd like to savor it as long as possible."

One of the policemen chuckled.

"Get up, Glass," Nunce said in his monotone. "Miss? If you please."

Matt stood and held out his hand to me. I took it and allowed him to assist me to my feet. He stroked my wet cheeks with the pad of his thumb. "I knew you would save me one day," he murmured. "I just didn't think it would be today."

"It wasn't me," I said. "I didn't tell them you were the Dark Rider." I wanted him to know. *Needed* him to know.

He touched my chin. "I believe you."

"All right then, out you go, miss," Nunce said, coming to stand beside us. "Constable Stanley will escort you."

I shook my head. This was all wrong. Matt couldn't be the Dark Rider. I had no evidence to refute his claim, except for the feeling in the base of my stomach. I rounded on Nunce. "He's innocent," I said. "You have no evidence against him, except some malicious gossip."

"That's enough from you, miss." He shooed me off with his hands.

"I will not leave! This is an outrage. You're holding an innocent man—"

"India." Matt grasped my shoulders and forced me to face him. He looked healthy, his color normal, but exhaustion still shadowed him. He needed to be home, resting properly. "There's no need to create a ruckus. Once Commissioner Munro knows I'm here, he'll see that I'm freed." He glared at Nunce. "As long as the commissioner is told, that is."

"The commissioner's too busy to listen to stories," Nunce said. "If I sent for him every time a perpetrator asked, he'd never get anything done."

Ruckus. I'd heard that word three times in as many days, whereas I'd only ever heard it used once before that, and it was in reference to a riot in America, reported in an English newspaper. The reporter, however, had been an American at the scene.

I stared at Matt. He stared back at me and frowned. "I know who it is," I whispered, feeling sick yet relieved too. "Ruckus."

At a nod from Nunce, one of the constables took my elbow and steered me toward the door. The one with the keys held it open.

"India?"

I glanced over my shoulder at Matt. He was still frowning, concern etched into every tired groove of his face. "You'll be free soon," I told him. "I know who the Dark Rider really is."

"Who?"

"Dorchester."

Matt's face darkened. "How do you know?"

"That's enough," Nunce said. "Get her out of here, Stanley."

I planted my feet on the floor and folded my arms. Constable Stanley didn't come closer. "There's a fellow going by the name of Dorchester," I told Nunce. "*He's* the Dark Rider." He *had* to be the Dark Rider and not the sheriff fellow. The sheriff had no need to hide his accent from the world and sneak around the city.

Nunce scratched his ragged beard. "Where can I find him?"

"Near Piccadilly, but I don't know exactly where. And even that might have been a lie."

"Why should I believe you, miss? Perhaps you're trying to trick me into releasing Mr. Glass, here. What evidence do you have of the Dorchster fellow's guilt?"

"He used the word ruckus."

He gave me a blank look. "So?"

"Ruckus is an American word, and Mr. Dorchester claimed to be English. From Manchester, in fact, although his accent was all wrong. I should have guessed from the beginning, but I...I wanted to believe him."

I couldn't meet Matt's gaze. I didn't want him seeing my shame. I'd wanted to believe that Mr. Dorchester liked me for me and not because I could give him something. I was such a bloody fool. Once again, I'd been blinded by charm and my own pathetic need to be liked. The truth stung but it didn't bring tears; only anger and a resolve to make Dorchester pay for his crimes.

"A word?" Nunce grunted. "That's not evidence, miss. Go on. Out you go."

"India?" The concern in Matt's quiet voice had me looking up as Constable Stanley took my elbow. "Will you be all right?"

I straightened my spine. "Of course. Now, if you gentlemen will excuse me, I have a commissioner to visit before he goes home for the day."

Matt smiled.

Constable Stanley escorted me to the station's entrance, but I stopped dead in the doorway. Mr. Dorchester stood at the counter, speaking with the bobby on duty. "That's him," I whispered, grasping Constable Stanley's sleeve. "That's the real Dark Rider."

The pimply faced youth eyed Dorchester. "You sure, miss?"

"Of course. Arrest him."

He glanced back at the door now shut behind us. "You heard the inspector. One word isn't enough to arrest a man. Besides, he looks decent enough to me."

"Can you not question him? Ask him what river flows through Manchester, or some other fact about the city that a resident should know."

"What river flows through Manchester?"

I sighed. "The Irwell. Go on. Speak to him."

He didn't budge despite my push. "I must follow the inspector's orders, but I'll get his current address off him, if that'll satisfy you."

I was about to tell him that it wouldn't when Dorchester suddenly looked our way. My heart leapt into my throat. I tried not to react, but he must have seen something in my face because he did not smile in greeting as the kind Mr. Dorchester would have done. He scowled at the constable at my side.

"Go on," I said to the young bobby. "Go and speak with him now."

I walked off and nodded a greeting at Dorchester as I passed him. He touched the brim of his hat. The exchange was so stilted and formal that I suspected he knew exactly why I was there and what I thought of him.

I rushed out, determined to get far away from him as quickly as possible. The sun had dropped behind the buildings, shrouding the street in eerie gray-green shadows. I glanced over my shoulder, but Dorchester had not emerged from the police station.

I turned on to busy Piccadilly Street, where I blended in with the other pedestrians heading home or to railway stations and omnibus stops after work. There were many routes to Victoria Embankment from Vine Street, some of which would have brought me to New Scotland Yard faster, but I remained on the busier streets for safety. Even though several glances over my shoulder proved that Dorchester wasn't following me, I didn't want to take the risk.

There was something comforting about the imposing edifice of the clock tower that housed Big Ben in its belfry. It was visible beyond the new headquarters of the Metropolitan Police, and stood confidently amid the bustle of carriages, carts and pedestrians below, just as it had done all my life. My father used to bring me to see it and explain how the giant clock operated on the same principles as my own pocket watch.

A pocket watch that suddenly chimed in my reticule. A watch that had never chimed before and wasn't designed to.

I opened my reticule, but something smacked into me from behind, propelling me forward. It happened so fast, that I managed nothing more than a gasp before a gloved hand clamped over my mouth. In the inky shadows of a deep recessed doorway, he pressed my back against the cold bricks. Although I couldn't see his face, the man had the same height, build and scent of

Dorchester. He must have known I would come here, and he had taken a quicker route.

"You stupid fool," he growled in a low voice that was very different to the one I was familiar with. It was hard and cruel with an American accent. "You should have kept your nose out of Glass's business. Out of *my* business."

How had I ever liked this man? I certainly was a fool to believe his story. I struggled against him but he was too strong, pressing his weight against me, grinding my shoulder blades into the stones. His gloved hand muffled my cries and, after a busy burst of traffic, the pavement was now empty of pedestrians.

Panic rose to my throat. I kicked out but my damned skirts got in the way. He pressed himself against me more, blocking my legs so that I couldn't kick at all. I was pinned against the wall, unable to move or make a sound.

"If you'd stayed out of it, I could have finally got my revenge on that scum. Yes, it was me who told the police he was the Dark Rider. It was the perfect plan. He gets arrested and tried here, well away from the friends who can help him. But then I learn he has the commissioner in his pocket too, so I know I have to act fast before he's released. I went to the police station to give him my parting gift." A click echoed around the stone doorway, followed by the whine of metal on metal. Something sharp bit into my neck above my collar. He had a knife—his "gift" to Matt, intended to go straight through his heart, no doubt.

I swallowed, shut my eyes and willed for someone to walk past, to see me at this evil man's mercy. But our clothing was dark and the streetlamps were not yet lit, and nobody passed by anyway.

"But they wouldn't let me see him, thanks to you, you little bitch. I know you told them about me. I could see it in that kid's eyes—and his chief's, when he came out. I only just got away after some quick talking."

I tried biting him, but only found a mouthful of leather glove.

He chuckled. His teeth flashed white in the darkness, and a glint shone in his eyes. "Do you know the man you're helping is a turncoat? He was an outlaw, too. He's got blood on his hands, has Glass. Lots of blood."

My breath hitched. My body stilled.

He chuckled again. "So he failed to mention it to his little lady friend, eh? He hates ordinary folk knowing. Hates that he's related to the Johnsons. But that ain't the worst of it, no ma'am. You think I'm bad, but he's worse. We've both killed men before, but at least I haven't murdered my own kin."

Bile surged up my throat. I choked on it, making my eyes water and my nose run. Tears pooled but didn't spill. He *must* be lying.

"Murdered his own grandfather in cold blood," Dorchester went on. "Glass could have got him arrested, like the others in the old man's posse, but he chose to shoot him instead. My little brother was one of Johnson's posse. Just a kid, he was, when they strung him up." He sniffed and wiped his nose on his shoulder. "So what do you think of that, Miss Prim? What do you think of your big handsome hero now?"

His hot breath scalded my forehead. The sharp point of his blade nicked my skin. Blood trickled into my collar. I whimpered and shut my eyes. My watch chimed again, louder this time. I prayed someone heard it and became curious.

But no one walked past.

"He ain't going to rescue you now," Dorchester said, chuckling. "He's all locked up, getting a taste of his own medicine. Pity he'll probably get out, sooner or later.

But when he does, he's going to find his pretty little friend was the victim of just another London murderer, right here under Scotland Yard's nose. He took someone from me, so I'm going to take someone from him."

I wanted to scream at him that I hardly knew Matt, that I wasn't important to him. But I wasn't sure it would have mattered. Dorchester hated me for being on Matt's side, for bringing attention to him now. He wanted me dead, and no amount of pleading would make a difference. With my mouth covered, I couldn't even try.

He pressed the blade again. Fresh blood oozed and trickled down my neck. I shut my eyes and prayed for my soul. There was nothing more I could do.

CHAPTER 16

Dorchester bared his teeth then leaned in and licked the blood on my neck. I gagged. He laughed, and did it again, enjoying my horror. Enjoying toying with the rabbit in his snare.

My reticule moved in my hand. My heart leapt and I gave a muffled cry, but I clung onto it. If I'd not heard the watch chime earlier, if I'd not heard the word magic bandied about, I would have thought a mouse had found its way inside. But a small, mad part of me knew my watch was trying to get out.

My arms were pinned, but my hands had some movement. I managed to maneuver the reticule and insert my fingers into its drawstring opening to stretch it wide. My watch found its way into my hand. The silver case, usually cool to the touch, felt so warm that I could feel it through my glove.

My mind flashed back to the night of the poker game, when I'd thrown that carriage clock to knock out my attacker. A strange thought settled, one that I couldn't shake—it hadn't been my good aim or the force of my throw that propelled the clock into Dennison's forehead. It had been the clock itself, changing course to hit him. It had been magical.

Dorchester laughed again. He licked my ear then pressed the blade harder into my neck. I cried out, not because of the sharp pain, but because the watch fell from my hand. I'd lost it! No, no, NO!

Dorchester froze. The pressure from the blade eased. Then his body began to shake violently. He released me and stumbled back, convulsing. He looked like he was doing a crazed dance. He tried to speak, but no words came out. His eyes begged me to help, but I did not, even though I knew it was my watch causing him to act that way. The chain wrapped around his wrist and the watch itself pressed into his palm.

He fell to his knees as if someone stronger had shoved him down. Then he fell forward onto his face, smashing his nose into the stones.

I ran. "Help! Help me!"

Three men hurried up to me, two of them uniformed bobbies, the other declaring himself to be a detective inspector from the Yard.

I pointed to the doorway. My hand trembled and my voice wobbled, but I managed to tell them that a man by the name of Dorchester was in there. "He's the American outlaw known as the Dark Rider, and he attacked me. He—he wanted to silence me."

I could just make out their incredulous expressions in the dim light. They must have had a dozen questions for me, but they all knew the most pressing concern was capturing my attacker. They carefully approached the doorway, batons raised. I followed, not sure what we'd find.

The constable at the front lowered his baton. "Is he dead?"

I stumbled, sick to my stomach. *Please don't be dead.* I knew he would be hung for his crimes, either here or in America, but I didn't want to be the one to pull the trigger, so to speak. I didn't want his death to be a result of my...magic.

The bobbies dragged Dorchester out of the doorway. He groaned and stirred. I breathed a sigh of relief and edged closer, taking a wide berth around him until I was at the opening of the doorway. My watch glinted in the shadows. I bent and scooped it up. It not longer felt warm, but like an ordinary silver watch.

"What you got there, miss?" the inspector asked.

"My watch." I showed it to him. "I dropped it in the scuffle."

He nodded, satisfied. "How'd you overpower him?" he asked as the two constables lifted the dazed Dorchester between them.

"I...I suppose it was a combination of luck and timing." I dropped my watch back in the reticule. "Excellent timing."

"So what's this about him being the Dark Rider?"

"It's a long story, and I must speak with your commissioner about it immediately. Is he in his office?"

"The commissioner's busy, miss."

"I don't care!" Good lord, the man was more inaccessible than the queen. "I have vital information about the Dark Rider to give him, and only him. Take me to him now. Please," I added, more demurely.

He eyed me then the retreating backs of his constables carrying Dorchester. "You can tell me all about how you came to know that man is the Dark Rider while we walk up to the commissioner's office."

I was so thankful, I clasped his hand. "Come on then!"

I gave him my name and Matt's address as we walked, but told him I wanted to save the details about the Dark Rider for the commissioner's ears.

It was dark inside the building, and the inspector commanded one of the constables on duty to hand him a lamp. It threw out enough light for us to see our way through the corridors of New Scotland Yard. The smell of fresh paint followed us. The brass doorknobs and hooks for coats gleamed in the lamplight. Unlike Vine Street Police Station, the windows were not covered by bars. I wondered where they'd taken Dorchester and if he had recovered.

We entered an office on the second floor with furniture polished to a sheen and a portrait of the queen on the wall. It was empty, but appeared to be only an outer office that led to another. The inspector knocked, and I was relieved to hear a gruff voice order us to enter. The commissioner had not yet gone home.

Commissioner Munro was a distinguished looking gentleman with white hair on the sides of his head and gray on top. His white moustache curled at the ends. He wore a uniform with impressively decorated epaulettes, and a cap hung on a hook beside another portrait of the queen. Shrewd eyes watched me, but with curiosity, not unkindness.

He rose and we shook hands. The inspector made the introductions and gave him a brief account of our meeting. The commissioner invited me to sit and directed the inspector to make me some tea.

"No, thank you," I said. "Tea isn't necessary." Anything that delayed the commissioner getting Matt out of jail wasn't necessary.

"Miss Steele, why are you certain this fellow who attacked you is the Dark Rider?" the commissioner asked. "Perhaps he's simply an opportunist who saw a young woman walking alone at dusk."

"Directly outside New Scotland Yard? It would take a brazen attacker to be so bold. No, Commissioner, he's the Dark Rider and admitted as much to me."

He leaned back. The leather of his chair creaked. He rested his elbows on the chair arms and steepled his fingers. "The Dark Rider has already been caught. He's currently being held at—"

"Vine Street Police Station. Yes, yes, I know all of that. But that man isn't the Dark Rider."

Snowy eyebrows inched up his forehead. "You're doubting my very experienced inspector?"

"Inspector Nunce may be experienced but he's a fool. He arrested the wrong man. I believe you know him, sir, and you can vouch for his innocence." I hoped I had that correct, and Matt's asking for the commissioner was an indication that this man could be trusted. Based on what Dorchester had told me, I was no longer sure who or what Matt was, but I did know he wasn't the Dark Rider. I also knew that he hoped the commissioner could help him. That was enough for me, for now.

"I am intrigued," he said. "Who is it?"

"Mr. Matthew Glass."

The commissioner lowered his hands. "Thank you, Toohey, that will be all."

The inspector, who'd remained standing behind me, left, shutting the door on his way out.

"I require the entire story," the commissioner said in a calm voice edged with steel. "Now."

I explained everything, where I had an explanation. I brushed over the use of my watch to escape from Dorchester and didn't speculate on how Matt might know the commissioner when he'd been in London only a week.

The commissioner rose from his seat before I finished. He plucked his hat off the hook and placed it under his arm. "It seems I have to visit Vine Street before I head home. Hopefully Mrs. Munro won't be too upset at my tardiness tonight."

He stopped in a downstairs office to speak with Inspector Toohey about keeping Dorchester well locked up, then commanded one of the constables to bring his carriage around. As we waited, Big Ben struck the hour. Its deep resonant gong thrummed through me. I breathed deeply, drawing the air into my lungs with what felt like my first proper breath since Dorchester's attack.

It was a short ride back to Vine Street, in which the commissioner questioned me about my connections, my background, and finally, he asked for specifics on how I'd escaped from Dorchester.

"I don't know," I said honestly. "I truly don't. One moment his knife was here," I touched the small cut above my collar, "and the next he was on the ground, convulsing."

"Epilepsy," he said with certainty.

I tucked my reticule closer to my body and pressed its soft sides until I felt the familiar shape of the watch. The familiar, comforting shape. That watch had saved me; I was certain of it. It had tried to warn me that Dorchester was near, with its strange chimes, but I'd not listened. Then it had leapt from my hand to his and emitted some kind of electrical current into him.

But how could that be? What logical explanation was there for a watch to act and *think* on its own? It was ludicrous. I must have been losing my mind to even consider it. Yet there I was, considering it very seriously. If it had been just my watch, and just this one incident, I would have been a little more skeptical, but it wasn't the first time. The clock on the mantel at the gambling house had also saved my life. My aim wasn't *that* good.

Perhaps all watches were magical and I'd never been in a dangerous situation to witness their power. But that didn't explain why people were murdered all the time when they carried watches on them, or were killed in the presence of clocks. The clock beneath Big Ben's belfry hadn't thrown itself upon my attacker, either. I smiled at the absurdity of it but it quickly vanished. I'd handled both the clock in the gambling house and the watch in my reticule. I'd opened them up and touched their mechanisms.

I was the key that set their magic in motion.

My fingers tightened around my reticule. The commissioner said something, and I had to ask him to repeat it. It wasn't until a constable opened the carriage door that I realized we'd arrived at Vine Street Police Station.

Policemen gasped when they saw the commissioner then saluted with a click of their heels. The police station was quieter, and Constable Stanley stood at the front counter instead of his gruffer colleague. He smiled upon seeing me, only for it to dissolve into open-mouthed surprise when he realized who accompanied me.

"This way, sir," he said, when Munro asked to see Matt. Not Detective Inspector Nunce, but Matt himself.

I followed, only to be ordered to remain behind by the commissioner. I considered arguing with him then decided to sit and wait. There were probably things he and Matt needed to discuss alone before Munro ordered his release.

If he ordered his release.

If he did not, then my attempts had been for nought. There was nothing more I could do.

It felt like an age before the door opened again, but according to the clock on the wall, only ten minutes had passed. Willie emerged. She caught sight of me and smiled. I grinned back, relief flooding me. I felt giddy with it.

Duke followed her, then Cyclops, then finally Matt and the commissioner. Our gazes briefly connected before an enthusiastic Willie embraced me, almost knocking me off my feet. She clasped me tightly, laughing.

"I knew you would rescue us!" she cried, giving me a gentle punch on the arm before letting me go.

"Liar," Duke said before he elbowed her out of the way so he could hug me too. "*I* knew you'd rescue us. Never had a doubt."

"Nor me," Cyclops said, folding me into his side and kissing the top of my head. "I see you brought him the watch too," he whispered, nodding at Matt. "Seems we need to thank you twice over."

They had to sign some paperwork before they were fully released, but it didn't take long before Willie, Matt, Munro and I climbed into the commissioner's waiting carriage, while Cyclops joined the driver and Duke stood on the footman's platform at the back.

Willie, sitting beside me, took my hand. She alternated between smiling at me and turning grim. I suspected there were things she wanted to say to me. Things that she felt awkward expressing. I squeezed her hand to let her know I forgave her.

I looked at Matt, drinking in his appearance, checking every inch of his face. He seemed tired still, but not exhausted or ill, thank goodness. He smiled and his hand fluttered to his pocket where he'd slipped his watch.

"Commissioner," he began, "I have to disagree with you."

I arched my brows. Clearly this was the continuation of an earlier conversation I'd not been privy to.

"It's unwise," the commissioner said, glancing at me. "The fewer people who know, the safer you are."

"Miss Steele is the soul of discretion. She won't tell anyone. I think she's proven herself worthy, don't you?"

The commissioner's lips flattened. I decided to make it a little easier for him. "Is this about you working for the American law enforcement to help them capture outlaws?"

All three of them stared at me. "Dorchester told me a little," I admitted.

Matt sucked in a breath. He stared at me, his body rigid. "What did he say?"

That you murdered your own grandfather. I looked away, no longer able to face him. It took a certain type of man to kill, and quite another to kill his own family.

"Do not believe everything that man told you, Miss Steele," Munro said. "Including his name. Scotland Yard will wire America for more information and send a sketch of that fellow we arrested for attacking you."

"Attacking you!" Matt bellowed.

Munro waved his hand. "She's perfectly all right, as you can see."

Matt couldn't sit still for the rest of the journey to Park Street. His fingers tapped his knee, the wall, the door handle, the seat. No one else seemed to notice except me.

"I think I might be able to help you with his name," I said. "He told me that Mr. Glass was involved in his younger brother's death."

"Could be anyone," Willie muttered.

Matt glared at her, and she shrugged before glancing at me and wincing.

"His brother was a member of your grandfather's posse," I said.

"So you know about him," Matt said flatly.

"I do."

He lowered his gaze and rubbed his forehead. After a moment, he turned to the commissioner. "Given that information, I suspect Dorchester is one Patrick McTierney. Have your men wire their sketch to the Lake Valley sheriff. He's a good man, and Patrick McTierney's family lives in his jurisdiction."

"God damn it," Willie said on a breath. She leaned forward, resting her elbows on her knees, and shook her head. "We always feared he'd come for you, sooner or later. Never thought it'd be here."

"You never met the fellow?" Munro asked.

"Not Patrick," Matt said. "It's true that his younger brother was part of our grandfather's posse." He spoke to me, not Munro. "My evidence got him arrested and he was hanged for his crimes."

"They were supposed to go easy on him, on account of his age," Willie said heavily. "They didn't."

There must be more to the story but I didn't ask questions, and Matt didn't offer answers. I may never get them. Never find out if he had killed his grandfather in cold blood, or how he felt about it. I wasn't sure I wanted to know.

The three of us climbed out of the carriage, but Munro held Matt back. "You may tell her as much as you think she needs to know. I agree with your assessment—she's proven her worth."

Matt nodded. "Thank you, sir. I'll be in touch."

"If you're staying in London, I have some work in mind for you." The commissioner touched the brim of his cap. "For now, enjoy your freedom."

The front door opened and Miss Glass stood there, back straight, head high. "Finally! You're home! Now, what did you bring me, you naughty man?"

Matt climbed the steps and drew her into a hug. She patted him gently on the back. "What do you mean, bring you?" he asked.

"From your travels," she said. "Harry, do you mean to say you've been all over the world and haven't brought me back so much as a hairpin?"

He hugged her again. "It's in my luggage, arriving tomorrow."

She clapped her hands and grinned. "Ooh, I can't wait to see what it is."

We all retired to our rooms to freshen up and change for dinner prepared by Polly. I didn't expect to see Matt at all, thinking he would go straight to bed to rest, but he was down before me, waiting by the dinner gong, alone.

"I haven't had a chance to thank you yet," he said quietly.

"There's no need."

"There's every need." He took my hands in his and my heart skid to a halt. He leaned in. He smelled like lavender and spices, a scent uniquely his. "Thank you, India. You saved my life today, and I will never forget it." His lips pressed to my forehead and lingered for far longer than decency dictated.

I didn't move. I was frozen to the spot. I clung onto his hands and felt his fingers squeeze mine. My heart lifted, but I quickly dampened it. This was real life, not a fairytale. He was grateful, yes, but that was all.

"I owe you an explanation," he said, pulling away.

I nodded, my heart still in my throat where it seemed to have moved permanently. "Do you work for that famous American detective agency? Pink something? I've heard about them."

"Pinkertons. No, I'm my own agent, but you could say my role is similar to what the Pinkertons do. I specialize in apprehending outlaws of the western states and territories. Because of my family connections, I have knowledge the lawmen don't. My mother's family is somewhat notorious, and I became embroiled in that life after I returned to them upon my parents' deaths. I got out eventually, as did Willie."

And now he was bringing them to justice. It was noble and yet sinister as well. They were his family, after all.

"It makes family reunions awkward." He smiled tentatively, as if trying to gauge my reaction to his dark joke. I smiled back, but it lacked warmth. I wasn't sure how I felt about his work yet. "I have contacts with the local law enforcers, so when I told them I was coming to London, one of them gave my details to Commissioner Munro, suggesting my services could be of use to him. Infiltrating criminal gangs is my specialty, you see, and he thought I might be useful while I was here. Munro hadn't taken up the offer, however."

"So the Dark Rider followed you to England, not the other way round."

He nodded.

"Was he the intruder too?"

"I believe so now, though I didn't suspect him at the time. I have no proof, however. I don't know how he knew where to find me. Perhaps he haunted the gambling houses where poker is played and followed Willie home, one night. I've sensed that we were being followed for some days."

"Hence your constant peering through windows." I'd just had a thought. Dorchester—McTierney—must have followed me too, after I came to work for Matt. It explained why he'd been outside the butcher's shop with an umbrella at precisely the same time as me. Ice chilled my veins and I shivered. "Why not just shoot you in the street?" I asked.

"Because he doesn't want to swing for his crimes. Having me blamed for them was the perfect scenario for him. Up until now, his face hasn't been seen. I suspect he's been behind some attacks on me in recent years, but I had no proof. His methods have been sly, cowardly, never openly revealing himself to be behind them."

"How awful. He truly did consider you responsible for his younger brother's death."

"In a way, I am. I'm responsible for a lot of deaths."

"Including your grandfather's," I said quietly.

His eyes fluttered closed. Tiny dark blue veins webbed the lids. He nodded. "I shot him in self defense after he shot at me. Perhaps one day I'll show you the scar his bullet made."

He'd been shot by his own grandfather! I searched his face. It was unmarked.

His eyebrows twitched mischievously. "It's in an unmentionable location."

My face flamed. He laughed, and I gave him a withering glare.

He took my hands again. His thumb stroked mine and his features settled, once again serious. "I know you have questions about the watch." He patted his pocket. "And I can see now that you must be told. Can we speak tomorrow? It requires lengthy discussion, and I don't want Aunt Letitia to know."

I also suspected he was too tired for such a discussion. I nodded.

"Good." He smiled again. "I'm glad you've decided to stay on as her companion."

"But—"

"I think I hear her now. Let's tell her, shall we?" He thrust out his elbow to me.

I hesitated then took it with a shake of my head. "You ought to be a politician. You have a knack for swaying people to your viewpoint."

"You're too kind, particularly considering you rarely believe me when I am being sincere."

I was about to protest again, but he gave me that crooked boyish smile and my insides melted a little. Besides, Miss Glass approached.

Matt informed her he had employed me to be her companion. She was delighted, in a reserved, upper class way. She patted my cheek, then insisted her nephew escort her into the dining room instead since she was the most important female member of the household and he the most important male. He simply thrust out his other elbow, which she accepted with a smile in her eyes.

"Tomorrow, Miss Steele, I will take you shopping," she declared. "If you're to be my companion, you require new dresses. Those are far too dreary."

CHAPTER 17

My watch looked entirely normal. I spent the morning pulling it apart and inspecting each tiny mechanism. Nothing was out of place. There were no hidden striking trains, hammers, gongs or repeaters. It couldn't possibly have chimed.

I put it back together, a familiar task I could do without even looking. It hadn't been the first watch I'd ever worked on, but it was the one I'd opened up the most. My parents gave it to me on my sixteenth birthday. The silver case was monogrammed with my initials, and a message congratulating me on my birthday was etched inside. It was my most cherished possession.

Somehow, it had saved my life.

A knock sounded on my door, and Willie called out, "It's me. May I speak with you, India?"

"Of course. Come in."

She opened the door just enough to squeeze through and leaned back against it. She bit her lip and looked everywhere but at me.

"Is there something I can do for you, Willie?"

She huffed out a breath. "I wouldn't really have cut you up, you know."

I pinched the back of my hand to stop myself smiling. "I know. Thank you for reassuring me."

"Matt says you're going to stay."

"I'm to be his aunt's companion." I hadn't had time to discuss the new arrangement with either of them, but I felt immeasurably lighter since the decision had been made. The weight of uncertainty over my future had been pressing down on me without me realizing.

She rushed forward and grasped my forearms. "You won't give up on finding the watchmaker, will you?"

"Matt no longer needs my help. We've called on every watchmaker I know. Cyclops is capable of taking him to—"

"No, *you* must help. You know London better than any of us, and you know watches too." She dug her fingers into my arms. "You've seen what his watch does, India. It's of vital importance that it gets fixed."

"It seems to work perfectly well. It...rejuvenates him when he uses it."

"It's slowing down." She let me go and perched on the edge of the dressing table where I'd been working. She lowered her head and some loose strands of hair fell over her face. "It no longer works for days, as it used to. It will stop altogether, one day."

"And there is no one else who can fix it?"

"None that we know of."

What sort of watchmaker fixed a life giving, magical watch? A magician, I supposed. The notion was utterly absurd, yet I couldn't shake it.

"I will help Matt whenever he requires it," I assured her. "Now, tell me, will you come shopping with Miss Glass and me later? We would enjoy your company."

"Why?" She plucked the fabric of her trousers at her thighs. "I'm a terrible judge of fashion."

"Or are you secretly hiding your femininity as a mode of protection?"

She screwed up her face in a most unladylike expression. "Not damned likely. Besides, I can't come shopping. I'm going to see Travers again to tell him I've decided to play for my locket."

"No! Willie, you shouldn't. You promised Matt."

She strode to the door. "I have to."

"How? You said you have no money."

"I don't need money."

"You've asked Matt for a loan?"

She shook her head. "He's got too much on his plate." She jerked the door open, surprising her cousin who had his fist poised to knock.

He stepped aside with a raise of his brows as she stormed past him.

"Why is she in a foul mood?" he asked. "She was contrite when I spoke to her earlier."

I sighed. "She's still upset about her locket." I didn't tell him she was planning on gambling to win it back. It was none of my affair, and she wouldn't like me to tattle. "How are you feeling this morning?"

"Better."

He did look better, but I'd come to expect to see the tiredness in his eyes now. "But not completely healthy."

A beat passed. Two. "I don't expect to be," he said.

My heart ached. What an awful thing to always feel tired, to be worried about one's health. No one should have to, particularly not a young, athletic and capable man like Matt.

"Don't, India." The low ebb of his voice washed over me. "Don't pity me."

Easy enough to say, not so easy to do. I studied the watch in my hand, tracing my thumbnail over the monogram. "Tell me about your magic watch, Matt. Tell me everything."

He touched his waistcoat pocket. Perhaps he didn't want to be parted from it for one moment, even at home. Having witnessed what happened when he was separated from it for too long, I could see why.

He closed the door and sat on the trunk at the foot of the bed. He leaned his elbows on his knees and looked at me. "So you believe in magic."

"I...I don't know yet. It seems so childish and fantastical, yet I've seen things. Tell me what you know. And tell me why I've never heard of such things as magical health-giving watches before."

"You've never heard of them because magic has been suppressed for hundreds of years. Magicians were almost wiped out in medieval times, after a small group committed heinous crimes using their magic. People panicked and attacked *all* magicians, not just the guilty few. Those who managed to escape have kept their secret all these years, out of fear."

I nodded, hardly daring to breathe. Could such a story truly be possible? "How do you know all this?"

"One of the men who gave me this watch told me about it. One of them was the watchmaker, known as Chronos, the other a surgeon. They saved my life."

"Surgeon? I think you need to start from the beginning."

He cast me a crooked smile. "I will, Miss Impatience. Five years ago, I nearly died from a bullet wound. The wound my grandfather gave me, as it happens."

"Oh, Matt," I murmured.

"No pity, India."

I pressed my lips together and nodded.

"I was in a town called Broken Creek, and the gunfight happened outside the saloon. A surgeon from one of the most prestigious hospitals in New York also happened to be in town."

"What was he doing so far away from home in a tiny backwater?"

"He was an alcoholic. He'd been given leave to dry out. Unfortunately for him, he didn't try very hard. Fortunately for me, I was shot at ten in the morning when the saloon hadn't yet opened. He was an excellent surgeon, even with a shaking hand."

"Was?"

"He's dead. I know that for certain because I went in search of him before I came here. I spoke to him just days before his death. Considering how much he drank, I was surprised he lived so long. I knew *his* name, you see, and I hoped he knew the real name of Chronos. They worked together on my surgery after the gunfight. I don't recall any of it, but Duke, Cyclops and Willie said it was both nightmarish and a dream come true. They told me Dr. Parsons worked on me on a table in the saloon. He'd removed the bullet but my life was slipping away and he hadn't sutured the wound yet. I was going to die unless a miracle could be produced."

"Or magic."

He nodded. "My friends told me that a small crowd gathered to watch Dr. Parsons work on me. Another man came forward. I'd seen him talking to Parsons some evenings in the saloon. He asked Parsons if he wanted to try his idea out, and Parsons replied that there was no chance of my survival using normal surgical methods. Duke told me that no one knew what the men meant, but Willie screamed at them to try whatever they wanted to make me live. They ordered everyone to leave, but Willie hid beneath a table in the shadows. According to her account, the man who called himself Chronos searched my person and found my watch." He patted his pocket again. "Willie almost revealed herself to accuse him of theft, but when she saw what he did with it, she remained hidden."

"What did he do?" I asked, breathless.

"Chronos held my watch in his hand, palm up, closed his eyes, and whispered some words. The watch began to glow, but neither man was alarmed. Willie thinks I stopped breathing at that point because Parsons shouted, "Now! It must be now!" Chronos took my hand and placed it over his, the watch between. As he chanted, Willie saw the purplish glow infuse itself into my skin and spread through my veins."

"I've seen it work," I said.

He arched one brow and grunted.

"Go on. Then what happened?"

"Willie tells me that Dr. Parsons worked on me again, sewing up my wound while Chronos continued to chant as he held the watch against my palm. When Parsons finished, he told Chronos it was done, and Chronos placed the watch over the wound. Dr. Parsons took over the chant and the watch suddenly flared. Willie said she thought it had caught fire, but the light quickly faded away to nothing. My veins ceased glowing too. That's when she noticed my chest rise with a deep breath. I remember everything from that moment on. It's so clear, like it happened yesterday. I sat up. They gave me a dram of whiskey. I was still covered in blood, but the wound had been sewn up. That's when Dr. Parsons handed me the watch. He and Chronos explained that it would keep me alive. Whenever I felt unnaturally tired, I should hold the watch in my palm and it would work its magic on me and bring me back to life. I thought them utterly mad and told them so. They looked at one another, sighed, then told me I could go to hell. They didn't care what became of me. But there was something in their eyes. Elation, I think, like they'd won a victory. They patted one another on the back and paid each other compliments. They began discussing the future of their discovery, and what it meant for the world, but they disagreed on whether it should be brought to light. I had no idea what they were talking about, but it seemed not to concern me. It was like I wasn't important."

"You just happened to be the closest dying man," I said. "They wanted to experiment with magic, and you were there at the right time." It surprised me that I'd accepted his story and the idea of magic so easily. But I trusted him, and trusted that he wouldn't believe without solid evidence. "What happened after that? Did you see the men in Broken Creek again?"

He shook his head. "I got up and left. Some time later, Willie found me. She was in shock. She told me what she'd witnessed in the saloon. None of us believed her at first, but a week later, when I began to feel exhausted for no good reason, she suggested I hold my watch in the palm of my hand and see what happened. I thought her mad and refused. I quickly became ill, weak, and close to death. The doctors didn't know what was wrong with me. Willie simply placed the watch in my hand one day, as I lay in bed, and I immediately felt restored to normal health. Not like you see me now, but completely better."

"The glowing veins didn't alarm you?"

"Terrified me. But I could feel the benefits to my health immediately. I didn't let the watch go until I felt completely well again. The four of us discussed what it could mean, how it had happened. Cyclops had heard stories about magic, but only in whispers. We asked his grandmother, but she refused to talk about it. She said magic was dangerous and was kept secret from the world for a reason. She did tell us that people were born magic, to magic parents, but it was a skill that required training to work efficiently. From Willie's account of the surgery, it was clear that Parsons and Chronos had worked together somehow, and they were both magicians. For five years, I used the watch whenever I felt unnaturally tired and it worked perfectly. But four months ago, its power waned, and I needed it more often. I knew I had to seek out Parsons and Chronos."

"Before it stopped working altogether," I said on a breath.

He gave a slight nod.

My throat clogged. I tried not to show pity, but I don't think I was very good at keeping my thoughts to myself.

He studied his hands. "I knew nothing about Chronos, but I knew where Parsons worked, so we went to New York. He was on his death bed, with only days to live."

"What did he say?"

"That he regretted experimenting on me."

"Why?"

"Because it was playing God. It was Chronos's idea to bring me back to life, and Parsons felt he'd been coerced into it. He hadn't seen Chronos since that day."

"Had he performed much magic before then?"

"Only rarely. He thinks he must have mentioned it to Chronos in his drunken state one day in Broken Creek, and Chronos, also being a magician, began to discuss mad theories and ways to combine their magic. Parsons explained that there were different styles of magic, based on one's profession or skill. As a doctor, his own magic helped him heal people, but he couldn't give them back their life, only extend it for short periods of time. He claimed it was almost useless, for that reason. An engineer can create superior strength steel, but again, it only lasts for short periods of time. A carpenter can infuse wood so that it doesn't burn, but it doesn't last more than a few hours."

"But Chronos had discovered a way to combine his magic with that of other types to extend it," I said. "My god." It was genius and thrilling. Yet so strange. Part of me couldn't believe I was discussing magic without giggling. Perhaps tomorrow I would wake up from this dream and laugh about it.

But Matt's grim nod was very real. "Chronos had never combined his magic with a doctor's before. Indeed, he'd only worked with carpenters and the like until that day in Broken Creek. Chronos knew he could extend the magic of other magicians, but extending the life of a dying man had never been tried, to his knowledge."

"It's quite remarkable. So Parsons put his magic into the watch too?"

"The magic from both magicians exists in the watch and in me. The two entities cannot be separated for long or the magic fades, and the watch cannot work on another human, only me. It's a part of me as much as my heart or lungs."

"That's why it doesn't glow when anyone else holds it," I said, more to myself than him. "Did Parsons tell you what happened between he and Chronos after they healed you?"

"After the euphoria of their success wore off, Parsons told Chronos that he had reservations. He said he would never work with Chronos again to save a life. Chronos flew into a rage. He said they were on the verge of something monumentally important to the human race. But Parsons was afraid of what could happen if the magic fell into the wrong hands. Chronos was furious. He'd never actually met a magical doctor before, and he feared he'd never find another in his lifetime. Apparently they're the rarest magicians."

"I wonder if he did ever meet another."

Matt shrugged. "Parsons couldn't help me fix the watch. As the problem is in the horology magic, not the medical magic, a timepiece magician is required to service the watch. No ordinary watchmaker can do it."

"What about a different magic watchmaker?" I asked, curling my fingers around my own watch. "One who isn't Chronos, but is a magician?"

"Parsons seemed to think only the original magician can fix it."

I looked down at my fist. My watch's case felt cool now, not warm as it had been the evening before, when McTierney attacked me. I swallowed heavily. My mind was a jumble of questions and theories, all vying for attention. I managed to sort through them. There was only one pressing point. What if Parsons was wrong?

"Matt," I whispered, looking up at him.

He crouched before me. His gaze searched mine, worried and yet curious too. "What is it, India?"

"Last night...my watch wrapped itself around McTierney's wrist and shocked him. It almost killed him."

I opened my fist and he plucked the watch off my palm. He inspected it and opened the case. "Did your father make it?"

I nodded.

"Do you think he could have been a magician?"

"I don't know. But that watch chimed and moved of its own accord. I think the clock in the gambling house saved me too." I told him how it had dipped unexpectedly when I threw it to knock over Lord Dennison.

"That reminds me," he said darkly. "I ought to pay him a visit."

"You'll do no such thing. The incident is in the past. Anyway, what I'm trying to tell you is, I handled that clock. I toyed with its mechanisms for something to do while Willie played. Just as I've taken this watch apart and put it back together dozens of times."

His eyes widened. "You think *you're* a magician? I admit that I have wondered. My watch feels warmer when you're near, as if it's responding to your presence."

I lifted one shoulder. "I don't know what to think. The entire concept of magic is so new to me, and so very strange. I know nothing about it."

He placed the watch back in my palm and closed his hand around mine. "I know so little as well."

"Matt...if I am...I might be able to help you." I placed my hand over the pocket of his waistcoat. His watch heated at my touch. We both felt it.

He swallowed hard and nodded. Then he pulled the watch out. "Take it apart. Do whatever you did to your watch and that clock and we'll see if it makes a difference."

I didn't tell him I already had done so before taking it to him at Vine Street Police Station. Perhaps now that I knew a little more, my magic would show me what to do. I set to work immediately. He didn't stay. I removed the parts and laid them out. I cleaned them, inspected them, and returned them to their place again. It was easy; the mechanism was uncomplicated. But I felt no strange pull, no magic at work.

Matt returned carrying tea and sandwiches on a tray. "Aunt is asking when you'll be ready to go shopping," he said, setting it down beside me. "You're finished?"

I snapped the watch case closed and held it out to him by the chain. He accepted it and closed his fist around it. It immediately glowed and the magic flowed into him, lighting his veins. I watched its progress up his throat, over his face to his hairline. He breathed,

breathed again, then returned it to his pocket. His color returned to normal.

"Well?" I prompted, no longer able to sit. "How do you feel?"

"Like I could kiss you."

My breath hitched. "So it works more efficiently now?"

"I don't know. I won't know for a few more hours, but I still want to kiss you." He smiled. He looked happier than I'd ever seen him. "I've shocked you."

"Yes," I said, turning away so he couldn't see my flushed face. "Tell me how you feel later."

***

Matt's watch was not fixed. He still needed to use it every few hours, instead of every week, like it had once been. He told me in private in the library after dinner.

"I just used it again," he said.

I clasped my brandy tumbler in both hands and stared into the liquid. My vision blurred. I swallowed the entire contents. "I'm sorry, Matt."

He plucked the glass out of my hand. "It's not your fault."

"I know," I said heavily. Yet I felt like I'd failed him. "Do you think my magic is different to Chronos's?"

"I've been considering that, but I honestly don't know. I wonder if your magic is simply raw. Perhaps, with training, you could extend the life of my watch."

But there was no one to train me. And with magic being such a deep secret, we were unlikely to find a magician in the newspaper advertisements. Even worse, we were unlikely to find Chronos himself.

"Perhaps if we discuss this development with the guild—"

"No." He slammed the glass down on the table. "No, India, you are not to mention magic to them. You saw their faces. They already dislike you. This will make it worse for you. Besides, from what Dr. Parsons told me, the authorities are the most fearful of magicians. We don't have guilds in America, but there are committees and other groups that govern trades and crafts. He claimed magicians are not welcome. They're reviled, in fact. You must keep your magic a secret, India. Understand?"

I nodded. "Since Abercrombie and the other members were fearful of me, they must have suspected I possessed magic," I said. "But how? Did they sense it, do you think?"

"Perhaps. Or did they know your father was magic, even though he didn't use it? Perhaps they learned as much when he was dying, since you said it wasn't until around that time that they became fearful of you."

"A little before, when he tried to get them to admit me to the guild," I said, absently. "But Father wasn't a magician. I would have known, or suspected. He was never anything but normal."

He refilled my glass from the decanter on the sideboard and handed it to me. "I'm sure there's a logical explanation."

I sighed. "I suppose there must be." I drank in silence, feeling his intense gaze on me but not daring to meet it. My cheeks were warm enough. "Tell me what you said to Abercrombie to get him to cease accusing me of theft. He claimed you threatened him."

"It was hardly a threat. I merely explained that I work for the police on two continents and am a personal friend to Commissioner Munro. As such, Munro is more likely to believe my account of events over his."

"That's it? There were no threats made to his person?"

"I may have used language and a tone of voice that seems to scare some people easily."

"Ah yes, *that* voice. I've heard it." I smiled. "Thank you, Matt. I appreciate it."

He waved a hand. "It's nothing."

It didn't feel like nothing, but I let the matter rest. "Do the others know that I tried to fix your watch?"

He nodded. "They've been urging me to ask you." He fished in his inside jacket pocket and pulled out an envelope. "There's another reason I called you in here."

"Oh?"

"This arrived for you while you were out. I wanted to give it to you in private."

It was a telegram, all the way from America. "It says that Dorchester is indeed Patrick McTierney." I read on and gasped. "The reward will be sent to me at this address in gold bullion!" I bit my lip but couldn't stop my smile. I re-read the telegram then looked up at Matt. He smiled. "I am to get the reward?"

"Of course."

"But...he was here because of you."

"You caught him."

"It's your job, and you have all these people to support."

"India, I'm a man of independent means. My father saw to that. He worked hard after he escaped his family here, and built a property empire that spans the globe. I don't need the reward money." His eyes sparkled as he perched on the table next to me. "So what will you do with it?"

"I don't know. How much is two thousand dollars in English money?"

"About four hundred pounds."

"Four hundred!" I downed the rest of my brandy in one gulp.

Matt took the glass off me. "Steady, India, or I'll have to carry you to your room."

I hardly heard him. Four hundred pounds was more than my father earned in a year. Was it enough to buy my own shop and equipment? Was it enough to buy out Eddie?

Perhaps, but I still couldn't be a shopkeeper. The guild would never grant me a license. I could buy myself a small house and rent out a spare room to lodgers. The possibilities were endless and rather exciting. Even better, I didn't have to make a decision yet. For now, I would remain as Miss Glass's companion and live at Park Street.

"Matt, do you know a man of business here in London who can help me invest the gold for the time being?"

"My father's lawyer will know someone."

"Nothing risky. I don't want to lose it."

"Then perhaps a bank vault for now, until such time as you need it." He lifted his glass in salute. "Congratulations, India, you are now a woman of independent means. You deserve it."

Warmth spread through me at his crooked smile. The brandy must be taking effect.

"Matt!" Duke shouted from just outside the door. "Matt, you in here?" He pushed open the door and grunted. "Good. Go and stop your hare-brained cousin from ruining her life."

Matt glanced at me and sighed. He set his glass down and pushed off from the table. "What's she doing now?"

"Going to meet Lord Travers to try and win back her locket."

"How?" Matt asked. "She hasn't got anything left to gamble with."

"She's wearing a dress."

"Hell." Matt stormed out of the library, leaving me wondering how Willie wearing a dress was a problem.

And then it struck me. She was going to offer *herself* to Lord Travers as payment.

I picked up my skirts and raced after Duke and Matt. I found them confronting Willie in her room. She'd applied some color to her cheeks and lips, and her hair flowed around her shoulders. She was beautiful.

"You look like a whore!" Duke snarled.

"That's the point," she shot back. She eyed Matt, standing with rigid shoulders, his entire body expanding with his deep breaths. I suspected the deep breathing was an attempt to control his temper, but it wasn't working particularly well. I was glad the hard gleam in his eye wasn't directed at me.

I stepped between them. "I'll lend you the money," I told Willie. "I have some coming to me shortly. Perhaps Lord Travers will accept a promissory for now."

Willie blinked at me, but it didn't stop her eyes filling with tears. "You would do that for me?"

"Of course."

"I can't accept it. This is my predicament, and I'll get myself out of it. Thank you, but I don't want your money. Or yours, Matt."

"I'm not offering you any," he snarled. "I'm going to win the locket back for you. Get your coat." He turned and marched out of the room.

"Is he a good poker player?" I asked when he was out of earshot.

"He's the best there is," Willie said quietly.

"Was," Duke said. "He hasn't played since the gunfight with his grandfather. He gave up all his gambling and drinking ways after that."

"It's not something you forget," Willie told him.

"You better hope not. Come on, let's go."

"I'll get my coat," I said, hurrying to my own room.

***

Mr. Unger agreed to the private game between Lord Travers and Matt. The hush that had descended upon our entrance lifted as excited voices eagerly placed wagers on who would win. All the games were suspended so everyone could watch. Unger rearranged the furniture and Travers and Matt took their seats.

Lord Dennison wedged himself between me and Duke. The scar on his forehead from the wound inflicted by the clock looked red and raw.

"What a pleasant surprise," he murmured thickly in my ear. "If your friend loses, will you wager yourself this time? I'll be tempted to play—"

He was suddenly ripped away. Matt held him by the collar, pulling it tight and high at Dennison's throat. Dennison's struggles only managed to give him a red face, and score a few laughs from the others at his expense. "Is this the fellow?" Matt growled at me.

I lifted my chin. "If it is, what will you do to him?"

Matt looked to Dennison then to me, then to the table. "Take him for every last penny."

"In that case, yes it is."

Excited whispers rippled through the crowd. They scented a dangerously thrilling game ahead. Matt shoved Dennison down onto a chair. "If you don't play, I'll take you out the back and flog you."

"This is outrageous!" Dennison spluttered. "Do you know who I am?"

"Enlighten me."

Dennison plucked at his collar and stretched his neck. "I'm Lord Dennison! The son of the Earl of Morecombe."

Travers snorted. "He's not important. Come now, let's play." He lit a cigar and leaned back in his chair.

"Stand," Matt ordered.

"Pardon?" Travers chomped on his cigar and didn't move.

"Stand up so I can see that you're not hiding anything."

"Check his pockets," Willie said.

"Bloody hell!" Travers muttered, but he pushed his chair back and heaved himself up. "Never been treated this way by an *Englishman*.

Duke checked Travers's pockets and the chair itself, and declared he'd found nothing untoward.

Travers snorted as he sat. "I'm not a cheat."

I elbowed Willie when she opened her mouth to protest. She shut it with a grumble.

"Deal," Matt ordered the dealer. "What have you got to stake?" he asked Dennison.

"Nothing," Dennison said. "Lost it all at hazard."

"Did you come in a conveyance?"

"Of course."

"Then I accept that."

Lord Dennison lost his conveyance on the first hand. He slunk away from the table, his head low, muttering how his father was going to rake him over hot coals when he learned what he'd lost.

"Stay where I can see you," Matt ordered Dennison, pointing to a spot well away from me.

Travers was a little harder to beat, but Matt did it with only a pair of eights after a mere ten hands were played. Travers could have won with his pair of jacks but he folded too soon. He handed over the locket.

Willie swooped on it and slipped it around her neck. Matt rose and nodded at the dealer and Unger.

"Wait!" Travers cried when he realized Matt was leaving. "Another game. Give me a chance to learn from you. Your skill is sublime. I couldn't get your measure at all, not even a little." He grabbed Matt's arm as he went to walk off, but missed and almost toppled off his chair. "Come now, sir, we can make it as interesting as you like. I'm a bloody rich man. Ask anyone here."

Matt gave him a look of utter contempt. "Good evening to you." To Dennison he said, "Come and point out your carriage and tell your driver he's no longer required."

Dennison followed us down the stairs, past the porters, his head low and shoulders stooped. Outside, a carriage came forward when one of the drivers recognized his master. Dennison gave him the bad news. The driver looked crestfallen.

"But I have a family! How will I feed them?"

"Work for me," Matt said. "I live at sixteen Park Street. Duke, go with him."

"I'll go too," Willie said quickly, eyeing Matt. She must have suspected she'd be on the receiving end of his temper for some time and wanted to ward it off for as long as possible.

"May I humbly request a ride back home?" Dennison asked.

"Walk," Matt growled.

He held the door of his own carriage open for me and assisted me inside. He followed me and closed the door. Cyclops drove off, the other conveyance behind us.

"You play well," I ventured after two minutes of taut silence.

He grunted.

"You won, Matt. So why are you angry?"

He'd been looking out the window, but he now turned to me. Some of the frostiness had already vanished from his eyes, but they were still cool. "I'm not angry."

I barked a laugh.

He rubbed his eyes and I felt awful for mocking him. The poor man was exhausted. "I possessed a lot of vices in my youth," he said. "Gambling was one of them, as was drinking to excess, usually both at the same time."

"You don't have to explain," I said.

"I want to. I want you to know that I stopped because I didn't like the man I became when I gambled and drank like that. I gave up after I was shot. Things tend to fall into perspective when your life hangs in the balance."

Neither of us spoke. The hissing of the carriage lamps and the *clip clop* of the hooves and rumble of wheels were the only sounds. The night air wasn't cold, but it was dense, confining. My corset felt too tight. "I'm sorry," I said finally.

"For what? None of this is your fault."

"For misjudging you. I see now that it's not anger but tension. You wanted to get out of there quickly."

"I didn't even want to be in there," he said quietly. "Sometimes..." He removed his hat and dragged his hand through his hair. "Sometimes I find it tempting."

"Yet you manage to have a drink or two without going to excess now. Why not a game of poker here and there?"

He shrugged. "I didn't want to risk falling into old ways. I haven't played in years."

"We could play at home. That might satisfy Willie too, and keep her from going out to find opponents. We don't have to play for money, but for something else. Matches or tokens."

His mouth hooked up at the corner, all mischief again. His tension vanished entirely. "You want to learn to play poker, India?"

"If you'll teach me, yes."

His smile turned positively wicked. "You'd better not wager anything you can't afford to lose."

I smiled back, even though my heart fluttered madly. "Nor had you."

His eyes turned smoky. "For the first time in my life, I think I'd like to lose."

THE END

LOOK OUT FOR

The Mapmaker's Apprentice
The second GLASS AND STEELE novel.

When a lad apprenticed to a mapmaker disappears, Matt is asked to investigate. But when he uncovers lies and magic, he knows he needs India's help. Meanwhile, time is running out to find his watchmaker.

To be notified when C.J. has a new release, sign up to her newsletter via her website: www.cjarcher.com

ABOUT THE AUTHOR

C.J. Archer has loved history and books for as long as she can remember and feels fortunate that she found a way to combine the two. She has at various times worked as a librarian, IT support person and technical writer but in her heart has always been a fiction writer. Her first historical fantasy series, THE EMILY CHAMBERS SPIRIT MEDIUM TRILOGY, has sold over 45,000 copies and garnered rave reviews. C.J. spent her early childhood in the dramatic beauty of outback Queensland, Australia, but now lives in suburban Melbourne with her husband, two children and a mischievous black & white cat named Coco.

She loves to hear from readers. You can contact her in one of these ways:
Website: www.cjarcher.com
Email: cjarcher.writes@gmail.com
Facebook: www.facebook.com/CJArcherAuthorPage
Twitter: @cj_archer

82596759R00181

Made in the USA
Lexington, KY
03 March 2018